D1518319

CARNIVOROUS CUPID

#1 in the "Angry Greek Gods" series

Copyright 2020 © Stephanie Rose

AUTHOR'S NOTE
&
ACKNOWLEDGMENTS

"CARNIVOROUS CUPID" is a project many years in the making. I've been obsessed with Greek Mythology for a *long time,* trying many times to write a story about how much I love it, with a modern twist.

Almost a decade later, here it is!

But publishing this wouldn't have been possible without the help of six fantastic women: **Sevannah, Vee, Ellysa, Natalie, Yasmine, and Kaitlyn.** You have provided me with so much advice and confidence to pursue this dream, and I appreciate the time and effort you all put into this story!

To my family, thank you for allowing me to follow my heart and for giving me ample time to write whenever I needed it.

To Just, for dealing with my mood-swings and my *need* to write—this is why I do it!

To all my online friends and authors who read Carnivorous Cupid in its early stages—*thank you!* Your feedback was essential in creating this work.

And finally, to those starting out in this field—don't give up!

‖1. HEARTS‖
???

Hearts.

Beating. Thumping. Thrashing. Pumping. He heard them all, knew which belonged to whom, and labeled them in the back of his mind for his personal knowledge.

He recognized them as they passed by, each pulsating at their own rhythms, as if communicating with him, or saying hello. He didn't look at faces or dig his eyes into their souls to get to know someone; he looked at hearts. That's how he identified each human he oversaw.

Now, he waited, concealed in the darkness of the late-night sky, his breathing leveled—steady yet anxious. He gripped his bow so tight his hands ached.

They should show up any minute.

His temples throbbed as strangers passed by, all oblivious to his dark figure hiding behind a dumpster. Rain drenched his black leather coat, and he shivered, droplets creeping under his clothes, rolling down his bare arms.

He kicked off the water from his boots and shook his head to free his hair of the weight. He smelled like a wet dog, but he didn't care.

They'll be here soon.

Skyscrapers surrounded the dingy dumpster and a gloomy navy blanket towered overhead, unleashing thick drops of rain. Puddles splashed as cars sped by, their loud rumbles awakening the crowds. People rushed to avoid getting wet, but most were unable to react fast enough. Drivers didn't seem to notice as they drove on, headed towards more passers-by to splash and soak.

He cackled, the bark of sound loud in the darkness.

Stupid humans.

He shifted to a crouching position, hoping to better hide from those passing him—no one could see him. Ever.

I can't be compromised or stopped.

Distant footsteps resonated in his skull, muffling every other sound around him. He perked up, keeping close to the ground.

That's them. They're near.

He pulled two arrows from the bag at his feet, and notched them. Blood dripped onto his shoes, making him frown; but he disregarded his disgust to focus on his upcoming task.

The footsteps grew louder, and the world around him became faint. The cars, the people, the rainfall; nothing affected him but the steps, like heartbeats. Faster, nearer, within reach.

Thump, thump. Thump, thump.

He lifted his bow, strung his fingers.

Thump, thump. Thump, thump.

He saw them at last. A man and a woman, walking in slow motion, their strides in rhythm with those in his head. Both wore raincoats and arrived from opposite ends of the street, oblivious to each other and to everything surrounding them. Lost in thought, likely hurrying to their destinations to dodge the rain.

He rose, and in the blink of an eye, he tugged the string, drew the arrows back, took a sharp breath, and released them as he puffed out his cheeks.

One embedded into the man's torso, knocking him back; the other charged into the woman's gut, hunching her over in pain.

He smiled.

The arrows disintegrated as they pierced the skin, disappearing in an eruption of black smoke that blanketed the two individuals. Within a few seconds, they regained their balance, shook their heads, and took in their surroundings.

When their eyes met, an invisible link established; like a thin, silver thread connecting them, drawing them to one another. They froze, mouths gaping, limbs straightening. They rolled their shoulders and marched up to each other, only stopping once their noses touched.

Satisfied, the archer slipped his weapon back into the bag on the ground, never taking his gaze off the scene.

It's time. Soulmates, unite.

The two humans emitted a low moan, an earth-rattling shriek. Others passed by them, ignoring them; no one paid attention to the couple stopped dead in the middle of the busy, rainy sidewalk. No one cared about the strangers and their sudden meeting, their purpose, their supernatural connection.

But they will all care soon.

The man ripped off the woman's raincoat in one fluid movement. The woman did the same to him, then tugged at his shirt, watching as buttons flew and fell to the pavement, in sync with the raindrops.

Still, not a single person passing by gave their extraordinary actions any attention.

He yanked her dress over her head, leaving her in her intimates, and high boots up to her knees. He let her undo his belt and drop his pants to the wet ground, and as he stepped out of them, only his boxers and shoes remained.

Finally, a few curious glances came from shocked citizens and tourists. The archer could only imagine their thoughts; would these two end up uniting right there, in the street, in public? What were they doing?

He smirked.

It's time.

As onlookers halted, trespassing on the situation, the man and the woman reached out—and plunged their hands into each other's chests. A blinding flash of light consumed the area as witnesses tumbled to their knees, weakened by the overwhelming brightness.

Some ran, splashing in the rainwater; slipping, falling, struggling to escape as fast as possible without a second glance.

Those who dared to stay had no choice but to witness the final event. The culmination of the archer's efforts; when his targets removed their hands, holding each other's beating hearts—and both pulsating members still attached to their bodies by a few thin veins.

So began the screams. The fainting, the retching in a corner, the desperate attempts to shield eyes; but no one could evade the horror. No one could tear away.

The man and woman dropped to their knees and, to a chorus of yelps from their audience, they lifted the hearts to their mouths—and sunk their teeth in.

Crimson liquid splattered all over, drizzling into the small ponds of water, exploding all over the poor onlookers.

As they chomped, tearing through muscle tissue, the crunching sound echoed down the street, bouncing off the walls in the alley and the surrounding buildings. Deafening chewing rang in the archer's ears, squelching as tender chunks of heart projected from behind their lips and glazed the slick ground. The rainwater on the sidewalk reddened, thickening as a foul stench escaped the zone.

Though everyone around cowered, unable to pry their gazes away, filling with revulsion, the two continued; munching down on every meaty piece until nothing remained and juices coated their faces.

And the archer watched, a sickening grin on his face.

"Do you love your little humans now?" He snarled. "Come and get me, Mother. Come and confess your mistakes."

With a growl, he arched his spine.

Then, and only then, will this Cupid stop the carnage.

He heaved his bag over his shoulder and ambled down the opposite end of the alley, chuckling to himself.

Behind him, the man and woman had finished their feast. In unison, they released their final breaths as they tipped backwards, sloshing into puddles of water, blood, and flesh. Their hearts eaten, their bodies decaying—they were no more.

The passers-by ran in all directions, yelling for help, calling the police, begging the skies for mercy; but it was too late.

Don't fuck with Eros.

‖ 2. HOTEL ROOMS AND WOMEN ‖
LUKUS

A woman lounged beside a man, lips pouting.

"So, *agent*. What's it like?"

He grabbed a lighter on the nightstand and flicked it, illuminating the end of his cigarette. It ignited, and nicotine entered his body as he inhaled. He blew out the smoke, relief filling his lungs.

The woman raised her eyebrows and dodged the vapors though she didn't seem bothered by them.

He sighed. "Being an FBI agent?" She nodded. "Constant traveling, reports and files, interrogations and drinking. Violence here and there. And lots of blood. That about sums it up."

She batted her thick-coated eyelashes, and swung her leg over his under the covers, rubbing her soft skin against him.

"Oh, come on, give me something good," she said, tracing along his arms with her fingertips.

Her bright red nail polish reminded him of the oozing blood he had seen earlier that day.

No, stop that! Get back in the mood!

He shivered. At this point, he would ask a woman to dress and leave, but he enjoyed this one's presence. He hadn't had such fun in a while, not when his mind was elsewhere.

He couldn't see himself requesting her to take off after such a passionate, exciting evening.

"What do you want to know?" He brought the cigarette to his mouth again. "How long I've been an agent? What my degree is? If I'm married and have children?" He blew more smoke out into the room.

It was a nice hotel—nicer than his usual. The FBI spoiled him for once—that, or he didn't read about the covered expenses for this case, and would have to fork out the money for this place on his own.

The wallpaper wasn't cracked, the carpet wasn't stained, and the bed didn't squeak while they played. There was a flat-screen TV, and a long list of channels to choose from, to keep entertained. Not that he'd have time to peruse them.

The lock on the door was functional, the curtains didn't have holes, weren't frayed, and didn't stink of smoke.

He felt bathed in luxury.

The woman nudged him and giggled, her voice making his extremities tingle. "No, not that. Play with me, *agent*. Tell me the dirty stuff. The shady hotels, the women, the crimes... *that's* what I want." Her tone, so husky, was the sexiest he'd ever heard.

He took another drag of his cigarette and kept his cool, unwilling to give in to her again just yet. "I don't stay in shady hotels. I stay in places like this." It wasn't like she would figure out the truth.

The woman shoved him again, seeing right through him.

"Okay, okay, *fine*. Dark, scary rooms with shadows that dance on the walls, creepy hallways, weird strangers walking down them at night... is *that* what you want?"

Her features lit up. The sheets barely covered her naked body, and he resisted the urge to jump her.

He almost cracked his cigarette from squeezing it too tight between his fingers. "Lots of women, like you. We meet in bars, we drink, we exchange glances. We don't talk, usually. You're *lucky*."

The woman feigned surprise. "Oh, little *me*? What a privilege. Tell me more." She propped herself up on her side, facing him.

The cover slipped and her breasts showed, almost warranting a gasp from him.

She's teasing me! That sly thing.

"More about the women? How we turn off the lights, slip out of our clothes, sneak under the blankets, and direct our hands to those special, secret places? Or did you want more about the shady hotel rooms and what they might contain?"

He hurried to finish his cigarette; her taunts had gotten the best of him, and he was ready for more.

She wagged her finger. "No, about the job, silly. The crime scenes. The investigations. The *criminals. Excite* me, agent, get me nice and scared!" The covers fell farther, revealing the rest of her upper body.

He gulped, unsure how long he could keep up with her 'game', and not lose his ability to think straight. He sensed a tightness below that he couldn't control, and consumed his cigarette far faster than he should, the nicotine swirling in his lungs, rendering him dizzy.

"I'm not at liberty to reveal such things, young lady," he whispered as he extinguished the cigarette in an ashtray, and turned to her.

She was a gorgeous woman. A classic beauty with big, scarlet hair, plumped, crimson lips, a fair and smooth complexion. Curves in the right places, and a deep, seductive voice he had been unable to resist when he met her in the bar hours before.

She frowned. "It's not like I'll tell anyone. I like the gruesome stories, okay? The weird shit. Gets me turned on, I don't know why." Her hand grazed his pectoral muscles, sending chills down his spine.

Beautiful, but strange.

She caught his attention earlier that evening, at the hotel bar. Sipping on a martini, looking his way, undressing him with every glance. He hadn't hesitated to approach her, and when he said he was a federal agent, her eyes sparked with lust.

Did she think he was joking? Role playing? Faking his job title to get laid?

Maybe she's an actress?

"I can't, though." He smiled as he caressed her face, memories of their rolling in the sheets preparing him for another round.

She pulled away. "It's just a *game*, Luke. You're not an agent, and I'm not a lonely housewife from the fifties," she said, looking over at her dress on the floor.

It wasn't a modern outfit, for sure. He realized now that she looked like she had walked straight out of an I Love Lucy episode.

Maybe *she* was roleplaying this entire time.

Who is this chick?

He cleared his throat. "The name is Lukus. And sorry, but I'm not playing. I am an FBI agent." He reached for his pants by the bed and yanked out his wallet, flashing her his official ID badge, gleaming in the gentle light from the bedside table.

She scoffed. "Well, shit." She tugged the covers up, concealing her milky skin.

He laughed. "What? Is that a turn off? Seriously?" His forehead scrunched, remembering how most of the time, his job was an instant attraction for women.

Was I not supposed to give out my actual identity?

She shook her head. "You'll get me in trouble." She slipped away, dropping onto the other side of the mattress. "You'll get me fired."

He looked at her in awe. "How and *why* would I do that?"

She reached for something on the ground, turning her back to him. She stood up, put her underwear on and marched to another spot where she'd dropped her bra. "I'm a *prostitute*, genius. You and I should not be seen together. I'm guessing you could lose your job too." She pulled her dress up along her perfect body and zipped it at the side.

There she was, the sexy lady he had plucked at the bar downstairs, just hours prior.

And she was a lady of the night, a forbidden fruit that would have cost him more than he could afford.

He smacked his hands to his temples.

Dammit. That explains a lot.

He shrugged, a sliver of anger racing through him. He understood how some needed to make ends meet—but he never mingled with women who got paid for sex. *Never.*

"I agree; we shouldn't have done this, but not because of my job. I rarely sleep with *your* kind." He lept from the mattress and dressed.

He chided himself for not being more attentive. Because he knew the signs; so why didn't he see *this* coming?

No prostitutes, Lukus.

The woman groaned. "Hey, everyone has to make a living, dude. *This* is how I make mine. Don't criticize. Trust me, I've heard it all before, and don't need a lesson from *you*." She arranged her expression into a sad, pleading frown. "And please, don't report me." Her tone was still displeasing; but she pouted her lips again, trying to seduce him as she had earlier.

She slipped into her black pumps and took a few steps to gauge her balance.

"Honey, I don't work for that department." He scowled at her as he buttoned his shirt. "I cover violent crimes, not whores. I have no business reporting you."

He thought about taking a shower to wash the night away; but his body begged for another drink. For *several* drinks. To wash away his shame, first.

"*Don't* call me a whore. That's rude, agent." She sneered as she searched the room for her purse. Once she found it, she sat on a chair, balancing the bag on her thighs. "I'm not sure why you're in town but you should leave. There are a lot of *my kind* in this sector, and they'll all come running for you. They *love* your type, the slick, smart-ass detective look. They'll be fooled like I was." Powdering her nose, she squinted. "You'll put us out of business." She added color to her lips and puffed up her hair.

"I *can't* leave. I'm investigating a serious crime in the area, and until I consider this town safe, I'm staying put. So, I guess I'll have to remain celibate for the time being." Lukus wrinkled his nose, realizing playtime in Chicago was over.

The woman's brows shot up. "A serious crime? Are you... talking about that *cannibalism* murder?" Her heels clicked as she made her way to the agent and stopped, staring at him with intrigue. "Is *that* what you're investigating?"

Lukus fought his shock, but leaned forward, her décolleté bringing him flashes of their fun under the covers from moments before.

Maybe she could help; maybe she had clues. It wouldn't be the first time he enlisted a whore to aid him on a case.

"Yeah, that one. Have you noticed anything that might be of use to me?" He slid backwards, out of reach.

She shrugged. "Not much. Just that it was bloody and disgusting. Nothing that you don't already know. It didn't happen in my area. And none of my clients witnessed it. I deal with tourists like you." She tossed her hair, sending a faint cigarette and cheap perfume scent into his nostrils.

He put his suit jacket on. "I don't know anything, that's the problem. Two people ripped each other's hearts out and *ate* them. How is that biologically possible? Is it a virus? Is it fucking *magic*? And why has it happened in other cities too? Why are people turning into cannibals and chomping down on hearts?" His voice cut out.

Fuck. I shouldn't have said that.

The prostitute put her hands up. "Whoa, *too much information*, man. I pretended to be into dark crimes to stay in character, but I don't want the details, okay? Especially if this is spreading all over the country. I'm out." She headed towards the door, taking her overly floral stench with her.

Lukus went to his wallet on the bedside table. "Wait," he said, and the woman jolted around. "How much do I owe you?" He hated her kind, but he wasn't a criminal; this was how she made a living, and he owed her.

Her lips curved into a crooked smile. "Consider it a freebie, sweetie. I can't have it known that an FBI agent paid me.

It won't look good. Someone will find out, they always do. Good luck with your case." She left without another glance.

Cursing under his breath, Lukus peered at the flat-screen TV.

Maybe I'll have time for channel surfing after all.

‖3. THE UNHAPPY GODDESS‖
APHRODITE

The sweet melody enveloped her senses as she lay on her bed. A thick, feathered fan rested in her hands, helping to cool her down.

Ah, yes. That's how I like it.

The delicate tunes escaping the harp gave her a rare happiness. Because these days, poor Aphrodite suffered; stuck in her quarters, longing for adventures and games, seeking romantic getaways to the beaches of the Mediterranean with her lover. Instead, her white paradise imprisoned her, with her cupbearers and fair maidens as entertainment while everyone else played.

When the tune deepened, its notes sharper, she glared at the harpist. The girl released a squeak as she reverted to the airy song she began with, unwilling to displease the Olympian princess where she lounged on the bed. Tossing a plump grape into her mouth, the latter smirked, sucking on the juices.

Her suite smelled of exotic fruits and the sea, like the contents of a suntan lotion bottle. Pearls and seashells accentuated every piece of furniture and appeared in all artwork, alongside swans and doves, tidal waves and tsunamis, beaches and tropical islands.

It *was* her happy place; but she wasn't happy.

The pastel pink curtains somewhat shielded her eyes from the overwhelming sun, but she almost wished it wouldn't. She preferred to burn; it would be more entertaining than her current boredom.

Dropping her fan with an exaggerated sigh, she reached for the bouquet of light red roses beside her.

She *hated* red.

What in Zeus' name is he trying to do?

Aphrodite tossed the flowers to the other side of the room, above the harpist's head, and they crashed into the wall. The harpist didn't flinch, nor did she stop playing; she knew better than to provoke her.

She stretched and reached for another grape. She squeezed it hard, releasing the liquid within, letting it drip all over her laundered white tunic. She watched as the purple stain expanded, covering her chest, and drops of grape extract fell in between her breasts, tickling her. A mixture of anger and pleasure took over her senses—and she imagined squashing *his* head just as she had the fruit.

That sensation provoked more delight in her than him.

Where is *he?*

She snatched the bowl of grapes and threw it too, right on top of her favorite seashell jewelry box on the dresser. And she gasped when she realized her mistake, rushing to the area to clean up her mess.

Her pearls spilled all over, falling to the ground, some going all the way to the harpist's foot.

Enough of this.

Aphrodite stomped over to the musician. "Get out!"

The harpist stopped playing, a look of protest on her face. "But, Your Highness, Miss Aphrodite—"

Holding her hand up, Aphrodite groaned. "I'm bored with you. Go find someone else to entertain. I'll have your harp sent to you."

The poor girl bowed her head and exited.

Virgins, all the same!

Aphrodite frowned as she picked up her pearls, put them all away, and closed the box. Her fingertips lingered on it as she stared at its intricate design, its glimmering shells pieced together in a measured and unique way. One of her husband's only talents: crafting beautiful *and* useful objects.

She tossed her long mane of hair as she returned to her mattress. The pale green satin sheets welcomed her body, sending waves of comfort through her limbs. But how could one be comfortable in a forced marriage?

She glanced at her reflection in the mirror on the ceiling above her blankets. Cliché as it was, she *loved* to admire herself, even depressed. She enjoyed caressing her soft, strawberry blonde hair as it glistened in the late afternoon sun, seeping in from the uncovered parts of her window. Her curves molded into her seashell shaped bed, longing for caresses. Not from her husband— but from *him*. The one who brought her red roses and ignored her for days on end; the one who was in big trouble.

Despite her brewing fury, images of her lover and their better times entered her mind. When they pranced around, with not a care in the world. When they ran down the moonlit palace corridors to escape Zeus' wrath. Or when they hid in closets to frolic about while others sat in the throne room and listened to the king's rants.

How could he make her so aroused and so angry at once? They had been at it for centuries; the excitement should have worn off.

As she imagined his defined muscles and licked her lips, someone knocked on the door, interrupting her only happy thoughts of the day.

"Oh, if it's that harpist, I *swear...*" She sat up and fixed her features back into a scowl. "*What?*"

The door opened to reveal a young maiden, wearing a boring tunic that covered most of her frame, her hair pulled into a bun.

Aphrodite stretched, grimacing. "Hebe? What do *you* want?"

Hebe, the cupbearer; the girl who hated her with every fiber of her polite, unemotional being.

Why would she be at my doorstep?

Hebe didn't recoil; she didn't fear Aphrodite's tantrums like others in the serving staff. "You're summoned to the throne room. At once."

Aphrodite's muscles tensed.

Was it him? Had he come home? And *why* would he want to see her out in the open?

Standing up, her legs slippery against the sheets, she pressed down on her dress, smoothing it. "And *who* summons me?" If it was him, she wouldn't hurry; he could wait.

Hebe's lips turned upwards. "The *king*." She sneered, spinning away from the door.

Zeus, summoning her in the heart of the afternoon? A part of Aphrodite prayed he had an adventure for her, a special task; she rubbed her hands together at the idea.

"I need a moment," she said, fixing her hair in the mirror above her dresser.

Once satisfied with her glowing self, she followed Hebe. Her long tunic flowed with her every move as she swayed—not walked—behind her adoptive sister, wondering what her adoptive father wanted. "Have you seen Ares today?"

The girl rolled her eyes. "No, I haven't."

Aphrodite huffed. "You're more hostile than usual, I see!"

Hebe strolled faster in response. They cruised through the copper corridors in silence, passing portraits of Greek heroes and gods, captured in their famous moments, all glaring back in disapproval. They slid by doors leading to other private quarters, libraries, dining areas, and ballrooms.

At last, the large opening to the throne room came into view—and Aphrodite's breath caught in her throat.

She saw not only Zeus, but the Olympian committee, all seated on their thrones.

What in Tartarus is going on?

Hebe grinned as she disappeared through a side door, leaving her alone to enter the vast space. It was open to the outside world, with marble pillars holding the ceiling, and beautiful vines full of exotic flowers flowing up and down, separating each throne.

Soft music normally played in the background, bringing a sense of tranquility. But she had stolen the harp *and* the harpist—there was no calm today.

A deep, rumbling voice drew her back to reality. "Aphrodite, step forward."

Startled, she looked to the throne across from her, in the middle of all others. She approached it and kneeled, bowing her head. "Your Majesty."

This can't be good.

She dared a peek to Zeus' right side; Hera, eyes piercing like daggers, her mouth ready to spit out the usual profanities, sat straight against her regal blue cushions.

And a few seats down... was none other than Ares.

That traitor!

Had he been home the entire time?

Aphrodite glowered at him, but he appeared unable to gaze upon her.

"I'm sorry to bring you here in such a fearsome fashion, but I had no choice," Zeus said, placing his hands in his lap. His curly beard moved as he spoke, his posture stiff and official.

Aphrodite stopped glaring at her lover to watch Zeus again. "What is it you need from me? What have I done, what can I do?"

It couldn't be about the affair; everyone already knew. Even her husband.

She noticed her spouse's position a few chairs down from Zeus; *he* hadn't warned her either.

What sort of betrayal is this?

Hera's choppy tone overshadowed her thoughts. "Your son is missing."

"Which one? I have *several*." Aphrodite much preferred to speak with Zeus, and not his crazy wife.

Zeus coughed. "Your *favorite*. Eros. He left Olympus and now roams Earth in search of... victims."

Aphrodite blinked. "So, he's working? Looking for *love* victims? You summoned me here to tell me he's taken off to go do his *job?* Where is the problem with this?"

Another stupid scam to get her in trouble for no reason and involve her children; Hera *had* to be responsible for this.

Poseidon, farther to Zeus' right, frowned. "He's *not* working," he said before Zeus nudged him. "What? She deserves to know!"

Crossing her arms, Aphrodite's gaze wavered between the two brothers. "Know what?"

Zeus' mouth tightened as he squinted. "My dear, your offspring is on a *killing* rampage."

Aphrodite couldn't contain her squeak.

"He has taken to Earth, provoking death among humans. We aren't positive how, but he's making them... *eat* each other."

Aphrodite sensed her face paling. "*Eat...* each other? H-how so?"

Did I misunderstand that?

Zeus sighed. "I don't know the details, only that he left, without warning, and started murdering humans. None of us can figure out why. We... were hoping maybe *you* could."

"*Me?*" Aphrodite tilted her head. "How would I understand what his problem is? We haven't had a job together in weeks. I... I didn't even know he was gone."

She realized that she hadn't seen him in the main dinner hall with his wife, nor had she come across his daughter, either. A sour flavor lingered on her tongue; and not from the grapes she ate moments before.

Hermes, towards the end of the row of thrones on Zeus' side, stood up. "I'm the only one who has information, as I've transported souls between realms to Hades." He shifted his feet, struggling to keep his chin up. "He shot his victims with *arrows* and provoked them into eating their soulmate's heart. That's all they told me." He lowered to his seat, eyes glistening.

Aphrodite froze. Her Eros, the god of love, her *sweet* boy; he would never harm humans. His arrows caused affection and tenderness, not cannibalism.

This can't be real.

Hades, who remained in the Underworld during Olympian gatherings, sat to Hera's left. "And *I* confirm this. The victims I received downstairs have said the same to me. They never met their soulmate beforehand." Hermes nodded, and in the distance, someone appeared in the shadow of the thrones.

A woman, stern and cold, in a long, gray, worn-out tunic, crossed her arms and stared at Aphrodite, her irises containing half the warmth her hearth did.

Hestia?

She quit the Olympian council eons ago; her presence only worsened Aphrodite's angst.

Zeus followed Aphrodite's gaze. "This matter concerns all Olympians, including Hestia. Her worshippers are afraid. The murders are all over the United States of America. Four to date, and it's likely more will come until someone finds Eros and *stops* him."

Aphrodite shivered, blood boiling; they blamed *her,* didn't they?

"And because I'm his mother it's *my* responsibility? What about his father, huh? Where is *his* part in this? He's the one with the aggressive genes." She pointed at Ares. "He's as responsible as

I am!" How he dared to cower behind his dad and not defend their son sent violent thoughts into her cranium. "And you aren't even *sure* the culprit is Eros, are you? Where is your proof?" Fury seeped into every vein in her immortal body.

Ares turned away, ignoring her, shame drowning his demeanor.

Zeus stood, turning everyone else still as statues. "It's your responsibility because *you* were closest to him before he left. And *you* might be the reason he went crazy, Aphrodite! Your centuries of making him do your dirty work might have finally come to bite you!"

She repressed the urge to scream. They were all hypocrites.

The 'dirty' work was for them!

Zeus' conquests behind his wife's back, Poseidon's rapes, Hades' kidnapping of Persephone—they forced her into helping with those. And Eros had no alternative, either.

What kind of sick joke is this?

Before she could raise her voice, Zeus grunted; a majestic, tremor-inducing sound all were afraid of. "We are certain it's Eros! Who else shoots arrows into human hearts without killing them? Sure, his twin Anteros could be a suspect, but we checked his cover story. *He* hasn't left Olympus."

Aphrodite huffed. "So, what do you expect *me* to do about it? You're the king of the Heavens, are you not? Aren't you the only one with the power to stop him?"

Eros wouldn't listen to her, stubborn as he was. She had no idea why he turned murderous, but it wasn't something she'd be able to resolve.

Zeus rubbed his fingertips over his bearded chin. "Though I am his king *and* his grandfather, I don't have the capacity to stop him—not without killing him. As his mother, your ties with him are our only hope. You *must* investigate, find out his motives, and consult with us so we may *all* decide how to confront him."

His brothers nodded, but everybody else remained silent, all agreeing with the plan. And not one of them caring how *she* felt.

Aphrodite jolted up from her kneeling position, her knees aching. Her heart raced, fueled with a fire she had hoped to extinguish with a simple sighting of Ares; but now her anger level went above the time they were first caught in their adultery, millennia ago. "*Fine*. I'll search through his room, and talk to Psyche and Hedone, figure out what he told them. Then I'll send spies down to Earth to get the scoop. All right, your Majesty?"

Her potential night of fighting and lovemaking with Ares slipped through her fingers; though he didn't deserve it, anyway.

Athena, on the exact opposite side of Ares, laughed—a cackle, resonating in the open space, raising hairs on Aphrodite's arms.

"Is this *funny* to you?" growled Aphrodite, as the other goddess gulped and halted her giggles. Her smile remained, and it filled Aphrodite with another wave of grueling rage.

Zeus snapped his fingers. "We are not here to fight!" All refocused on him. "You will descend to Earth, Aphrodite. You will oversee this investigation, on your own. And you *will* uncover the reasons behind your son's erratic behavior, or suffer my wrath. Do you understand?" His quaking timbre almost shattered the marble pillars.

Aphrodite dropped back to her knees. "Yes, your Majesty."

Eros, I will kill *you.*

‖ 4. CHICAGO ‖
EROS

The glass hit the counter harder than he intended.

But Eros had no remorse as liquid splashed, inundating his napkin, falling into his lap, spilling all over his favorite leather pants, dripping onto the tiled floor like a leaking faucet.

The bartender would clean it up; he had enough to worry about.

He ignored the pool of alcohol and took a handful of peanuts from a bowl that luckily didn't get wet. Stuffing the nuts into his mouth, he didn't bother to close his lips as he chewed. The crunch drowned out the sounds of the hearts beating around him, and he enjoyed the salty taste, matching his mood.

He looked up at the TV screen above the shelves full of booze.

"Another gruesome murder scene, right here in Chicago, similar to the other three discovered in the past three weeks. Like in San Francisco, New York, and Miami, the victims seem to be missing their hearts. Witnesses claim the victims ate those hearts, but we're unable to get any comments from police or FBI to

confirm this. We'll keep updating as this case continues, so please stay tuned."

Eros hid his smile, watching the local news station reporting his glorious, gruesome work. His attitude shifted, pride radiating from somewhere within him; he was on a television device. How *cute!*

And I have so many more cities to provoke and destroy.

With a long list of soulmates to ruin, he would soon move on to Europe—closer to home. But for now, the United States was a perfect spot to work.

He tossed a few more peanuts into his mouth. Though he *did* like the flavor, he wasn't used to it; and within a few seconds, he wished to spit the pieces out.

What he required was ambrosia. The more he swallowed bits of human food, the more disgusted he became.

If only they made ambrosia-flavored nuts.

He checked the pay-as-you-go phone in his pocket, revealing the time; one forty-three a.m.

Only one god could sneak ambrosia out of Olympus for him; Anteros, his brother.

He finished his drink—rum and coke, a despicable excuse for a cocktail—and deposited a few dollar bills on the counter, waving at the bartender. He shoved his cell into his coat pocket, heaved his bag over his shoulder, and chuckled as another human on the television told her side of his gory crime.

"It was awful. So sudden. We... didn't really see what happened, they... they just took each other's clothes off and ripped each other's hearts out!"

Eros proceeded out of the bar, but not before the reporter appeared on the screen.

"The pictures from the scene are too brutal to show, but we'll let you imagine the extent of the crime. We're not yet sure if we're looking at a serial killer, or a toxin contained in certain foods that might be causing such reactions. Folks, be on the alert, and go nowhere alone. From what we understand, the FBI has no leads..."

Eros opened the door, breathing in the post-rain air. It wasn't comparable to his home; it was toxic, polluted. Plagued with murder, sex, and blood. Olympus had a clean air; mountainous and fresh. And pure. Air he missed though he might never be in it again.

Weak in the knees, he focused on locating ambrosia. Gods weren't supposed to be down on earth so much; he couldn't risk turning mortal and not finishing his task.

I must gain some, and quickly.

He walked, unsure of where he headed. Chicago was stop number four, and he needed to decide which big American city would come next.

He cackled; Americans were so easy to rouse and provoke. So easy to test. Exploring the country hidden beneath his hood, he appreciated the landscapes and buildings; but found the place tainted. And *that* crude atmosphere attracted him if only for his mission.

Zipping up his jacket, a slither of worry weighed on his heart.

He had to find her. The more people he tortured, the closer he got to answers. The deaths fueled him, made him stronger—and that was the only way.

He stuffed his hands into his pockets and looked around. The streets were busy, despite the late hour. Honking cars swerved by, late-night adventurers ran down cross-walks without waiting for their turn, tacky commercial signs dangling from dizzying buildings blared bright lights in his face. He listened for anything to give him a hint of what came next, but the sewer and fried food odors from nearby made his stomach rattle.

How could they continue on with their lives when his hung by a thread? How were they all so oblivious? Humans only cared about themselves.

He closed his eyes, holding in the pain tearing through his soul. He missed *her*. To end the madness, he had to find her, and fast. Before he got too carried away.

When he opened his eyes again, the street was empty. He reveled in the rare moment of silence before more humans appeared to interrupt him.

And when they did, he moved out of the way, to stand against a building for a better view of what surrounded him.

The skyscrapers, the bright lights, the museums and shopping centers. The rumbling caused by the various forms of transportation, and the remnants of the rain, dripping from rooftops.

Rain.

He liked rain. Though he preferred for it *not* to drench him when he shot his targets. Where else in the United States did it rain this much?

He wasn't familiar with American geography and weather, but he dug deep within, hoping to remember his lessons from Mount Olympus, centuries ago, as a child. The things Auntie Hestia taught him about the world.

Relaxed, he concentrated, tuning out everything around.

Seattle.

That was where he had to travel next. She would have liked it.

Returning to life, he scurried towards a trashy side alley a few streets down, making sure he was alone.

Large, white wings erupted from his back, through his leather jacket. A few feathers fell to the ground, drowning in the puddles of rainwater.

Eros bent his knees and sprung into the air, shooting into the night's sky.

Goodbye, Chicago.

‖ 5. THE SAME ‖
LUKUS

Damn, that's a lot of blood.

Lukus had become accustomed to seeing crime scenes. Three years of special police work and five years with the FBI gave him sufficient details to make a successful horror movie. Rapes, murders, assaults, violent and lethal attacks—he was no stranger to gore and guts, and it no longer disgusted him.

But he had seen nothing like this.

He enjoyed visiting Seattle. Nice people, good food, weather that pleased his moods. He loved seeing the Space Needle and didn't mind the constant rain. And the coffee was out-of-this-world, of course. But today, he regretted his arrival in the city. Nothing warm or welcoming about a crime scene—and this one less so.

The flashes from the forensics photographer's camera brought him to the present.

How is this possible?

He kneeled over the two bodies on the ground.

A man and a woman, next to naked, partially disintegrated—and their hearts missing. They lay in pools of blood and rainwater, side by side, eyes closed, limbs spread out.

Lukus looked up, sucking in a breath to calm his nerves. Giant office buildings surrounded them, and curious onlookers gaped out of windows, desperate to understand what happened.

Me too, guys. I also want to understand.

He lowered his chin, returning to the scene. The victims' fingers—or what remained of them—were stained with a crimson liquid, which matched their mouths, chins, and chests. The rest of their bodies were burnt; ashy and black as coal, as if they escaped from an explosion, or lava had washed over them and caked their skin.

Witchcraft?

He groaned.

No, that shit doesn't exist.

What weapon had the power to provoke such horror? Lukus leaned in for a better look at the torso where the male's heart was missing.

Dumbfounded, he waved at an investigator to approach him. "What did the witnesses say, again?" He removed a small notepad and pen from his coat pocket, jotting down a description of what lay before him. Turning to the investigator, he narrowed his eyes.

The young man shrugged, wrinkling his nose. "One guy said he saw them snatch each other's hearts out and eat them. Unsure if we can trust him though; he was the only witness, and he's some alcoholic homeless dude." He teetered backwards, his upper body twitching as he curled his lip.

Every person involved in the investigation appeared to be in a trance, on the verge of being sick—yet all were familiar with the gruesome grime of crime scenes.

Lukus shook his head. "I'll receive all the information available. Have the coroner collect and autopsy. I want access to everything they find out, so have the coroner call me with the results." He rose, leaving room for the forensics teams. "And take the witness to the local station. Get him some food or coffee, sober him up a little. I'll stop by to talk to him soon."

He snapped a few pictures with his cell to analyze the bodies again later; alone, and in the comfort of his hotel room.

I must compare these with the others.

He distanced himself from the scene, from the yellow tape and the curious bystanders. The crying citizens and loud-speaking onlookers drove him crazy as they begged police officers for details. Lukus couldn't take it. All feared for their lives, wondering if they were next. But the killer remained unidentified, and the suspect list was bare.

And it's all my fault.

He looked at his notes, and reviewed the ones from Chicago, a few days prior. All the same; the gory situation, the bloody aftermath. He was certain the witness accounts would match, too: a flash of light followed by disturbing heart-eating.

He flipped the pages to the first murder observations and compared. Again, it all matched. Whoever did this—or *provoked* it—was meticulous and detailed. But who would have time for such planning? What sick bastard had the imagination and ability for such cruelty? And what would be his motive?

No one deserved to die like that.

Lukus wasn't sure if he *could* suspect anyone. The more scenes he investigated, the more he realized how inhuman they appeared. Losing faith in his competence, he closed the notebook.

A virus? Zombies? He chuckled, rubbing his forehead. Those were only in movies.

But the hearts—*that* was something he could look into further. His sister was a cardiothoracic surgeon; if strange viruses lurked about, she would know.

With a start, he grumbled. "No, I can't call her." He knew his sister well; she'd alert the entire family and order a reunion.

This is my job, my problem.

He scanned the area, searching for a place to sit and gather his wits. A nearby coffee shop caught his eye, and he wandered away from the crime scene to erase the image of brain-eating monsters.

Did zombies eat *hearts* too?

The shop was quiet despite the craziness. He ordered a latte, added sugar, and found a table close to the window, far from the customers. He dipped a plastic spoon in the beverage and stirred, his thoughts twirling around with the caffeinated liquid.

There had to be a connection, an explanation, a *reason*; there was always something logical behind the insanity. He sipped his coffee and peered through the glass as the forensics teams and detectives hustled about the scene. It wasn't his first rodeo. He had dealt with obscure cases before and solved them. This case wouldn't be any different, right?

His lead tended to assign him the unsolvable situations. The ones any other agent would've given up on or believed impossible. But Lukus always succeeded because he knew the supernatural didn't exist. He only followed logic.

Lost in his thoughts, he spilled his coffee. "*Shit!*" He lurched back before any of the liquid reached his shirt, pants, or jacket.

Watching the beverage trickle down the edges of the table, he snorted. Who was he kidding? Everything about the case turned on the warning lights in his skull. He had nothing. How could two people rip out each other's vital organs and still be *alive* to eat them? How could they still breathe after killing each other?

Something doesn't add up.

Maybe the witnesses were to blame. Maybe they'd exaggerated all of this. But whatever the case, a flaw lingered— and he swore he would find it.

In the past, he'd come across conspiring witnesses and murderers; if he had to dig deep to uncover a similar plot, he would.

Sipping carefully, he shrugged, realizing he'd have to re-interrogate every witness. And this time, he'd play *bad* cop. He didn't care if he had to travel back to all five crime cities.

I will get the facts.

He returned to wrap up the scene and give out final orders; clean the blood, sweep away the ashes, zip up remaining evidence. Eradicate any trace of the crime.

No one needs to wander down here and be reminded of what happened.

As he decided to go to the police station, to speak with the witness, the weather turned dreary. Clouds covered the sky, threatening to release a storm—and Lukus looked forward to it. As his cab passed tall buildings and busy sidewalks, he let out a heavy sigh. It was all the same; overwhelming, stressful. He'd rather be elsewhere, but his job always brought him to the same big city settings.

Yes, he liked Seattle; but not today.

Why there, why those two individuals? And why cannibalism?

He didn't get it. He didn't see the connection between the cities and the victims—or if there was a connection at all.

Once they arrived, he paid the driver and made his way into the police building, waving his badge—granting him access despite the dirty glares of the officers. Most didn't appreciate having a *'fed'* on their turf; but the situation went beyond their abilities.

Lukus found the witness in the interrogation room—panicked, holding a plastic cup of coffee. He rubbed the back of his neck as he sucked in a big inhale and approached. He hated having to be cruel, but it was the only way to scare the guy into telling the truth.

Barging into the cramped space, he slammed the door behind him. The poor man almost dropped his drink into his lap.

"Cough it up, buddy. What did you really see?" Lukus leaned over the table that separated them.

The homeless man gulped. "Like I... said to the officers, sir. A big, bright... flash of light. They took each other's hearts outta their chests. And... ate 'em. Swear to God."

Though the man's eyes widened in petrification, Lukus grunted. "No, I don't buy it. You're covering up for the murderer." He pressed his palms harder against the metallic surface between them. "Or, *you're* the murderer. You think stupid horror stories will save you, huh? Think you can get away with this? What's in it for you? Money? A job? Success? I'm not dumb, so tell me the truth and maybe we can work something out." He threw his badge onto the table. "Comply. It's your best option."

The witness side-glanced at the gleaming badge. He then raised his shoulders. "I didn't ask to see this, sir. I ain't lyin', I have no reason to. And I don't want money or success... wouldn't mind a job, though."

Lukus winced to hold back his real emotions and slanted farther forward. "You think homeless life sucks? Wait until you go to prison. You know what the penalty is for lying to a federal agent?" He smelled the mixture of alcohol and coffee in the man's breath, making his stomach churn.

A knock on the door interrupted them. Before Lukus could answer, a man in uniform slid his head inside. "A word, agent?" He had a dominating air that would intimidate many; but not Lukus.

The police chief?

The man glared at Lukus, who grumbled at the witness. "I'll be back. You think about what I said." Following the chief out into the corridor, he closed the door. "*What?*"

"Look," the officer squinted and scratched at the stubble on his chin, "don't be so hard on the guy, okay? I heard you yelling from my office. Jimmy is... well, he may be an avid drinker and homeless, but he's not crazy. He's a regular around here and he's done nothing wrong."

Lukus pinched the bridge of his nose. "So, you *believe* him? You want me to take his account and report it in my notes? You think what he says adds up? Are *you* crazy?"

Officers in the surroundings perked up, listening.

The chief cleared his throat, and all resumed their duties. "I don't know *what* to believe. This shit's insane, that's why they called you in. But Jimmy wouldn't lie about what he saw, so if I were you, I'd stop the asshole agent act, take his word for it, and go. No need to cause a ruckus in my department! I don't care who you work for. We value respect in here."

Lukus pursed his lips, rage burning through his veins. He wanted to smile at the chief's defiance, but instead kept quiet.

I'll address that later.

He came back to the interrogation room, fingernails digging into his palms. "Did someone write your statement?"

Jimmy nodded. "Fine. You're free to go. Don't get caught up in any more business like this, understood?"

The man rushed out, and Lukus left soon after, too embarrassed to stick around.

I'm an FBI agent, for fuck's sake!

The chief's behavior didn't sit well with him, and he planned to warn his supervisor when he got a chance.

Strolling towards his hotel—only a few blocks from the station—he let the fresh air wash over his cheeks and soothe him. A faint coffee aroma fizzled up his nostrils; something that would usually make him smile, calm him.

But he *wasn't* calm. Nothing made sense, and until he understood these murders, he'd be unable to control his temper. He pulled out a pack of smokes and his lighter from his coat. Selecting a cigarette, he lit the end of it, relieved to inhale the nicotine he craved all morning. He ignored the noises and smells as he focused.

A beam of light—was that some magic trick? It couldn't be zombies or sorcery; there *was* a logical explanation. Hopefully, the autopsies would provide more insight than the last four.

San Francisco, Miami, New York, Chicago—those victims confused the coroners. All four crimes too puzzling, with autopsies that provided no clues. Stumped doctors and scared officers left Lukus desperate.

Maybe Seattle was the clue; maybe he would regain faith in one of his favorite cities.

He finished his cigarette quicker than expected, and arrived in front of his hotel, dreading the hours of waiting to come. He remembered the situations before, stuck in his shabby suite for what felt like an eternity. Especially in New York City where he had to stay hidden to avoid letting his family know he was in town. If the murder had been in Queens, his mother would have found him. He *hated* New York, even more so after visiting it under such dire circumstances. And now, he began to hate Seattle, too.

When you visit a city for a crime, it changes your view on things.

His home in Washington DC had never been so appealing. After three weeks of constant death and blood, he was ready to kick his feet up, get pleasantly drunk, and forget about it all.

But not until I close this case.

He entered his hotel room and drew the curtains. Sitting at the desk, he put down his notes and pulled out his cell phone with the pictures.

Will I ever catch the culprit?

‖6. GOODBYE, OLYMPUS‖
APHRODITE

My son murdering humans. What in Zeus' name has gotten into him?

Aphrodite's suite was less welcoming than before her summons to the throne room. None of her usual trinkets took her mind off the matter at hand. The seashells, the ocean smells, the pretty pearls; all insignificant now. Her satin sheets weren't smooth, her belongings didn't comfort her or bathe her in luxury.

Her heart ached.

No, she wouldn't kill her son—she couldn't. But she would shake the truth out of him. Her baby boy on a killing rampage?

Unbelievable.

She thought about packing a bag with some of her favorite items to remind her of home; a few of her elaborate outfits, her sensual fragrances, her exquisite jewelry. But then again, she didn't *want* to think about home, did she? A place full of so-called family members who betrayed her, pushed her into a corner and blamed her for her son's behavior?

She shrugged; it was best if she established *new* memories on earth, instead.

Changing her stained tunic, she combed her mane and selected a simple seashell necklace from her jewelry box. No one gave it to her; she made it herself. It would be her prized possession to keep on at all times, a reminder of her *real* home: in Cyprus.

As she admired her depressing reflection, the bedroom door opened. She pivoted on her heels and found her husband limping in, a gloomy expression on his face.

She cringed, racing over to throw him out. "Hephaestus—"

"—I'm sorry," he whispered, passing the threshold before she could stop him. His dark gaze sparkled. "I mean it."

Aphrodite groaned and resumed her self-admiration.

"I couldn't change their minds. I even offered to find him myself, but since I have no affinities with him, it would be of no use."

Aphrodite tossed her hair. "Just... go away. Please."

He walked over and put his hands on her shoulders. Seeing him in the mirror, standing behind her, she had to refrain from gagging. Though not as ugly as most of mythology portrayed him, Hephaestus was still the least attractive amongst all gods. His crooked smile and hunched spine, his weak posture and scarred features; all brought bile to her throat.

And as he admired her, devouring every inch of her skin, she wondered if Anteros shot her with one of his unrequited love arrows.

I will never care for my husband, no matter how hard I try.

She escaped his grasp. "What's done is done, right?" She adjusted her tunic, letting it flow over her body. "I'm forced, once more, to do something I shouldn't have to. I'm becoming used to it."

Hephaestus grunted and lunged towards the door. "Let me go talk to him again."

Aphrodite blocked him. "There's no point. He's too stubborn, and everyone's mind is made up. I'll... deal with it."

He wobbled closer, his expression softening. "You don't *have* to." But when he moved in to kiss her, she avoided his lips, allowing him to graze her cheek instead.

Nausea bubbled in her gut as she gave him a last look before leaving the room, abandoning him as usual—lustful and unwanted.

Sadly, meandering through the halls was just as dreadful as staying in the bedroom. The decorated heroes in the paintings gazed, as always, pointing invisible fingers at her. Reminding her how bad a parent she was. Laughing and yelling at her for failing as a goddess.

It's not my fault!

She passed the empty throne room and didn't stop to admire it as she usually would. It only ignited rage in her chest— fury she didn't prefer to dwell on anymore. Entering the main corridor opposite from where she came, the large golden doors shined; calling her name, beckoning her to exit the palace and wander out into the unknown.

The area was empty. No one showed up to escort her or wish her luck. No one cared.

After marching past the glittering arches lining the main hallway, fighting the urge to *not* throw balls of energy into them and knock them down, she pushed open the grand doors and light peered through, blinding her. Slipping outside, she breathed in the fresh air of the heavens. Took in the beauty of the blue skies, the tranquility of the chunks of clouds surrounding the property, the quiet from their above-earth location. Where she was going, there would be no silence and godly landscapes.

She started towards the stairs; but an echo resonated behind her. Another set of footsteps descending after her.

Do I have a departing committee after all?

Spinning around, she frowned at the sight of Zeus. Cursing under her breath—she had hoped to avoid him and sneak out to start her task—she lowered into a quick curtsy.

"I'm glad I caught you before you flew off," he said, striding up to her. "There are a few things to go over first."

She fought the impulse to roll her eyes.

Zeus scoffed. "You can't leave before I brief you on the details! Especially since I must *remove* your powers for the duration of your stay on earth."

"*What?*" Her knees buckled. "Remove my powers?" She stomped her foot. "And *how* am I expected to succeed without them? Have you gone mad, my king?"

Ignoring her offense, Zeus crossed his arms. "You have to be incognito. There can be *no* suspicion of who you are, from humans *or* from Eros himself. I do this for the benefit of us all."

Aphrodite's back muscles tensed. "But... my powers—"

"—*yes!*" He let out a snort. "You? Unleashed down there with your full godlike array of abilities? That's almost more dangerous than your son's killing rampage."

"*Fine.*" Her lower lip puffed out. "Take them all. See how I fail!"

"You'll keep your godly intuition," he said, leaning near her, "meaning you'll sense his energy and know if he's nearby. You'll also keep most of your seductive auras, as I'm unable to remove those. Aphrodite, you must be careful and not let your behavior get out of hand. *No one* can find out you're on earth."

Rolling her shoulders, Aphrodite huffed. "You think I can control how alluring I am? I can barely manage it around gods, imagine with *humans*."

Zeus chuckled. "Well, I will lock your girdle up, so that should help. Learn to regulate your impulses, or they'll be your demise."

All faith lost, Aphrodite's chin tipped down.

Zeus lifted his arms, closed his eyes, and a small jolt of lightning crashed over her. Her powers slipped from her being. Air filled her lungs, blood pumped into her veins, and tingles reached her extremities as her mind overflowed with questions she never dared ask.

Humanity.

She dropped to her knees, humanity weaning its way into her heart and brain, taking over her bodily functions. Her bones cracked, her nerves fired up, her skin lost its glow. "*Ugh.* This is worse than I expected."

"You'll accept it." Zeus reopened his eyes, not a trace of sympathy in his tone. "You are not to approach Eros until you've figured out a motive and you have clearer details on his plans. He's dangerous, even for you. And you're mortal now, though only partially. I will grant your powers once you've discovered the truth, and then you can confront him, calm him. But you *must* contact me first, so I may decide if the time is right or not."

Aphrodite sighed, struggling to adjust to her new feelings. "Understood. And... where am I going? What's my backstory if I am to remain undercover?" She was eager to leave.

The blood flowing through her was foreign and uncomfortable, and an uneasy fatigue drained every fiber of her being.

Zeus put his hands behind his back, pacing by the door. "You will infiltrate the *FBI*, which, as you might remember, is a massive, anti-criminal squad within the United States of America. You will pose as a rookie, and work on your son's case with an experienced agent, giving him hints and helping him. *Discreetly*. I don't want him anywhere near Eros. He is not to die, and that's imperative. We've lost enough humans as it is." He craned his neck to glare at her. "I'd rather this agent not know who Eros is, so be careful how you help him. Make sure he stays safe, and you're the one to confront your son, are we clear?"

"Yes, I'll protect the human." She waved her hands. "But *where* will I live? Have godly accommodations been prepared for my arrival?"

What does human luxury even look like?

She hoped for satin sheets and maidens delivering trays of fruit and ambrosia.

Zeus cackled. "You think you *deserve* that?" Tears formed in his eyes as he doubled over, smacking his thighs. "Truly?" He straightened up, wiping his forehead. "You'll be like any *regular* rookie in the FBI! You'll travel a lot anyway, so you'll see more hotel rooms than an actual home, to be honest. Do not expect luxury, or you'll know disappointment."

Aphrodite cringed. "I... don't know how to live like... a *human.*" She remained on her knees and bowed her head. "Please, your Majesty... is there *any* way you'll reconsider? Give me assistance, someone to go with me? Let me have *some* of my skills? I implore you. I can't see myself succeeding in this mission. It's not what I was created to do!"

She prayed for his mercy; prayed all he wanted was for her to beg.

Well, I'm begging!

Zeus set his finger below her chin and lifted her though his expression was far from gentle. "Your son has caused too much damage, and you're the only one he'll listen to. That's my hope. This needs to end before he provokes a war. It's against his nature and his oaths, and if I go after him myself, I..." His jaw clenched. "I would kill him without a fair trial. But you will use your better judgment. I don't mean to punish you, Aphrodite, though you deserve it. So, view this as a new adventure to regain the trust of all Olympians and restore balance on the planet."

Rubbing her eyes, hoping to prevent any sign of sadness from washing out her perfect features, she nodded. "U-understood."

Zeus patted her on the back and gave her a set of handwritten notes. "Here are further directions. Your *backstory,* as you called it. It'll be confusing at first, but it's for the best. Adjust and camouflage." He slid backwards, and with a quick incline of his head, he pivoted into the palace. "I'll be waiting."

Her emotions were out of control as her immortality poured out, replaced by an unwanted humanity she dreaded. Sniffling, she turned to finish her descent when yet another figure emerged from behind the golden doors, its shadow reaching her.

"What now?" She jolted around, wrinkling her nose. "Can't I leave for my suicidal mission in peace? Who would—"

She immobilized at the sight of Ares, clad in his scarlet and iron warrior attire, his helmet in one hand, a wrapped gift in the other. "My love, I—"

"—oh, *now* you want forgiveness?" Her non-godly feelings threatened to pour out and drown her lover. "And what's this? A parting gift? How thoughtful!"

He dropped his helm and reached out for her hand. "My love, my dear, true love, I'm *so* sorry." He squeezed her fingers.

She sneered at him. "Broken record, Ares. Hephaestus beat you to that apology. You must come up with something more *creative.*"

He brought her palm to his lips and kissed it, sending wave after wave of lustful shivers down her spine.

No! I won't give in to you!

"But I *am* sorry. I had no choice. They wouldn't let me interfere. Our son... they're afraid my temperament will only make him worse. Your love is what he requires." He planted kisses all over her skin, his grip firm as he tugged her closer.

Her flesh burning as her heart hammered in her rib-cage, she retracted and shot backwards. "No!"

Eyebrows raised, Ares thrust the wrapped box against her belly. "But I have a gift for you, my sweet! Created by your husband and perfected by me. Please, take it."

Aphrodite hesitated, but snatched the present and ripped the paper. Inside was a box with a heart-shaped lock over its top.

"Only *you* can open it," said Ares, gaze grazing the ground. "It contains special god tranquilizing bullets that should aid you in immobilizing Eros. Father... doesn't know."

Aphrodite's fingertips caressed the box's smooth surface.

"You can put them in any regular handgun. They'll... stop him from doing any more harm. These are a last resort, so conceal them, and only use them if Eros finds *you* before you find him. He can also sense you, don't forget that."

Aphrodite tightened her grip on the box. "Hephaestus helped *you?* He hates you."

Ares chuckled. "Yes, but he *is* my brother, and we both care about your safety. You'll be vulnerable down there, and... Eros is angry. Who knows what he could do?" He caressed her cheek, his calloused hands scratching her skin but waking all sorts of repressed emotions in her gut.

She trembled at his touch, and, despite her bubbling anger, she grabbed his chin and dragged him closer to her. "He would not kill his mother." His breath, heavy with ambrosia, washed over her cheeks. "I... don't know what his problem is, but I'll find out without dying. Mortal or not."

Ares' presence somehow infused her with courage. And as he pulled her into a passionate kiss, she let him. He weaved his fingers through her curls and rubbed his chiseled chest against her cleavage, leaving her breathless and yearning for more.

And just like that, he slinked back into the shadows of the palace.

Teary-eyed, Aphrodite peered up at the white marble structure, the sun reflecting on its walls, its heavenly scent and warmth calling to her.

She didn't know if she'd ever be back, but she vowed she'd do her best to return.

Goodbye, Olympus.

‖ 7. MEET YOUR PARTNER ‖
LUKUS

"Agent Arvantis, speaking."

"Lukus! I'm sending you back-up," said the familiar voice of Lukus' supervisor, yelling from the other end of the line.

"Back-up?" Holding in his surprise, Lukus thwarted a cough. "Uh, okay... may I ask why?"

His boss grunted. "You may *not*, and she'll be arriving at your location within a few hours."

Lukus pursed his lips. "*She?*" He refrained from snorting. "I didn't know we had current female operatives at HQ. New hire?"

Women were fine agents, but he hadn't heard of any in his department. He rarely worked with ladies as much as he loved them—preferring to keep business and pleasure separate.

Wow, I'm a pig.

The supervisor scoffed. "A rookie, yeah. I figured I'd stick her with one of my best. And anyway, to tell you the truth, you're drowning. You could use another set of eyes."

Lukus' ego shattered to pieces. "Really, boss? A rookie, on this case?" He sighed. "I don't think that's a good idea. It's hard enough as it is, and if I have to watch out for a *newbie*, it won't help me solve this."

"It doesn't matter what *you* think. Her plane will land at Tacoma International soon, and then she'll head your way. Be nice, and look sharp—she's not what you expect." The supervisor hung up before Lukus could add another word.

He sat up from the bed where he lay glaring at his phone screen. "Great! Her name would have been helpful, boss!" He rubbed his forehead and checked the time.

Five-fifteen. Too early for a cocktail?

He splashed his face with water, spritzed a drop of his signature cologne, and changed his shirt, before checking his reflection as he dashed out of the room. Twirling a strand of ebony hair around his finger, he realized he needed a haircut. He shrugged and headed downstairs to the hotel bar, ready to drown his sorrows in alcohol.

* * *

So deep in conversation with the bartender—a lovely woman whose eyes were bluer than his—he started when someone tapped on his shoulder.

"What?" He jolted around, bracing to spit out some choice curse words—but the person standing before him was a bellboy, no more than eighteen years old. Lukus fixed his frown and flashed a weak smile. "What is it?"

The boy shifted his weight, chin tugging down. "Someone is waiting for you in the lobby, agent."

Lukus nodded and swiveled on his chair to gape at his drinking companion behind the bar. "Duty calls, doll. Maybe... we can continue this conversation later, closer to my room?"

The bartender blushed. "I can't sleep with guests," she whispered, her adorable shy grin tugging at Lukus' heartstrings.

Lukus winked. "I'm an FBI agent. I can compel you to comply." He deposited cash on the counter, his insides warming at the woman's gushing. She was too beautiful to be a barkeeper, and as he walked backwards out of the bar, he winked at her again. Once he'd concluded this business, he'd return to finish seducing her.

He pivoted in time to reach the hotel lobby—and to find it empty. "Uh... where is this person?" He searched for the bellboy, but he had disappeared.

Instead, Lukus caught sight of a woman standing near the glass doors, her rear end to him. Long, strawberry locks slid down to her waist, partially covering a brown trench coat that stopped below her knees. Her limbs were bare—she must have been wearing a skirt.

That's not who's waiting for me, right?

He couldn't see her face, but he had a knack for guessing if a woman was good looking from the back or not—and this one made his extremities tingle. They were alone; the rookie he expected hadn't arrived yet. Was the bellboy mistaken? Blowing into his hand to check his breath, he perked up and strolled up to the woman—forgetting about the barkeep he flirted with seconds before.

She spun around, almost in slow motion, and her face was glowing, gorgeous, *heavenly.* Lukus' heart stopped at her eyes, so bright he saw them from feet away. Green as shining emeralds, deeper than the sea. Her pale skin, creamy like silk, and her delicately flushed cheeks. And of course, his gaze settled on her lips—plump, rosy, slightly parted as if inviting him to press his against them.

Gulping down his initial shock, he arched his spine. "Well, well, hello there sweetheart—"

"—Lukus Arvantis?" Her voice, raspy, gently provocative, cut him off.

Her coat was open, revealing a fitting green dress, the same shade as her irises. It stopped above the length of the raincoat, showing off her gorgeous figure.

She knew his name, like an angel straight out of his imagination. His mouth watered as he fought to control his emotions—and urges. "Y-yes? Who's asking?"

Please, don't let me wake up, if this is a dream.

The nearer he got, the less confidence simmered in his gut. Each step he took brought him closer to her, and an aura of perfection floated around her, turning her iridescent. Every curve on her body made his pants tighter. The surrounding lobby faded, leaving only the woman and her glowing gaze violently digging into him, speaking to his soul.

"Agnes? Your new partner? I thought your boss told you about me." Her tone shifted to one sweeter than caramel dripping from a candied apple.

Lukus licked his lips. He focused on the swaying of her jacket, the way her legs rubbed against one another, calling him over to caress them. She batted her eyelashes, and as she sent her palm to rest on her hip and blinked at him, he found it impossible to breathe.

For a second, he hesitated. Was she another role-playing prostitute? And *how* did she know he was expecting the rookie?

She's too good to be true.

Maybe she overheard him talking at the bar. He ambled closer, in a trance, unable to stop. Every cavity in his brain filled with images of her smiling, biting her lip, lifting her finger to beckon him—

"Hello? Lukus? Are you okay?" She waved at him, but his gaze remained glazed. "You seem nauseous."

He peered at her legs again, then lingered on the brown high heels she wore. He *loved* high heels. His belt would burst off his pants at any moment, he was certain. But he couldn't react; he was on a cloud, his steps padded, his brain turned to mush as he let her absorb him.

The delectable lady snapped her fingers as she stomped up to him. "I'm not here to play games."

"Huh? What's happening?" He shook his head, and the hotel lobby in all its shabby shades of brown and gray came back into view—along with *her* frustrated expression.

"Where is the real Lukus? I need to meet with him." She crossed her arms. "I'm Agnes, the new agent assigned to his case. Our boss wanted me to get up to speed as soon as possible."

Lukus' lucid thoughts weaved into his skull—and he gasped.

"She's not what you expect..."

"*Shit,* that's what he meant?" He dragged his palm over his face.

The woman tapped her foot to the ground. "Excuse me?"

Wow, I've already made an ass of myself. What a great first impression!

He descended from his cloud, his temples throbbing as if he smacked his head on the way down. With no clue how she enraptured him so, he extended a hand, forcing an embarrassed smile. "I'm *so* sorry. Long day, lots to drink. Agnes, it's a pleasure to meet you."

Agnes' concerned features changed, and she smiled as she reached out to his fingertips. A jolt of electricity coursed through his veins as their hands touched. All Lukus' earlier sensations returned. She was *hot*. The most gorgeous specimen he'd ever seen, by far.

But when she pulled away, the cloud of lust hanging over him dissipated. "*Charmed.* Is there somewhere we can sit and talk? You must have plenty to fill me in on."

He shook away his perverted thoughts and witty comebacks, and nodded, showing her the way to a table near the hotel bar. "I'm sure you'd rather get some rest, no? I could take you up to your room instead." He cringed, realizing how crude he sounded.

Lukus, she's your partner, dammit!

Agnes stepped around him, heels clicking on the tiles. "No, I'd rather not waste time. I slept on the plane."

He followed her into the bar, and as she sat on one of the stained cushions before the rickety table, she passed her right leg over her left. Lukus shivered as she tossed her hair side to side and pouted.

Fuck. Fuck, fuck, fuck.

"Where did you travel from?" He fought his instincts and averted his gaze to her eyes. Sparkling oceans of pleasure, causing a stiffness in his lower body—

Stop! Look away—Anywhere but at her!

"Boston." She slipped her raincoat to the back of her chair, revealing her porcelain, baby doll skin. "I don't get out here often, I wasn't quite prepared for the weather." She picked up a drink menu and flipped through it.

To keep his cool, he waved at a passing server. "Aren't you transferring to DC?" He ordered a beer and waited as Agnes requested a complicated cocktail he would never remember the name of.

"I did, a few weeks ago." She reached for something in her coat pocket. "But Boston... I was, uh, visiting family there." She pulled out a small notebook and a pen.

Lukus squinted at her, drumming his fingers on the table. New agents didn't have time to visit family, of that he was positive. Between training and being on the job, rookies barely slept.

"Anyway, let's get started," said Agnes, her voice official, sharp. "What are we looking at?" She seemed unaware of the power of her beauty and tapped her pen on the paper. "Murders, right?"

Lukus cleared his throat. "Uh... allegedly. No murder weapon or motive yet, though, and no connection between victims so far. No connection between the locations either... it's weird, even for me."

Agnes jotted down a few words without looking down, her gaze fixed on Lukus. "How many? And where have they occurred?"

Lukus' head slipped backwards as he gaped at her. "Ah, uh..." He stuttered, unsure if he should be turned on by her professionalism or freaked out by her striking potential. "*Five*. San Francisco, Miami, New York City, Chicago, and now, Seattle. Hopefully that's it, but... they all happened out of nowhere, no warning."

Their drinks arrived, and if only to keep his hands occupied, he snatched his beer. The freezing glass chilled his burning questions, and he tipped the bottle to his lips, pinching his eyes closed.

"Murderers don't warn you before they kill you," said Agnes, writing a few more sentences. "Any traces of poison, toxins in the blood?" Lukus shook his head. "And no murder weapon? Not even a clue what it could be if there is one?"

Lukus couldn't catch his breath. Why was she so eager to hear it all now?

Can't she wait until tomorrow?

He'd gladly hand over all his files and notes; but tonight, she needed to relax. Sink that lovely body of hers into a bubble bath—

Shut up!

"I mean, if you consider the victim's hands as weapons, then that's it. They snatched each other's hearts out, according to witnesses." Agnes didn't flinch, and Lukus raised his eyebrows. "Whoa... that *doesn't* freak you out?"

"Cannibalism? Well... no. Disgusting as it is. This case is... interesting." She scribbled and turned the page. "But no sign of someone provoking it or aiding the victims to eat each other, I assume? No specific wounds like a bullet hole or scrapes in the arms resembling *needle* injections?"

Lukus concealed his surprise by downing half his beverage in one large gulp. Despite her unwavering beauty, she'd piqued his curiosity—who was this overqualified bombshell who looked nothing like an FBI agent and had no qualms about working on such a fucked-up case?

Something doesn't smell right.

"None of that, no… well, we're not sure about the provocation part, though." As his body screamed to press into hers, he leaned forward over the table. "Say, Agnes, how much experience do you have? You seem to, uh… know your stuff."

Agnes narrowed her eyes. "Enough to realize you're dealing with something you've *never* dealt with, and your boss wanted you to have help." She closed her notebook and sipped from her drink using the neon yellow straw provided. As she smacked her lips and licked a few drops from the corners of her mouth, Lukus' thoughts went wild. He chugged the rest of his beer to not drop his jaw at the perfect creature sitting across from him.

He deposited the empty bottle on the table and considered ordering another. "I mean, you don't *look* like an agent. That's… not the typical outfit, even for women. I'd say you're a professor, or a lawyer." He admired ladies in his field—but she didn't appear as one. Not that he was complaining; he only hoped she was as capable as she sounded.

That dress on the job… might be dangerous.

Agnes snorted. "I'm revolutionizing female FBI agent outfits, then!" She sat up straight, her lip curling. "But if *this* disturbs you, I promise I have more fitting attire in my luggage." With a huff, she slurped up every ounce of her refreshment. "On that note, maybe I should head to my room. I expect to go over all the gruesome details in the morning. Does that work?" She stood up, plastering a polite smile on her face as she grabbed her coat.

Great, she already hates me. So smooth, Lukus.

He was about to reply when his cell phone rang, interrupting their exchange. Removing the device from his pocket, he grimaced at the unidentified number.

"Hold that thought, would you? I'd like to walk you to your room, just give me a second," he said as he pressed the green button to pick up the call.

Agnes groaned, but nodded.

"Agent Arvantis, speaking."

I hope it's the coroner's office this time.

"Agent, thank you for answering. This is Sheriff Rodriguez, Las Vegas Police Department. I'm sorry to inform you that there have been two more victims in your cannibalism case."

Lukus filled his cheeks with air, then released with a moan. "Uh... great, hang on." He pulled the receiver away from his mouth. "Don't bother going up to your room yet. Looks like we'll be heading to Las Vegas."

I loathe Las Vegas.

‖8. AGNES/APHRODITE‖
APHRODITE

Aphrodite sprawled over the small bed in her hotel room as flashing lights from the Strip below poured in through the window.

That was intense.

She had never been so drained, confused, and disgusted. Even as a goddess, she had encountered nothing like... that.

Throwing her shoes off, she breathed out. "Those things *hurt!* How in Tartarus do women wear them?"

Rubbing the soles of her feet, she closed her eyes, hoping to relax—and instead, her mind swam with all the gruesome details from the crime scene she and agent Arvantis viewed moments before.

Those poor souls.

Two bodies—one male, one female. Their skin burnt—*gone* in the chest area—and their hearts missing. Ounces of blood on their clothes, bellies, arms, and all over the concrete.

She shuddered, dropping her foot onto the scratchy covers. Even Dionysus's frenzies never caused so much horror.

None of the beasts Heracles faced provoked such fear. And she doubted Zeus himself ever witnessed such brutality.

But she kept her cool, the whole time. She showed her *skills*, analyzing the scene, taking efficient notes, remaining discreet. And Lukus' impressed expression proved she did her job right.

She smiled; despite all the terror, she knew she could pretend to be an FBI agent with decency. Lukus put her in charge of witness accounts while he further examined the bodies and the scenes. And the comments rang in her skull, making her temples throb.

"A flash of blinding white light came out of nowhere."

"They shoved their hands through the skin of their chests. Through the skin! They pierced it! What the hell?"

"Oh, they ate each other's hearts. I saw it. It was nasty business. Ate the whole damn thing until they collapsed."

Her skin crawled imagining it all. Her breath caught in her throat as the voices filled her mind—repeating, resonating, deafening. The gods didn't endorse cannibalism. Aphrodite went as far as calling this *carnivorous* though not out loud.

That was no human's doing.

But no godly creature she knew of was capable of snatching hearts like so, either.

She stretched, her muscles tight for the first time in her long life. Her body ached in ways she wasn't aware were possible, and the pronounced pain in her scalp reminded her of her new condition.

Partially human.

Horrendous.

She chuckled, reviewing Zeus' hand-written instructions in her head.

Agnes.

It made her cringe. Yes, it was Greek, and yes, it started with an A; but it was *repulsive*. Her name was Aphrodite—a powerful, ancient name that inferred love and awe whenever it was uttered.

But no one would utter it down here.

"*Ugh,* I need a bath!" She stood and stripped her clothes, and the soreness in her legs amplified with her every move. How she wished she could call a cupbearer to draw an ambrosia and rose petal bath for her; sending heavenly scents around the room, accompanied by the soft hum of her favorite harpist.

Arriving in the hotel bathroom, she sneered—*that* was the tub she was to bathe in? Grimy, grossly green-colored and barely big enough to fit her? It was so close to the toilet and sink she wondered how anyone could move about in the tiny space. And upon turning on the light, she noticed the peeling, brownish wallpaper and the off-white tile, stained in areas, broken in others. Nothing like the glorious gilded opulence of her bathroom in Olympus—its diamond encrusted marble glittering under the flickering chandelier than dangled over her ten-seater tub. This was *not* the luxury mega-hotel on the Strip she had hoped for.

Welcome to Las Vegas, Aphrodite.

Lukus hadn't warned her of the dire conditions FBI forced their agents to live in during their travels, and she missed the copper-inlaid Olympus hallways more than she wanted to admit.

With a sigh, and thankful for her basic knowledge of earthly machines and inventions, she prepared her own bath, stretching as she waited for the tub to fill. Unpleasant as the bathroom was, Aphrodite stopped complaining once she slipped into the scorching water. It soothed her aching limbs as she soaked, rehashing the events of the week.

Deprived of most of her powers, thrown down from her home, given a new—and fake—identity, and told to investigate her son's murderous activities.

Fabulous, no?

She moaned, pulling herself underwater.

Eros had turned lethal, there was no doubt about it. And whatever his issue, he had a *lot* of rage. She had never known him this way; so furious, so wrathful. So, what would compel him to use these emotions on earthlings?

She couldn't shake the image of the blood. Splattered everywhere, oozing, thick; at first, it appeared so abundant that Aphrodite thought it might have splashed all over her dress when she arrived on the scene. Then her humanly senses took over, prompting her to panic.

She hated human emotions. Too intense, overbearing, frustrating. When in goddess form, she had enough feelings already; but now, as *Agnes*, she had to learn to control her urges and paranoia all over again. And also conceal them.

A few bubbles popped on the water's surface, and she looked down at her perfect curves.

I should tone down my aura...

She gaped at her legs, her arms, her breasts, recalling how men ogled her at the crime site, almost drooling—and how Lukus had a constant jaw-dropping air about him whenever she had stood too close to him.

Zeus was right, though she hated to admit it: her charms were too much for humans. Poor Lukus could barely keep it in his pants in Seattle. When he first found her, he looked ready to burst.

She giggled. As the goddess of love and beauty, it was her *goal* to arouse such pleasure—but as the boring mortal Agnes, she had to be careful.

As she blew the bubbles from her skin, she smirked. Her heart belonged to Ares, yes; but Lukus was *cute.* His attraction was flattering. His tousled ebony tresses, his piercing navy eyes, his olive complexion—he had the appearance of a god. And she enjoyed his attention though she wasn't here for that.

He snapped into professional mode after the call about the Vegas murder, but his interest lingered in his gaze. She had to keep her coat closed and leave several inches between them at all times to avoid temptation—which had been difficult on the plane ride.

A twinge of shame forced itself into her gut as she realized she may struggle to work with someone so handsome. And yet, despite it all, Ares was the only one who had access to her heart. The only one she dreamed of at night. Her Olympian prince, her soulmate.

And I'll only see you again if I fix our son's mess.

She had no time to waste on romances with mortals.

She exited the bathtub and wrapped herself in a rough towel. And padding over to the bedroom, she threw her suitcase onto the bed and pried it open, hoping to discover something to wear for bedtime.

She had no idea what was *in* it. Zeus had it waiting for her when she dropped into Seattle; that, and the hand-written instructions were all she had to navigate this adventure. She didn't even have a last name.

Digging through the contents of the case, she prayed for something comfortable, and also for a less provocative outfit for tomorrow. It relieved her to uncover a pair of simple beige trousers, and a white, long sleeve and collared shirt—though she had no other shoes aside from those she wore with the dress.

I can't wear those monsters anymore.

She rummaged through the suitcase, desperate. She needed new pumps. How would one go about getting some before tomorrow, without leaving the hotel? And at such a late hour—it had to be well past two a.m.

She dropped onto the squeaky mattress with a huff. In Olympus, she'd only snap her fingers, or summon a cupbearer. But as a mortal... she was powerless. So how did *they* get things?

As she massaged her scalp, racking her brain, something on the nightstand caught her eye. She moved closer to it and picked it up—a menu of services offered by the hotel.

"Room service. Laundry. Bellboy. Concierge... *Concierge?"* She turned to the indicated page. "That sounds familiar. Can't *they* go fetch me whatever I need?"

One service had to be some type of *servant.* All she needed was payment.

That's how individuals get what they want.

She grumbled, unsure if she had any money. She didn't recall finding any in her suitcase and doubted she carried any in her coat pockets either.

"Damn humans! Damn airplanes and cars and hotels! And damn clothes and shoes... and *money!"* She shot up, stomping about like a raving lunatic. "Why can't they imitate us? We only wear sandals! We don't use currency, we eat ambrosia, we drink delicious wine!" She moaned. "Where did Zeus go wrong with this lot?"

In all her stomping about, her purse toppled over by the nightstand—the purse she had when arriving at the hotel lobby in Seattle. And from within it spilled several items—one of them a small leathery folder. Her eyes widened as she lunged over to grab it.

A... wallet?

She vaguely remembered these shabby little things—they contained money. With a squeak, she snatched the smooth auburn-colored folder and took a deep breath. There had to be something of worth in it. Zeus wouldn't leave her human *and* poor, would he?

She snickered. "Oh, he *would.*"

Her features relaxed when she found several cards in the wallet—credit cards. One was black, with an *American Express* logo on it, and a sticker on it saying *Company Card.*

"Ah... does that mean it's from the FBI? And I can use it for... work-related purchases?"

She stared at her high heels across the room. Their discomfort *was* a work-related issue.

Convinced, she picked up the phone on the bedside table and dialed the number for the Concierge. "I need someone to buy me shoes. *Now.* It's important."

The man on the other end laughed. "Yes *ma'am*, I'll send someone up to uh... get your size and requirements." He chuckled more and coughed as he hung up.

Did these humans think she was *funny?* Her situation was no laughing matter.

Returning to the suitcase, she fished out something suitable to wear as nighttime attire—a T-shirt and shorts—and lay on the bed.

Perhaps human behavior was why Eros snapped. He grew sick of them and their twisted humor, their rudeness, their unwillingness to cease wars and get along. Maybe he couldn't take it anymore and believed humans didn't deserve his love; so he killed them to make a point.

Plausible as it was, she shook her head. "No, not my Eros."

She recalled her sweet boy, learning how to shoot arrows with his brother, Anteros. Playing in the gardens of Olympus as other gods watched in awe at his skill. Her little angel, his fluffy wings batting as he learned to fly. The strong, handsome youth who grew into a gentle and caring adult.

She held back the tears forming on her lash line. No, Eros wouldn't attack humans without a *real* reason.

Waves of sadness slid under her skin, and she huffed as she brushed away the water swelling in her eyes. If she showed weakness, if the agent saw her like this... he'd become suspicious. And he couldn't be. Not before she found Eros' motive—and stopped him.

She sat up straight. "Tomorrow, you will be Agnes, and you will play your part. You will be a *real* human and pretend to know what you're doing. You'll do everything you can to help Lukus and find out what Eros is doing and why."

A soft knock startled her, and she scrambled up from the bed, fixing her face into an angry glare. Under her breath, she hissed. "But tonight, you're *still* Aphrodite—and you need shoes." She tiptoed to the door, grabbing the brown heels on her way.

A young man waited, features sunken, hollow, almost sickly. But his eyes were kind, and he perked up when he glimpsed her. "You... requested assistance, ma'am?" His pupils bulged as his gaze wandered over the forms beneath her T-shirt, landing on her bare legs.

Snapping her fingers to get his attention, she lifted the horrid pumps up to his face. "I need comfortable shoes! Same size as these!" She thrust them closer to him and then shoved her form of payment under his nose. "And I can pay! I have a *credit card.*"

The bellhop barely caught the card before it fell to the ground and held the shoes against his chest. "So, like... flats?"

She cocked her head. "Uh... *flat,* yes! No heels!"

"Okay... and did you want a specific c-color? Brand?"

Aphrodite paused. Colors and brands—how would she know this?

Servants don't ask questions, they obey!

"I-I... don't care! Basic, something that goes with everything! And *definitely* no heels, those things are Hades incarnate!"

The boy inclined his head, but didn't move as he examined her, his mouth parting.

"What are you waiting for?" She pointed at the heels and credit card in his possession. "I need them *now!* Hurry! You have my form of payment, so go!"

Sick of his hesitation, she slammed the door; and when she heard him run off, she exhaled—though she was far from relieved. She spooked the hotel staff.

Maybe I should be Agnes tonight, too.

‖ 9. A GODLY PRESENCE ‖
EROS

Flying high above the clouds, Eros sniffed the air. Was that *her?* He couldn't tell. As his wings flapped, keeping him far from the ground, he sighed. It was almost sunrise, and he had the best of views; he refused to burden himself with negative thoughts—not right now.

And yet, as the yellows and oranges and pinks filled the sky, an eerie thought slipped into his mind, troubling him more than he wished.

He *did* feel something down in Nevada. An energy he was familiar with, a powerful presence—but *was* it her? Was she in Las Vegas?

Did she sense me, too?

He stopped in mid-air, wings rising and lowering, his body suspended. He crossed his arms and closed his eyes, drawing strength from the breeze and the clouds to better focus.

Maybe I should go back.

If that godly sensation he had was really who he thought, he should turn around. She needed him, and he couldn't leave her there on her own. But the bow in his backpack, heavy, coated with blood, reminded him of his burden. Wincing, he knew he had no choice. He had to move onward and finish his task.

He opened his eyes and uncrossed his arms as a tear fell down to his chin. His wings yanked him higher, the wind catching in his hair, splashing all over his face. The tear vanished as quickly as it appeared.

There's much to do.

Eros resumed his journey though still unsure of his destination. He dipped, soaring lower, farther from the rising sun and closer to the horrible place he compared to Tartarus. He found it *worse*. Earth; the terrible planet that allowed humans to live, their heartbeats sickening the more he encountered them. Flying was his only—albeit temporary—escape. But he wouldn't stop now, despite his disgust. He wouldn't tolerate interruptions. His final goal was to find *her*, but his torture of humans had to proceed. His persecution of the gods had to resume.

I must make them all pay.

Overcome with pride at the mastery of his plans, excited at the satisfaction the squelch of blood gave him, he grinned from ear to ear. She would thank him, he knew. She'd be flattered. What he did was to save them all, and soon, they'd see it too. They'd understand it was for the greater good.

I'm not the bad guy.

He pushed his golden curls out of his eyes. Gods didn't care about humans. No, they made it clear—he'd instigated the slaughter of six pairs of soulmates, and yet they lingered on their thrones, uncaring. Likely plotting which new goddess to rape or capture, which hero to send on an impossible mission, which cupbearer to abuse without remorse.

These gods—his family—were evil, and he planned to punish them. But he didn't blame them all equally; one, in particular, would receive a higher, more painful punishment. He'd make sure of it.

He cackled, pleased that no one would hear him.

Realizing he needed to see the world below, he plunged through a cloud. And as the smoky, almost silk-like substance caressed his cheeks, a sudden surge of panic took over him.

Dread like this *never* coursed through him, and yet now, it sunk into every inch of his soul. What if he was mistaken, and what he sensed *wasn't* her? Did the gods send someone down? Someone who caught onto his pattern?

I need to be more careful.

His irises fluttered about as if searching for a solution among the blurry landscapes. The power he had perceived was real, substantial, intimidating. *She* couldn't be that strong. It had to be someone... higher up.

An Olympian?

An unwanted tension spread to his shoulders, and his wings flapped too fast, rendering him dizzy, unsteady. His pupils darted back and forth, glancing at the horizon, desperate for answers.

But no matter his unease, his killing spree had to go on. He needed to make a point before they caught him. Whoever trailed him would expect him to sense them, but he had to stay one step ahead. Always. If someone hunted him, he was in deeper trouble than he anticipated; which meant he needed a new city. *Now.*

Expelling a heavy breath, he dipped below another layer of clouds, camouflaging inside the vapors. He peered beneath him, piecing together where he arrived; by watching the sights, taking in the scenery, inhaling the air.

Louisiana... is this New Orleans?

He rubbed his hands, pleased—a new town had surfaced as if on command. As if fate desired him to continue his plot. New Orleans would become city number seven. And perhaps he'd stay here a little longer if things went as planned. Not out of enjoyment, but out of duty—he smelled the sin from miles away.

He shot downwards, aiming for an empty alleyway in one of the worst and roughest areas of town. He directed himself with his wings, buzzing past buildings at a frighteningly dizzying speed. Here, his rugged appearance would go unnoticed. His crime wouldn't seem so unlikely. A place so full of lust and blood—not unlike Vegas—that his murders wouldn't appear so horrendous.

They might blend in.

He landed on the ground and brushed dust and dirt off his leather ensemble, readjusting the strap of his bag over his shoulder. His wings shrunk and eased themselves back inside his jacket, slithering into his skin. He smirked, glimpsing the street that awaited his footsteps. Loud music erupted down the alley as he sighted half-dressed women hanging from iron balconies lining brick buildings, still full of life despite the early hour. Inebriated passersby hobbled from sidewalk to sidewalk in search of a drink, a party, and a new friend.

"Come and find me *now,* Mother. I dare you."

‖10. MYSTERIES AT BREAKFAST‖
LUKUS

When she arrived in the lobby the next morning, Agnes had transformed her appearance. Lukus eyed her as she approached, her hips swaying with every movement, her hair straightened, long, flowing behind her, and her demeanor much more understated, almost relaxed. But he saw through the act; she was nervous. Her gaze unfocused, her shoulders tight, her steps uneven.

Poor rookie.

Though she controlled the crazy aura that used to surround her—he no longer got the unexplained urge to *jump* her—her wrinkling nose further showed her discomfort. Ditching the sexy look, she wore beige slacks, a white shirt, comfortable flats. And the tunic was *definitely* see-through... but an improvement.

She had the airs of an FBI agent.

Lukus struggled to hide his happiness as he ambled closer to her, pleased to concentrate on something other than her voluptuous frame, and hoping this time, he wouldn't get absorbed in some weird trance.

He smiled, and though she smiled back, the gesture was far from enthusiastic.

"Good morning," she said as her eyes met his, lighter than before, but shining all the same.

He'd drown in them if he allowed himself, so he glanced askance as he nodded. "How... did you sleep?" He adjusted his collar. "Was your room up to your... standards?"

The pull wasn't as strong—but it *was* there. He saw her black bra through her shirt, and, perking up to shake away all the bad thoughts slithering into his mind, he turned from her again. He didn't hear her response as he led her outside.

"Would you like breakfast? I was thinking of grabbing a bite and going over case notes with you," he said.

"Sure," she said, her voice solemn, her hair bouncing as she walked beside Lukus.

He fought to stop himself from weaving his fingers through her strawberry blonde strands, from staring into her eyes and pressing his lips against hers, slipping his hands under her shirt—

Jeez, Lukus, calm down!

He exhaled and called for a cab.

Unable to look at her, he sensed her presence beside him; a strong perfume he didn't recognize. Yet it filled his nostrils and expanded into his lungs, making it hard for him to breathe. How was he supposed to act normal and chit-chat with her when every ounce of him almost begged him to *take* her? Even though she exuded less confidence than last night—she appeared shyer, smaller, a little less prepared—her body so close to his only roused his desire.

Knock it off!

He shifted beside her, awkwardly searching for a way to start a conversation. "So, uh..."

"I'm not too fond of Las Vegas," she said, her gaze pointed towards the street ahead. They were at the end of the Strip—the bad part of it—and cars zoomed by, in a rush to reach their destinations. Surrounded by famous skyscraper-style hotels with flashing banners and promises to win jackpots, Agnes seemed swallowed by the scenery as she waited for their ride.

Yearning to help her relax, Lukus turned to her and grinned. "Ah, we can agree on that." He waved at the cab pulling in. "I would've preferred to stay in Seattle."

Even as they marched to the vehicle, he realized something had changed in her. So outspoken and passionate the night before, she was now calm and poised, a different person. Overwhelmed by the immensity of the city, she wasn't as intimidating.

Maybe all she needed was a good night's sleep; being a rookie was exhausting.

They ushered inside the car, and Lukus gave the address of a breakfast place he frequented whenever he was in town, his stomach growling in anticipation.

As the cab rolled on, they talked, avoiding anything relating to the job. Agnes was friendly but reserved; which made Lukus question her ability to perform on this case, despite her shocking abilities from the previous night.

She seemed so young. Barely looked above twenty-two, fresh out of school, innocent and unknowing. Was the boss sure this fieldwork would do for her? Did he need her to start with such a hard case?

Lukus drank in her features. He hated for such things to swirl in his mind, but she appeared so delicate and sweet, in her revised outfit and calmer nature. Did the boss want to test her? Scare her? Be sure she chose the right path?

Once they arrived at the restaurant, Lukus requested an isolated table away from any curious customers and ordered coffee for them both.

"Oh, crap." He groaned. "I'm sorry, I didn't mean to *order* for you. It's just... they have the best brew in town, so I assumed..."

She flashed him a tiny smile. "It's fine. I'll try it."

He placed his briefcase on the chair beside him and set up paperwork all over the table, handing a few files to Agnes, who sat across from him. She took the documentation, and the face she had worn the night before reappeared—trepidation, eagerness, and a hint of excitement.

Lukus cleared his throat. "So, here's the deal. Though all five murders—six, if we count yesterday—are similar, I can't prove that there is a connection ."

Agnes reviewed the menu with one hand, and held paperwork in the other, switching her eyes between the two. "Why not? Were there not enough similarities to link them?" She wrinkled her nose a few times, an air of disgust in her expression as she perused the food selection.

He cocked his head, torn between fascination and wonder at her demeanor. If she'd worn high heels today, he would have pounced on her, he knew it.

Unwilling to relive his hiccup from when they first met, he ignored the heat spreading across his cheekbones as he pulled out another document and handed it to her. "There are *many* similarities, yet something doesn't add up. The locations, the people, the time of day... *these* are different, and make it difficult to figure out a motive or a true link."

Agnes set down the menu and took the paper. "So, six different cities... twelve individuals with *no* connection... and all murders committed in various areas of each city, at random times."

The coffee arrived, and she glared at it for a time, as if angry it had interrupted her thinking process.

Lukus snatched his mug but watched her as she hesitantly added a splash of cream to hers and brought the cup to her mouth. She sipped, sneered, then placed the drink back down.

"Oh my, that's... well, I suppose it must do." She licked her lips all while scrunching her eyebrows, discomfort plastered all over her expression. And before Lukus had a chance to comment, she fixed herself and lifted the documents up to better see them. "And I'd say whoever the murderer is, wants to play games. He or she is purposely screwing around to confuse us. Choosing victims who *appear* to mean nothing, to not be connected... which would keep us out of the loop, keep us searching as he... or *she*... plots more assassinations."

After a shrug, she pushed the mug away and slid the document onto Lukus' side of the table.

He blinked, hoping his jaw didn't show how close it was to dropping. Maybe he had misjudged her—*how could she not like it?*—and she was wittier than she looked.

Unable to stop his curiosity, he squinted at her mug. "Do you not drink coffee?"

Agnes chuckled. "Oh no, I love it. But not this *crap*," she retorted, almost making Lukus fall off his chair.

He wasn't sure whether to laugh or take offense—or be turned on by her language. "How... I mean, why? Are you saying my... taste in coffee *sucks?*"

She smirked, and Lukus had to hold in a squeal at her adorable cheeks puffing and her flustered complexion. "I'm sorry, I... prefer it from Europe. I'm picky. To each their own."

Lukus relaxed his face, but his intrigue remained. "Are you *from* Europe?" In truth, he wanted to ask how the FBI had found her, and how she ended up here, with him. Such an exotic beauty who liked foreign coffee and spoke as if she had been an agent for years—though appearing so cautious and quiet on the outside.

He sipped his beverage, and for a moment he wondered if he *did* enjoy the flavor.

Pursing his lips, he held in a snort.

She's a snob.

She nodded. "From Greece. Born and raised."

Lukus' eyebrows inched up. Greece? He recalled his own Greek roots and wondered if *that* was why the boss stuck Agnes with him.

Did he put us together to see if we would get along because of our origins?

He shook away the feeling, and they ordered food.

As they waited, Lukus showed her pictures of the first five crime scenes. "The *situation* is similar," he said, handing each picture to Agnes for her to analyze. "Though the areas of each town were different, the murderer made sure it happened near crowds or busy streets. The bodies were recovered in the middle of massive tourist spots, and it was hard to contain the area and avoid curious eyes."

He pushed the images towards her, gauging her reactions. Agnes checked each photo, and as gruesome as they were, she didn't flinch, gag, or panic. Her face was bland, devoid of emotion, stone cold.

Lukus contained his confusion, but he struggled to understand how she wasn't disgusted. The night prior, when they arrived on the Vegas crime scene, she hadn't flinched either. He had worked with the FBI for years, and yet the bodies unsettled *him.* Had she seen this kind of case before?

Is that *why the chief sent her to me?*

She took out her notebook and flipped it to a new page. "Always a man and a woman?"

He guzzled down a few swigs of the caffeine, again wondering *how* she couldn't like it. "The second case was two men, actually, now that I think about it. Which threw me off... but I didn't have much time to further look into that."

" *None* of these victims have any connection amongst themselves. Curious." She hummed, staring between the pictures and her notepad. "Interesting. Well, as I said, it *could* be random, or... premeditated. Made to *appear* random though it's not. I say... we'd best dig into the victim's pasts and make sure we didn't miss anything. Even the most insignificant detail could lead us to the killer, or show a connection we might have missed."

She jotted down a few sentences, but Lukus wasn't able to see what.

He shrugged. "I've done that. And full autopsies on the bodies to determine if anything else was missing, besides the hearts. The results were inconclusive."

Agnes glanced up. "Then you didn't dig deep enough. I'm not just talking about a connection between the twelve victims, I'm talking about the two at *each* crime site. What is *their* connection? Why them? *That's* what we should dive into."

Lukus wanted to nod—but instead he gulped, helpless to stop his gaze from zooming over her notes and wondering what she recorded on each page. Smart and witty, sure; but did she not realize this was the *sixth* murder in the case? How could she not assume he explored all options?

"I agree, but that's *also* something I've looked into, to no avail." He crossed his arms, upset that she would question his training. He was the lead on the case, after all; who was *she* to tell him how to proceed?

Agnes shoved the pictures towards him. "You're missing something, agent. There's more to this than you think, I know it. There *is* a connection, and you may have to step outside the box if you want to find it."

Though compelled to put her in her place, Lukus instead filled his cheeks with air and tilted his head back to gape at the ceiling. Giving him orders and telling him how to do his job?

I don't think so.

He slammed his half-empty coffee mug on the table, a few drops spilling onto his hand. "If I may, what *is* your training? Your background in this type of work? Do you believe you have more experience than me?" When Agnes didn't bat an eyelash and instead cocked a brow, Lukus regretted his outburst, realizing how unprofessional he had sounded. "Agnes, I—"

"—I don't *believe* that's any of your concern," she said, clasping her hands on the table. "Your superiors esteemed me good enough to join you on this case, and whatever my experience is shouldn't matter. I'm here to provide fresh insight because, let's be honest, you're drowning."

Lukus' jaw fell, and he did nothing to stop it. Seconds ago, he wanted to apologize for being so rude, but her condescending tone convinced him otherwise. "Who are you to talk? You have *some* nerve!"

Agnes shoved her palm against his mouth to silence him. And though his eyes widened, and shock spread through him like lightning bolts in a dark stormy sky, he had no choice but to wait for her to speak.

Who the fuck does she think she is?

"Listen here, agent Arvantis. Six murders in six different cities in three weeks. You've found no connection, no murder weapon, and you have no leads on a suspect. Would you say you're doing a good job?"

Lukus raised his shoulders, powerless to speak thanks to her lotioned hands.

And crazy strength.

He battled to push her away and grumbled before moaning in displeasure.

She leaned in closer. "That's what I thought." Her nails dug into the skin around his mouth. "I'm not trying to tell you what to do, I only hope to guide you in the right direction. *You* are the lead, and I won't take credit for your findings, but there will *be* no credit if you don't step out of your comfort zone and research new outcomes and options. Do you get where I'm going with this?"

Lukus shrugged again.

I get that you're psycho, and that's all!

She dropped her hand. "Lukus, you may be dealing with something... *different*. These murders... you might not be able to explain them, but *I* can. Let me work with you, and hear me out, okay? Don't dismiss me." Her voice turned smoother, and she peered away, biting her lip.

He replaced his jaw. "What *are* you?" Wiping his mouth, he stared at the mysterious beauty seated across from him, her features impossible to read. "And what the fuck are you talking about? Are... are we *not* dealing with a good old serial killer, according to you?"

Though he could have had her fired on the spot for such behavior, he couldn't help it; she intrigued him, and he needed to understand what she saw in the case.

Agnes shook her head. "We are, but... not a human one."

Lukus' jaw dropped—again. And this time, he thought he might have broken it.

‖11. PROVE IT‖
APHRODITE

Shoot.

If she didn't recover quick, Lukus would get suspicious.

"I... I mean non-human as in *animal*." Her voice came through as less than confident, but she prayed he'd believe her.

Luckily, their order arrived, breaking the moment—pancakes and eggs for him, egg whites and turkey bacon for her. She crinkled her nose at the aspect of eating *human* food, but at least it would halt their discussion.

As his breakfast steamed before him, Lukus lowered his eyebrows. "I... well..." He huffed, snatching his coffee to take a few sips.

Peering down at her fork and nearly choking at having to eat the blobs of color on her plate, she sighed. "Think about it. The hearts missing, the gory scenes... I *can't* explain the flashes of light, but an animal attack *would* be plausible, wouldn't it?"

She picked up her utensil and slid a bite of the liquid-like, squishy egg stuff into her mouth. Doing her best not to cringe, she chewed and swallowed, wondering why she didn't sneak ambrosia out of Olympus when she left.

The substance turned plastic.

This is horrifying.

Lukus drenched his pancake in maple syrup, and Aphrodite held in the bile rising in her throat as the sickeningly sweet scent crept up her nostrils.

"I... suppose," he said, putting the syrup on the table. "But what kind of animal does *that?* Eats human hearts? That's so specific and... *carnivorous.* I didn't realize we had any animals of the sort in the United States." He took a bite, and though he smiled at the flavor, hesitance sprinkled across his features as he looked at Aphrodite.

She forced the rest of the egg whites down and attempted the bacon. She beamed as the crunchy meat slid over her tongue, the salty, savory flavor pleasing her.

If only all human food was like this.

"I've... never read of such animals either, so... we should do further research." The bacon crunched and its taste filled her with happiness. "Could it be something someone brought home with them from a foreign country to keep as a pet? Isn't that a trend nowadays?" She washed it down with water and watched as Lukus devoured his pancakes.

He didn't make a mess as she would have expected. Instead, he chewed with his mouth closed, cut his food into small pieces, and drank lots of water between bites.

A healthy-appearing human; this impressed Aphrodite as she once believed they were all *pigs*. She hid her laughter as the waiter took away their plates, and Lukus settled the bill.

She sat up straight in her seat. "Where should we start, then? Library?"

"Library? What century do you—" His phone rang, interrupting them. He frowned when he peeked at the screen. "Uh oh."

"Uh oh *what?*"

He lifted a finger to silence her. "Agent Arvantis, speaking." He went quiet, and she heard a voice on the other end, yet was unable to decipher the words. "Uh huh... yes... the same? And... but you're *sure?* New Orleans?" He rolled his eyes. "Of course, we'll be there shortly."

She set her napkin down and hunched over the table. "Another murder?"

Eros, are you not done killing innocent people for your unknown motives? What is it you want?

Lukus snuck his phone in his pocket and stood up. "Yeah, you guessed it! We have more work. *It* struck in New Orleans, so we have to get there now."

Aphrodite also got up, grabbing her handbag before helping Lukus put away his scattered paperwork. She followed him outside, and they stopped after passing the threshold. Stuffy, sticky air hit her cheeks and she grimaced, missing the pure breezes of Olympus.

"I'll take care of our plane tickets, if you don't mind calling a cab," he said, stepping a few feet away, dialing a number on his cell.

Brows raising, shoulders locking, Aphrodite panicked.

Call a cab?

She didn't even know if she had a phone included in her *human starter* package. She weaved her hands through her purse, desperate to find something looking like Lukus' telephone device. Soon, she sensed a thin and long box with a screen on it—and when she pulled it out, she released a sigh of relief.

She touched it, admiring its odd composition; they didn't need phones in Olympus, but she remembered seeing them and wondering if she'd ever use one.

Great... so how do I call a taxi?

She had no trouble deciphering appliances and other pieces of technology in her past, but a cellular device... was something new.

Pressing buttons instinctively, she prayed to summon a cab-car to their location.

* * *

Hours later, after a grueling plane ride and racing through the New Orleans airport, the cab screeched, stopping feet away from the yellow tape and flashing cop car lights. She would have much preferred to *teleport* there; the airplane was packed with children screaming and men ogling her and teenagers bypassing rules behind their parents' backs.

Gulping down her angst, Aphrodite escaped the vehicle and allowed the muggy atmosphere to engulf her, to coat her skin in sweat. It *was* a pleasant contrast to the dryness in Vegas—she preferred damp areas, anyway.

She got out her notepad and pen, mentally preparing herself for the brutality to come. Lukus threw bills in the front seat, and they exited, headed straight for the uniformed men guarding the crime scene.

They stopped her at once. "Authorized personnel and detectives only, miss," said one of the officers.

Crap.

Aphrodite reached into her purse, digging for her wallet—she hadn't needed to flash her badge last time, since Lukus got them both through. But this time, she had beat him to the area as he paused to say something to another detective.

"Just a... just a *minute*..." She winced as she fished through her wallet.

Lukus arrived, his badge whipped out in seconds. "She's with me. A rookie." He glared sideways at her before jutting his chin at the two cops. "Take us to the bodies."

She swallowed; his eyes, usually so clear and comforting, had turned dark blue, laced with anger.

He nudged her as they marched behind the officers. "Don't embarrass me like that again. *Always* have your badge at the ready, got it?"

She nodded, wary of blowing her cover. If she didn't appear to know what she was doing, Zeus would *kill* her. She'd done so well, so far, but she only knew so much about humans... and so much about working for the FBI.

Zeus, I despise you!

She breathed in and continued with Lukus towards the two lifeless beings on the ground. Both lay in puddles of blood, surrounded by ashes, pieces of flesh, and clothing scattered nearby.

Like last time.

Eros, what are you doing?

She kneeled, and Lukus handed her a pair of gloves. The metallic stench of death was overpowering, but she fought against the rising nausea, afraid to make Lukus look bad.

"Go ahead, take a deeper look," he said, pointing at the bodies. "See if those wounds look like animal wounds to you."

Aphrodite put the gloves on and inhaled, struggling to hide how the odor caused her to choke. She angled closer to the first corpse, a female, and placed a hand on the chest. With a silent prayer, she inched nearer and squinted at the details—and found a hole, several inches wide, and deep, where the heart should have been.

Daring to tip farther, she noticed the veins were perfectly cut, not a single piece of the heart remaining. All surrounding organs were intact as if never affected despite the heart being gone.

"This is... *wow.*" Lukus hadn't let her get as in-depth at the Las Vegas crime scene, and her arms shook, though she held them close to her sides, hoping he wouldn't see. "I don't understand it."

"So now you grasp *my* dilemma." He crawled closer to the next body—also a woman. "This might be a bit much for you, but... if you're okay with it, check this one, too. Tell me if they match."

Without glimpsing him, she obeyed, moving on to the lifeless creature beside this one. And sure enough, after a quick examination, she concluded the bodies were identical—down to the size of the hole in the chest.

How is Eros able to do this?

She remembered each of his powers... and none would allow him to kill someone with such precision.

"So, do you think an animal did this, Agnes?" Lukus snapped a few pictures with his cell, changing angles, zooming in. "Is it a possibility?"

She shrugged, her hand still placed on the second woman's corpse. "I... I don't know."

No, an animal couldn't do this.

But Eros didn't have that ability, either. And if he obtained it... how in Tartarus had he become so gruesome?

Lukus helped her up. "Not even a skilled cardiovascular surgeon could perform such an operation. No experienced killer or veteran military pro shooter would leave such an open wound, lacking a heart, and such intact organs. *None* of this makes sense. So, tell me again how I am drowning? Tell me again how I need assistance? And how could *you* assist me?" Their eyes connected, his like a night sky, enveloping her in ways no human's gaze ever had.

"I... I don't have a clue," she said, her voice softer than expected. As a goddess, she had seen nothing like it. She drew a deep breath, turning from the bodies, Lukus still perched near her.

She had to keep her cool, be professional, stay in character. The next few moments would be crucial to the rest of her fake career; she needed to *act* like Agnes, but with a touch of her goddess-like wit and stubbornness.

"Should I... interview the witnesses?" She peered at Lukus, whose eyes softened. He cocked his head and crossed his arms. "To... give you more time to take pictures and notes?" she added, unsure what his posture meant.

He rubbed his chin for a moment. "Well… sure, sounds good."

"*Then* we can panic, okay?" Tempted to pat him on the back, she recoiled, realizing how out of place such a gesture would be.

But if he saw her hesitation, he didn't point it out. He waved her off with a shy smile. "Get to it, then!"

Not wanting to linger in his presence and make him mad, Agnes sauntered off towards one of the officers. "Are there any witnesses to speak with?"

He shrugged. "Yes, but unfortunately they... are all *intoxicated*. There was a festival going on nearby, and the people willing to talk have alcohol in their blood."

Aphrodite sighed. "I'll take whatever I can get. Are they still here?"

The officer pointed at a small café across the street. "We sat them down and gave them coffee, to sober them up. They're all yours, agent."

She thanked the man and headed towards the coffee shop. But once inside, she tried not to gag; the space reeked of alcohol and cigarette smoke, causing an intense nausea to swirl again in her gut.

How she longed for the sweet ocean smells in her room, the blooming roses in the gardens, the ambrosia peppering the air—

"Are you the witnesses?" She walked towards a small group of individuals slouching in a booth, plates of greasy French-fries and half-eaten burgers on the table, surrounded by cracked cups of java. Some of them giggled, while others were half-asleep against the plastic-covered cushions.

"*Yup,* that's us... the... *witnesses,*" said one of them, followed by a hiccup.

She showed her badge and prepared her notebook. "Tell me what you saw and leave no detail out."

* * *

Lukus was speaking with a high-ranking officer when Aphrodite returned. She stopped next to him, clutching her notepad, as he turned to her. "Ah, the witness accounts. Anything new?"

She shook her head as he dismissed the detective. "All the same. They took their clothes off and ripped each other's hearts out, but not before the crazy flash of light blinded everyone and sent most of them running. These kids... they were all *drunk.*"

"Well... they're still witnesses." Lukus wiped his glistening forehead. "Thank you, Agnes. You're... doing great."

Aphrodite blushed, aware she was failing. She had no clue why her son killed innocent humans—though they ate strange food and smelled like booze, they had done nothing wrong.

But she *had* found a connection between the victims, thanks to the witnesses. Coughing into her hand, she caught Lukus' attention before he walked away. "Agent, I'm seeing a pattern."

Lukus froze, then pivoted on his heels to squint at her. "Ah? And what is it?"

She slid her hands in her pockets. "I mentioned this to you earlier, but... it's becoming clearer. The victims... may have a different connection. Not friends or family, or acquaintances. It could be... uh... *supernatural.* A more spiritual link, one binding their... souls.

Lukus' entire upper body went rigid. He remained silent, glaring at her as if she had discovered the cure for cancer, but it required him to chop his arm off. And then... his face brightened as he let out a loud laugh. "Oh, Agnes, you're hilarious." He squeezed her shoulder, the contact making her shiver. "Thanks for that. I needed to smile." He scoffed. "*Supernatural,* huh? Spiritual. *Linked souls...* jeez, that's creative. It's cute, really. A great idea for a novel, but... no, I doubt it." His fingers slid down her arm as he retracted his palm. "Come on, some local news stations want to ask some questions. And then we'll go check in at the hotel, okay?"

"Okay."

As he hastened to where a crowd of interviewers awaited him, Aphrodite's heart sank.

She had no way to convince him without revealing herself.

* * *

Sitting on her bed, staring out the window overlooking a dumpster, she grumbled. "Lovely hotel with a *lovelier* view."

At first, she'd found New Orleans fascinating, the fried smells hunger-inducing, the festive aura intoxicating; but locked in her tiny, cheap room, she'd changed her mind fast.

Gripping her phone, she glanced at the business card in her hand. Going behind Lukus' back could get her in big trouble; but her hunch urged her to not care. Urged her to do what she thought best.

Sighing, she flipped the card around, gazing at the intricate patterns above the name and the number inscribed. She bit her lip, ready to rip the thing up—but her son's image popped into her head. His golden locks, his amber eyes, his childlike face.

Screw it.

Dialing the number, she brought the phone up to her ear as it rang.

"This is agent Arvantis' partner, Agnes. I need to talk to the coroner about today's murders, the cannibalism ones," she said, when asked about the reason for her call.

Waiting to be put through, she considered hanging up, to beg Lukus to do this himself.

He should trust me and my instincts, right? Haven't I proven myself?

The coroner answered the line before she changed her mind. "Miss Agnes? What can I do for you?" He sighed, his voice weighted, dreary. "I received the bodies; I was preparing for the autopsy."

Back tensing, Aphrodite closed her eyes. "We... have an additional request for you." She cringed at her tone, aware that it didn't sound professional enough. "I... *we* need you to check around the victim's rib cages for anything... out of the ordinary."

He chuckled. "*Everything* about this case is out of the ordinary, miss. What exactly am I looking for?"

"Scars... marks... engravings. Don't ask questions, just do it, okay? It's what agent Arvantis wants, and I do as I'm told."

After a few minutes of debating, the coroner agreed, and promised to call her with the results.

Aphrodite hung up, an undulating sensation of guilt creeping into her body, floating in her abdomen.

She dropped the phone, her limbs trembling, her throat scratchy, her breaths hitching.

"I know what you're doing, Eros... but I need to prove it to Lukus." She held her head in her hands, images of the dead bodies haunting her. Men and women, men and men, women and women—Eros would never discriminate. "You're... killing *soulmates.* The ones it's your mandate to unite," she said, sinking her face between her knees. "If we find those markings... *that'll* be the proof. I'll show Lukus... and he'll believe me."

She fell backwards on her bed, ambrosia liquor dreams swooping into her mind, picturing herself drowning in pools of the sweet nectar until the pain in her temples stopped.

"And then... we'll stop you."

‖12. SHE'S HERE‖
EROS

Eros shivered, slurping the rest of his drink—a chocolate-flavored martini he quite enjoyed—masking his rage. The sweet flavor, though a little strong, burned on its way down his throat, but the smooth rich texture made him smile whenever it traveled through his mouth.

He wasn't mistaken this time—another god had arrived in New Orleans.

I smelled it.

He considered ordering a second cocktail, satisfied with the taste, resembling a drink he had once concocted by himself in the kitchens of Olympus.

But if it *was* her, he needed to be sharp. Prepared. She likely had no joy in being on earth, and he'd have to justify his actions when they met. He'd have to explain why everything he had done… was for her.

He looked around, taking in the atmosphere of the bar. Unlike the prior dive bars he frequented, this one had a fancy feel to it—dimmer lighting, a softer ambience, non-stained tablecloths, and no liquor splashed all over the floor. He couldn't help but bob his head to the jazzy music, enjoying the calm in this unlikely New Orleans location.

The old Eros would have loved it. Back when he cared about making humans happy and setting them up with their soulmates; back when he put their needs and desires first. When he didn't want to kill them all for revenge.

He blinked as a new tune played—choppy, rhythmic, exciting. A few patrons stood and danced, sloppy and noisy, spilling their drinks as they sang along.

They'd disturbed his pleasurable peace.

No more nice guy.

The drunken, shameless creatures littering the space near him had tainted the gods. Gods who had turned rusty, lazy. His family let its guard down—and now, humans had to pay for it.

Though they're not the only ones responsible.

He watched two men in a corner booth, sharing a large, electric-blue drink in an oversized glass, bright pink straws bringing the alcohol to their mouths as they giggled.

Eros considered, for a second, trying one of *those* drinks, before the TV screen above the bar caught his attention. The catchy news report jingle cut off the music.

"The Cannibal Murderer strikes again, right here in New Orleans. Though we still don't know if the criminal is eating the victim's hearts, our sources disclose that investigative teams have come to no other conclusions. We believe it's fair to assume the worst."

Smirking, he sipped his alcohol.

They reported his work, again. And he had a nickname, too. He sensed his cheeks heat as he waved at the bartender and ordered another drink.

Might as well indulge, to celebrate my exploits.

She was there, but he had time.

As he waited, a handsome man appeared on the screen. His ebony locks needed a trim, but his sharp, blue eyes and his crisp, navy suit intrigued Eros. He cocked his head, admiring the man's figure, the bulges in his biceps area under his clothes.

His mood changed—he hadn't seen such an attractive guy in a long time, especially not a mortal one.

"Lukus Arvantis, lead FBI agent on the case, claims he has nothing to report to us... yet."

Eros' eyes widened. The handsome man was the one investigating him, following him around. He licked his lips, staring at the television hungrily, unsure if he wanted to slay the investigator... or play with him.

As the agent spoke, Eros watched his body language, listened to the words he chose.

Lukus Arvantis... well, if that's not a Greek name, I'm no longer the god of love.

His new drink arrived, and Eros moaned with pleasure as the chocolaty liquid passed over his tongue, warming his insides. Humanity coursed through him, but for once, he didn't care. His godly powers remained intact, and his murderous urges intensified by the minute.

In the process of setting his cup down, he peeked up at the TV again, catching a woman in the background, behind agent Arvantis.

At first, Eros was aroused by the sight of her. Her voluptuous curves enticed him, even from a distance. She nearly glowed, her frame so perfectly round, her posture that of a confident queen, her tunic transparent enough to show the black bra over her cleavage.

The camera then zoomed in a little, showing her better as she stood close to the agent, revealing her strawberry blonde hair flowing in a gentle breeze, her eyes greener than the Caribbean ocean, her lips plump and rosy—

Eros gasped.

His martini glass shattered in his hands, and brown liquid exploded all over, spilling onto the counter, drizzling down his leather coat, smearing onto his leather pants. Small droplets of crimson slid from the lines in his palms, coating his hand in a sticky metallic substance he usually enjoyed.

Not now. Not when it was *his* blood.

His face twisted into an evil snare. The goddess he sensed... was the presence he feared most.

My mother?

Wrinkling his nose in disgust, he apologized for his mess and deposited several twenty-dollar bills on the dampened counter, wrapping his hand with a napkin. Without another glance—at the patrons, the bartender, the television screen—he hurried out, praying for somewhere more private.

He was panting, his breathing ragged, choppy—something he wasn't used to.

This whole time, his mom had been on his tracks. And though he *did* want her to find him eventually, he wasn't ready yet.

The alcohol pumped through his veins, clouding his vision.

I'm too weak.

Blood soaked through the cloth covering his palm. He winced—he wasn't supposed to bleed, especially not from a broken martini glass.

If someone sent his mother to stop him, he knew what he needed.

Ambrosia.

He had little time to finish what he started, but for that, he needed full god strength.

He dashed into an alleyway, and after making sure it was empty, he pulled out the pay-as-you-go phone from his pocket. He searched through the contacts and pressed the buttons, pulling the receiver up to his ear.

"Eros," said a deep masculine voice on the other end.

"*No.* Not tonight. We'll get caught."

Eros frowned. "Brother, *please.* I'm so close. *Too* close to lose now. She's here, and she'll tell me where *she* is, but only if I'm strong enough to *defeat* her."

"And that's *exactly* why I can't help you. *Mother.* She's there, she's following you, on Zeus' orders no less. Stop this madness." Fear laced the man's tone, resonating in Eros' ears.

"Anteros." Eros' heart stopped. "Mother *betrayed* me. Mother *hurt* me. Help me get retribution. Help me find my wife. I need ambrosia. Psyche is missing, and it's all Aphrodite's fault, I know it. *Help* me."

‖13. SUPERNATURAL‖
APHRODITE

Seated at the hotel restaurant—if one could call such a scum-filled space a *restaurant*—papers sprawled all over the table in front of her, Aphrodite huffed.

"There *is* a pattern," she said, scowling at the words jotted down, letting them swirl in her vision. The dim room, with a few decrepit tables and chairs spread around, had an old cigarette stench, often causing her to cough. A handful of other hotel guests sat at the worn-down bar, drinking beer and watching a sports game on the TV above the dusty shelves of liquor.

Aphrodite saw all human sports as pitiful, full of theatrics and cheating players hyped up on drugs to compete better. And the *commercials.* She grimaced.

They call this entertainment?

Lukus was in his room, far from the ashtray smell, but Aphrodite couldn't stay locked up—even if that meant she had to deal with the horrid stench, and the yells of the men as their teams scored points.

She closed her eyes and shook her head, picturing a tranquil beach. Seagulls flapping above her as she lounged naked on the sand, an ambrosia cocktail in one hand, holding Ares' with her other.

But the vision didn't work.

The nightmare she sat in was real. The FBI didn't allow luxury; she understood that. But this bar, this hotel, this *area* was disgusting, distasteful, and *inhuman*.

I wish Lukus would let me pick the inn next time.

She re-opened her eyes, her heart threatening to break into thousands of pieces, realizing she didn't *want* a next time. Eros needed to stop, and the only way to make that happen... was with her confronting him.

She stared at the documents once more, repressing another cough as a wave of smoke slithered towards her.

"I must hurry."

The pattern she envisioned weaved before her. Two victims—most times a male and a female, though the pattern once shifted to two men, and here, in New Orleans, to two women— about the same age, similar interests, living in the same city. So, what would provoke Eros to kill *them?*

Rubbing her forehead, she sighed, not used to the pain constantly nagging her there. "Soulmates, right? I know it, Eros knows it... he's *not* killing at random. But... why?"

Nobody heard her mumbling over the screeching of the sports commentators on the television. So, she searched through the documentation for the third time, hoping to find something to back up her hunch, her ears wrestling against the noisy hotel guests. Lukus wouldn't listen to her until she had palpable proof. He made it clear he didn't believe in the supernatural, and he wouldn't buy her expose as it was now.

I have to be more convincing.

The group of men at the bar cheered once more, prompting something to fall off the counter and spill onto the floor, splashing all the way up to Aphrodite's feet.

She jumped, ready to screech choice Greek profanities, but remembered her place and her lack of powers. Instead, she threw napkins on the ground to sponge up the mess. No one else would clean it; not in this filthy location with these filthy humans.

This is horrific.

She rolled her eyes. "So... soulmates. Eros can identify them easily, that's his job, but..." Puffing up her cheeks, she leaned closer to the notes. "But how can *I* find them first? I granted him the power... but it's not my forte." She exhaled. "How do humans... search for their soulmate?"

She thought to times when she spied on mortals. Remembered their games, technology, skimmed through her brain for images of their movies, their TV shows; surely *something* contained a clue to help her.

She froze as a few movie titles passed through her mind.

Romantic comedies.

She enjoyed watching humans' fake feelings, play with all outcomes, break hearts and rebuild them. Along with a few drama books she had stolen to keep busy while her lover was away, she educated herself in all manners of love on earth... and slowly, she realized her ancient knowledge wouldn't work here.

This world was technologically driven... so technology was the answer.

She peered over at the men perched on their stools watching the screen. One of them hunched over the bar, fiddling around with his phone. Though she couldn't see what he looked at, she cocked her head.

Is he on... the 'internet'?

They used it a lot in films as of late. For research, to order items or food—and in one movie, a woman used it to seek love.

She tapped her fingers on the sticky table, attempting to get a closer peek at what the man with the phone did—but without her powers, she saw nothing.

"So... how does one use the internet to meet a soulmate? *Argh,* I am clueless about the world wide web."

A loud commercial flashed on the television as the men shouted and yelled in complaint.

"Busy? Socially awkward? Need to find love but don't want to go out for it? Fret not! Loveonlineforbusypeople.com has your back. Sign up today. Your first week is free!"

A light bulb switched on above her head.

Websites.

She remembered that term and then recalled the word 'dating'. She snapped her fingers. "Dating websites..."

Were the victims on *those* sites? It was a common habit among humans to obsess over laziness and computers.

She smiled. "Dating... for lazy people. For *busy* people. That's what the commercial said, right?"

If she found their information... their *profiles*... and linked them, Lukus might be more inclined to accept her theory. All she needed was a computer.

She packed up her paperwork and headed to the shabby hotel lobby instead, trying to ignore its desecrated floors and peeling wallpaper. The clerk on duty pointed her towards a closet-like room containing a chipped wooden desk and a beat-up, old school machine he referred to as a *desktop.* And though she knew little about computers... she wasn't sure the thing would function.

Shrugging, she arrayed her notes on the desk and turned on the device, her instincts guiding her. The computer rumbled, shook, sounding like a choking motor; and as it appeared ready to explode, the screen flashed blue and soon led her to a main menu.

"Has *anyone* ever used this?" She set her hand on the mouse and clicked on a few links before finding the *internet.*

Thank goodness for my basic knowledge from spying on humans.

Glaring at the keyboard, she focused on her recollections from movies. It took her a few minutes to understand the system, but once she did, she typed away, opening browser windows and choosing a few dating websites—including the one from the commercial.

She created online profiles on several applications, and then researched the deceased based on their looks and names, thankful for all the pictures Lukus had in the file.

Soon, she found out her hunch prevailed—the victims *had* visited multiple sites.

Aphrodite then called the website managers, and after spending what seemed like *hours* on the phone, she gained access to each victim's profile—and discovered who their matches were.

Lists arrived in email format—she had to sign up for one of those, too—and she analyzed them, cross-referencing the names with her own information until her eyes burned from staring at the screen too much.

Each pair of victims from each city were potential *matches*.

Bingo. I'm good at this FBI thing.

If she showed this to Lukus, he'd *have* to open up. And then, they could really start investigating.

* * *

The burnt plastic stench in the corridor snuck into her nostrils—though compared to the scratchy smoke from downstairs, this was tolerable. The outdated flower patterns on the walls had holes, and Aphrodite gulped the longer she stared at them. Getting closer to Lukus' door, one hand gripping the printed notes to reveal the connection between victims, she blew out her cheeks. With her other palm, she tapped on the scratched wooden barrier.

Be Agnes, the FBI agent—assertive, confident, human.

Moments later, Lukus answered. He had removed his jacket, standing in the doorway in his long-sleeved white shirt untucked from his navy-blue pants. His belt, loose, drooped down by his thighs, and he yawned as he scratched his cheek. "Agnes?"

Damn, I woke him up.

"What's up?" He opened the door to let her in, rubbing his neck with another yawn.

She flashed a shy smile and entered, surprised at the fresh cigarette smell and the grayish cloud hovering around the area.

"I'm... sorry to bother you. I could come back later," she said, turning to Lukus as he closed the door.

He winced, but a tiny grin formed as their eyes connected. "It's okay, I needed to wake up anyway."

She gulped again. "I, uh... I found some interesting information to advance the case."

Struggling to raise his eyebrows, Lukus motioned for her to sit on a chair. "Did you, now?"

Though his room was identical in size to hers, it was dimmer; the floating smoke cast it in a gloomy atmosphere.

He groaned as he grabbed a squashed pack on the nightstand and removed a cigarette from it. He slid it into his mouth and snatched a lighter to light it up. An expression of relief flooded his features as he studied Aphrodite. "What?"

She frowned. "Those things *will* kill you."

Lukus chuckled. "Well, they haven't so far, so mind your own business." Aphrodite's brows shot up, but he ignored her as he paced away from the nightstand. "So, what did you want, then?"

Someone's grumpy.

"I..." she waved off the smoke slipping over to her, "... found a connection between the victims."

He took another drag, and more fog filled the room, hiding him from view. When he resurfaced, a smirk spread across his lips. "Fine, I'll bite. Go ahead, tell me what you think you discovered, Agnes."

She clenched the papers tighter in her hand. "They were *all* on dating websites. I doubt they met yet, and I'm not sure they talked, but... I called the companies and it seems they were matches. These people were... *meant to be*."

He squeezed the cigarette between his index and middle fingers. "And you trust an online dating website to give you this information? To prove someone is *meant to be* with another? According to you, *this* is relevant to the case?"

She scoffed. "And you don't think so? This is a legitimate connection, Lukus. Something we can use to identify the killer's motives. To assume he targets... soulmates."

Lukus almost spat out his cigarette. "First off, those websites are *shit*." He inhaled a large puff as Aphrodite crossed her arms, scrunching the reports against her chest. "But okay, let's pursue this. According to your theory, *every* person on them is a potential victim."

Holding in a cough, Aphrodite nodded.

"Okay, so... how the hell do we protect millions of people against a threat we haven't even identified?" Lukus' body stiffened as he stood by the bed, narrowing his eyes. "Tell me, Agnes, how do we approach them all and warn them that they *might* die because they *might* have a soulmate, and someone is targeting them? How is any of this plausible?" He huffed, took a drag, then stomped his foot. "And *who* would go after soulmates?"

Before Aphrodite could answer, he grunted as he smashed the cigarette in an ashtray, then dropped onto the bed, sliding his head in his hands.

Eros, you moron! That's who.

Insides burning, Aphrodite watched him huddling over the mattress. "Can't you at least recognize it's an option? It's not much, but it's a start. With this, we can look into the databases, search for related crimes, contact other criminals with similar motives and get into their heads, obtain more leads... don't you see that?" Admitting it was supernatural would only push Lukus further, so she held in that information—for now.

Lukus looked up, his pupils red, his lips thinning. "Agnes, listen... I'll admit you may be getting somewhere. Maybe the murderer targets lovers. But if he or she knows who these lovers are in advance, *we* don't." His fists bunched. "We'd have to look further into the victim's acquaintances and families, we'd have to seek details about their dating profiles and *anyone* they met on them. It *is* a lead, but... it's not one we should prioritize. Too complicated, and unlikely. I appreciate your efforts, though, I do."

"But this is it! It *has* to be." Aphrodite refrained from throwing the papers at him. "This killer has something against love, against soulmates and he... or *she*... wants to prove a point. He or she can tell in advance who these lovers are and—" She clapped a palm over her mouth, but it was too late; she'd stepped into supernatural territory.

He will for sure think I'm crazy now.

Lukus stood, squinting as he approached her. "What... are you saying?" Concern washed over his features. "Are we trying to apprehend a killer skilled in *hacking?* Did he or she hack into websites to target matches to prove some weird point against love and soulmates?"

She flinched, unable to deny his formulation made sense. "Well... I'm not saying no, but I was inclining towards something more... supernatural."

His eyes turned dark. "*Ugh,* there you go with the spiritual crap again! A psycho killer who just... *knows* which soulmates belong together? You're serious about this?

Aphrodite backed away. "I... I guess so." She lowered her chin, the documents sliding out of her clammy hands, though she managed to scrunch them to stop them from falling. "Nothing else makes sense. My animal theory was a bust, so I analyzed all your notes. You've... hit so many dead ends, so this... is your only remaining option."

Something akin to fear bubbled in her belly. She hadn't wanted this, but she had no choice. He'd dismiss her, she'd be on her own...

Zeus will be so mad...

Lukus marched past her and slammed his fist into the wall by the door, denting it. "No." He kept his back to her, his breaths labored. "Absolutely not."

Biting her lip, Aphrodite dared a stride forward. "Lukus—"

He whirled around, his irises laced with fire, his shoulders hiking up. "Your fantasy world of witches and wizards and angels and demons doesn't exist. I have no clue where the boss dug you up, nor what you grew up with in Greece... *ha,* you probably believe in those *stupid* Greek gods and their insane stories!" He pointed at her, his arm shaking, then at himself, jabbing his finger into his torso. "But not me. Not this, not on my case. There *is* a human, logical explanation to all this, and I will find it, with or without your help."

Against her will, she growled.

He insulted the gods. Called them names. He had no idea he hunted one of them, and was only alive because *she* allowed it, ordered to make sure he didn't die.

Ungrateful, spiteful, pitiful human.

"You call them *stupid*, but there are truths to certain myths, agent Arvantis." A confidence she had no control over wavered into her voice as she straightened up, no longer intimidated by his height. "You'd do well to inspire yourself from them if you want to get *anywhere* in your investigation."

Every inch of her skin tingled, and her guts filled with a dangerous lava. She marched up to him, her cheeks in flames, her tongue turning acid with fury.

Though the anger once showing on Lukus' face dissipated, he held his ground. "Inspire myself from *fake* crap like that?"

Aphrodite let out a tiny chuckle. "You're Greek, Lukus. I'm not saying most Greeks believe in that *crap*, as you call it... but speaking like that makes you a little bit of a hypocrite, no?" She charged past him, stopping an inch from the door before whirling around. "Have you even *tried* to think like a killer? To analyze the potential motives?" She slid a hand onto her hip. "Why two victims? Why take each other's clothes off and devour each other's hearts? *Cannibalism?* Does any of that seem human?" Lukus didn't reply, didn't move; and she didn't care. "No? Well, you have yourself a great day trying to figure out what *does* make sense."

She stormed out, slamming the door behind her.

Once several feet down the hallway, bile rose to her throat as she dropped the papers, catching her breath.

"Have it your way, Lukus..." she said, between inhales of the dusty air. "Make this difficult. But I might have more proof soon."

She thought of her call to the coroner and kneeled down.

Patience, Aphrodite.

She walked away, praying Lukus would see reason and research the Greek myths. That he wouldn't stay stuck in his beliefs. If he wanted to solve the case, he *had* to open his mind.

‖14. GREEK MYTHS‖
LUKUS

Lukus lit another cigarette, hands shaking, nerves sending him off the edge. Agnes stormed off fuming—but *he* was more entitled to anger.

She's fucking crazy and trying to make me swallow her outrageous stories!

He coughed up smoke, hardly able to take a drag without choking. His rage swirled in him, consuming his insides like fire, making him want to throw something. Break something. Punch *someone.*

He wondered how she knew of his Greek origins. Had the boss told her? Fists forming, he held his arms close to his ribcage, wary he'd attack anything in his passage. He wasn't usually so violent, but her behavior brought out parts of him he'd never encountered.

How did she believe in such things? The paranormal, Greek gods? What would persuade her that something non-human was responsible for this mess?

He huffed, kicking the mattress. "Nope, I don't buy it."

He put out the cigarette and lay face down on the bed, inhaling and exhaling, steadying his mind. The smoky stench imbued on the sheets filled his nostrils, and gross as it was, its familiarity soothed Lukus' heavy heart. Agnes was *his* partner—they were stuck together. But he worried he'd have to call the boss to warn him she was a psycho. A nut-job. An under-qualified chick who sought imaginary solutions to real problems.

What should I do? Think, Lukus!

He could barely breathe, but he didn't care. Suffocating seemed like a better idea than dealing with the craziness. Her voice ringing in his eardrums brought back violent thoughts once more. Turbulent visions of her sped up his pulse, and his extremities weakened, a dizzying rage coming over him.

"She's not what you expect." He should have known then. He should have listened.

Pounding his fist on the mattress, he groaned when the muffled sound gave him no satisfaction. He had expected a professional wanting to learn from the best—not some weirdo claiming the killer wasn't human. Who *was* she? With her pretty dresses and high heels, her gorgeous face and voluptuous lips. And her eyes—with special man-eater contacts, maybe? Too unreal.

She's not an FBI agent. She can't be.

He growled, sick of the images rolling through his brain. Sick of her unexplained attractiveness and how it clouded his instincts, buried his reflexes.

He pushed himself up and sat with his back to the wall, eyes closed, breathing in and out. "There *is* a logical explanation. She's veiled by fairy-tales." He pounded both fists on the bed; still no pleasant feeling waking within him. "I'll take what she said... with a grain of salt."

If he let her insanity drive him crazy, he'd never make a break in the case. He had to look for a *real* motive. Opening his eyes, visualizing her features, her determined attitude, rehashing her words... he feared she *might* have had a point. She found a connection between the victims—and though insignificant; it was a start. They were all looking for love, signed up on dating websites, wanting to connect.

As he rubbed his forehead, pain spreading past his temples, raging on behind his eyes, a migraine took over. His fatigue and stress got the best of him, and the harder he tried to clear his mind, the stronger the violent sensations taking over him became. Yawning, he took off his shoes, deciding to take another nap. He slid his belt off his pants and snuck under the covers, hoping for peace and quiet, for his thoughts to halt, for his head to stop hurting.

* * *

He jolted awake twenty minutes later, eyes watery, throat dry and raspy... and his head thumping away as if it had never stopped. Sitting up, joints stiff and body tense, he cracked his knuckles and stretched. He blinked a few times, peering around the dingy room, as if expecting someone to be watching him. He checked the time, and furrowed his brow, recalling his blurry dreams full of dark figures, alleyways, blood. The things he saw and heard drove his curiosity, but he got no answers.

Did Agnes cause his insomnia? Did she... know more than she claimed? Aware of something he wasn't? No, she couldn't have more information than him. But she *had* been more intuitive than expected; she might have stumbled upon something that could lead them to the truth.

The gruesome images from his dreams proved his subconscious was rattled, shaken up... and more affected than he thought.

"*Is* she on to something?" He stood up and brushed his hair, running his nails through the strands. "Not supernaturally, but... logically? Maybe..." He snapped his fingers. "The *murderer* is the psycho who believes in the supernatural! Not Agnes!" He scoffed. "Nah... she's not all there, either."

A lightbulb shined down on him, illuminating his ideas.

"The murderer assumes we'll research strange occurrences and myths, *that* was what she meant the other day at breakfast! Because he wants to *push* us in that direction." Watching himself talk in the mirror near the closet, he rolled his shoulders. "Agnes was right; he... or *she*... doesn't enjoy dating websites. Or love. Targets innocent people matching online..." He puffed his chest out, a smile tugging at his lips. "Is that it? Did I solve part of my case?"

Heart weighing less than it had minutes prior, Lukus fastened his belt around his waist, then searched for his suit jacket and threw it on. He grabbed his key and left, heading for Agnes' room a few doors down the hall. He had no intention of apologizing—she *was* crazy and had unexplained strength, as he recalled from their breakfast—but there had been truth to her insane words. And without realizing it, she might have uncovered a myth-obsessed killer.

If she knows anything about those legends, she has to tell me.

He tapped on her door. "Agnes, it's Lukus." Silence. "Agnes? Open up, I need to talk to you."

Still, no sound escaped from the cracks beneath her door. He squinted at the wooden barrier. Was she sleeping?

This is worth waking her. She needs to hear it.

He knocked again, a little louder. "Agnes! Open up, we need to talk!" He shrugged. "Come on, don't be like that. I... look, you *might* be onto something, and now I have a hunch and I'd like you to help me with it."

No movement.

"Agnes?" His voice carried down the corridor, resonating off the stained walls. "Is she... even in there?"

A man opened the door across from Agnes' and glared at Lukus. "She ain't in there, pal," he said, booming voices coming from inside his room. He wore a robe covered in dirt, open at the top, and a cigarette hung from his mouth. His hazy gaze and sullen skin made Lukus recoil.

"And *you* are?" Creeped out by the man's knowledge, Lukus wished he had his gun with him.

The man grumbled under his breath before removing the cigarette, revealing his faded pink gums missing a few teeth. "No one, no one. I saw her leave fifteen minutes ago, that's all. Stop knockin' and makin' noise, some of us are tryin' to get privacy here!"

He slammed the door before Lukus could retaliate.

Defeated, Lukus huffed as he peeked around the gloomy hallway, as if it would answer him. But he figured out what he had to do—he'd have to look up the myths... on his own.

I must discover this murderer's next move.

He paced in front of Agnes' door, considering finding a computer to research—but it wouldn't be enough. He needed full access to everything, a plethora of documents, someone knowledgeable to give him the right books—

Chuckling, he regretted mocking Agnes earlier for mentioning a library. He pulled out his cell and looked up local bookstores and libraries, and screenshot a few addresses. Seconds later, he scurried downstairs and called a cab.

Unable to let go of Agnes' disappearance, he searched the lobby, and even stepped into the dreadful bar, wondering if she'd be there. But she was gone—and he didn't want to ask any of the grungy weirdos sitting at the counter if they saw where she went.

Hoping she hadn't wandered off to investigate leads on her own, he slid into his taxi, and the man drove him to the closest, better-reputed library of the area. Swerving down poorly lit streets and past dingy alleyways, Lukus chose to not look outside and focused on his cell phone, sitting on his lap.

I hope she's okay.

They arrived at a small historical place near the center of the city. Far from festivals and parties, it was a relief to breathe in fresh, non-alcoholic air as he exited the vehicle.

The building, its foundations ancient but sturdy, was welcoming. He climbed the steps leading to the front door, happy to see that the location was open twenty-four seven.

The librarian on duty directed him to the mythology section and helped him choose a few books that would give him an idea of what myth the murderer could be imitating. Perhaps it was a copycat killer, wanting to slay humans like a god or a hero from the mythical fantasies. Agnes had implied it—that might have been the reason she mentioned myths.

He went through pages and pages of mythological history, rediscovering stories he had read in his childhood, and learning about more he never knew existed. His mother's tone buzzed into his memory; she had read these to him before bed, wanting him to remember the lessons in life and apply them. And his dad, one of the rare devout Greek-god believers in his hometown, insisted on her doing it.

I'm sure these legends are tattooed on his brain. I could call them...

He shook his head, almost twisting his neck. No, he wouldn't involve his family. He left New York City for a reason; he didn't need to get wrapped up in their hopped-up beliefs and their constricting criticism. So, he'd handle the case on his own, with the books... and maybe with Agnes, if she came around.

* * *

Closing the last book in his stack, he checked his watch. Hours had passed, and what did he find? No myths involving cannibalism or even carnivorous in nature. Except for Dionysus and his frenzies, no gods had such sickening histories. Was the killer trying to imitate Dionysus?

No, he doesn't link with soulmates. Must be something else.

Another name had popped up several times in his research. Eros, god of love. And *he* was affiliated with hearts and soulmates. Did he inspire the culprit? Did this sick person have an obsession with this god, thinking he *was* him?

Twisted, but I've seen stuff like that before.

He sat up straight and gulped, an uneasy sensation of dread developing in his stomach. The killer might believe he had the right to decide who is whose soulmate, then execute them. An evil, dark cupid? He recoiled at the grueling idea, no matter how plausible. But it flashed as more logical than Agnes' supernatural crap...

He returned the books to their places and paused to ponder the situation. Concealed between bookshelves, he paced back and forth. "What if this dude or chick is a stalker... found out these people were matches online... and is jealous?" Keeping his voice low, he paced faster. "Or angry? And found and murdered them before they met? What if he sets them up and tricks them, traps them... watches them perish?"

A chill ran down his spine, prompting him to pivot on his heels and gape at the empty area behind him. As if someone had been watching, or standing nearby, stalking *him*. He shivered again. No one was there. Nothing supernatural—that shit didn't exist.

It's just your imagination.

He distanced himself from the isolated space, away from the people, and outside into the fresh night air. His brain melted, over-saturated with images of gods and goddesses, their fairy tales and immortality, their far-fetched adventures. How could such things influence a human being and drive them to madness?

No matter how sick, it might be true. Lukus realized it didn't explain the cannibalism, but... what if there were two killers? One doing the murdering, one stealing the hearts. Though not matching the witness descriptions, he feared maybe those seeing the scene had gone mad, too.

I've got some thinking and analyzing to do.

He hailed a cab and waited, inhaling the muggy but soothing air, emptying his lungs, relaxing his thoughts. Out of nowhere, something whooshed against the back of his neck, forcing him to veer around and gawk at the emptiness behind him. As if something brushed past him, a soft wind touching his arm, grazing his skin.

"*Ugh,* I'm losing my fucking mind!" He smacked his hands onto his cheeks and groaned, wishing Agnes had never mentioned all her crap. Her insanity seeped into his veins, transforming him. He didn't need this, not now; not with what lurked in the dark killing innocent people. He wouldn't have two insane agents working the case; one of them had to keep their head out of the clouds.

That'll be me.

The taxi arrived, and Lukus glanced at the library one last time. Agnes had been right—his Greek roots *did* have the answer.

‖15. HUMANS‖
EROS

Handsome, but clueless.

Eros watched as agent Arvantis, anticipation in his expression, crept into a yellow car that would take him away from the small municipal library of New Orleans. Twice, he stood behind the man; and twice the agent brushed him off like a mere figment of his imagination. Eros wasn't even at full strength, and yet he fooled the human into being certain he didn't exist.

Not the believing type, it seems.

He pulled the hood of his jacket up over his head, concealing his face and hair. A muggy breeze whipped at his cheeks and under his clothes, and he cringed. He'd always been more of a mountain-dweller, enjoying the crisp altitude air and the colder temperatures nipping at his skin. New Orleans was *not* for him.

His godly powers were depleting. Like they poured from his veins, gushing from his fingertips. To conserve whatever energy he had left, he turned off his invisibility charm. Groaning, he realized he used too much power trying to follow Lukus around.

But it was worth it; he had to be positive the man wouldn't instantly figure out what was going on. And thanks to his spying, Eros concluded Lukus… was harmless. He couldn't help Aphrodite—not in excess, at least.

Fiddling for his pay-as-you-go phone in his pocket, he checked for messages from Anteros.

"Hurry, you *fool.*"

If Lukus visited the library alone… where was Aphrodite? She might be out looking for Eros now, and if she found him before Anteros… Eros was screwed.

I'm not strong enough to deal with her.

He descended the steps leading to the street and crossed, headed towards a tavern he remembered seeing before entering the library. It was simple, under the radar, and able to provide him with the mortal-style cocktails he had somehow gained a craving for.

Stupid human.

Lukus would never believe in the paranormal. Never realize the world he lived in was full of gods, demons, creatures of darkness, unspeakable dangers. Never grasp that he was being watched at all times, his life never safe. Did he assume his position as an FBI agent would always save him? He was wrong.

Handsome, but utterly clueless.

Eros entered the bar, welcomed with loud cheers. A horde of hungry women ran up to him, squealing as they showered him with unwanted attention. One wore a sash around her tight-fitting dress, reading 'Bachelorette—gettin hitched'. Eros had to hide his sneering as she tried to rub up against him.

Filthy humans, get away from me!

He wished he held enough power to shove them all off, but as he didn't, he huffed, and marched up to the bartender, struggling to erase their desperate cries of disappointment ringing in his ears. He had no interest in *stupid,* pre-marriage games. Because he wasn't there for that, and besides, he was committed to someone else. He snorted; he'd *never* mingle with such despicable creatures.

The women, embarrassed by the rejection, returned to their adventures, leaving Eros alone to order a drink off the chalkboard menu and brood in peace. Eager to finish his task and leave this insane planet, he watched the bartender pour the contents of his refreshment in a large glass and place it in front of him with a smile.

"Thanks," he mumbled, barely glancing at the man who served him. He closed his eyes, hoping to rid himself of the image of the grossly dressed women, their glazed, intoxicated gazes, their smeared makeup and foul-smelling perfumes.

They were all the same—obsessed with money, booze, and sex. Sure, he was responsible for the latter, but he never meant for humans to get so out of hand. These people had no time for real love; they abused one another, raped or killed each other.

Is that what Zeus created them for? To auto-destruct? To ruin themselves?

He refused to believe it. Sipping on his beverage, his appetite for alcohol diminished with each negative thought floating in his skull. He recalled his mother when he saw her on the TV before—standing tall beside Lukus, her admirative eyes flitting all over him, devouring him whole.

Eros' stomach churned. Why would she waste her time with a human like him? With the FBI? What kind of game did she play and who was she trying to fool?

His gaze darted around the room, ensuring Aphrodite didn't hide amongst the intoxicated humans to spy on him. He couldn't sense her, but his abilities had drained. As far as it concerned him, she might be nearby, and he wouldn't know.

She figured out he murdered the mortal creatures, right? She had to have concluded it by now. So why hadn't she come to find him? Confront him? Taunt him with his wife's location?

Aphrodite had a plan, she always did. Knowing her, it was necessary for him to stay focused, clear, and not get too pompous.

She's a wrathful, angry bitch—and if she's here to stop me, I should prepare to fight her. He slammed the glass on the counter a little too hard, and a few heads turned to stare at him.

"Sorry, sorry," he muttered, getting out money to pay the bartender.

Aphrodite took Psyche to spite him. So, he knew what she was capable of. The goddess enjoyed causing suffering, causing Eros' enraged behavior. But this time, he hoped his rage would help him. Despite his fear of her, her ruthless actions strengthened him; turned him into a monster. He stared at his drink, wondering why she hadn't shown up to argue with him yet.

To ask him to stop, to negotiate the return of his wife if he stopped killing.

Why weren't things going according to plan? She had done *nothing* he expected her to.

Eros hesitated, curious if another sip of alcohol would soothe him... or make him angrier. Human delights such as these tended to bring out the worst in him, and though his fury fueled him, he needed to prioritize real, godly strength. Ambrosia came first, no matter how much he enjoyed the cute, tasty drinks served by the human bartenders.

Leaving dollar bills on the bar, his mind made, he dashed off before anyone else could give him another confused glance, and before the *bachelorette* and her crew could assault him again. He had to attract his mother elsewhere.

He walked past a couple, their tongues swishing inside each other's mouths, drooling, as if eating each other. A sight that would usually please him, almost arouse him; but here, it only inspired more violent ideas and brutal torture tricks.

The best way to draw Aphrodite to him... was to kill again. Get her mad, get her attention. She had to be as mad as him; *then*, they'd be able to talk.

Only once she understands my anger can I treat with her.

He nodded, satisfied with his decision. Would he execute *this* couple as they slurped away on each other's saliva, hands digging into inappropriate spots? Their guttural sounds only made bile rise in his throat; no, not them. Not yet.

"You took my Psyche, Mother? Well... I'll take *everything* from you, too. Starting with... your credibility." He smiled, returning to the shadows outside the tavern, lingering by the door as he contemplated his new plans. "You'll never return to Olympus; I'll make sure of it."

‖16. COPYCAT KILLER‖
APHRODITE

"Please, Zeus, *please.* I found him; I know what he's doing. Give me my powers and let me stop him. You said I was the only one who could. He *will* kill again; I can feel it."

She peered up at the painted windows of the church she'd stolen into. It was deserted, thank goodness; but it wasn't a building she should have been in. Its spiritual leaders didn't respect her family, her beliefs, didn't speak in the same tongues. But places that still followed her traditions, that allowed the worship of her brothers and sisters, cousins and lovers, were few and far between.

Leering on her knees, she clasped her hands as tears streamed down her face. Her palms ached, her voice trembled. She didn't recognize herself and hated for her comments to be so desperate, so *low.*

"Bring me home and let Ares confront him. He's better at this than I am. Or Athena, *she's* the wise one, your favorite. She'll know the proper words, have ways of soothing him, options none of us have. Maybe I'm *not* the ideal goddess for this mission." She choked back a sob. "But I did what you asked! I played my part! So please, deliver me!"

Her squeaks echoed around the empty space, and she prayed the priest on duty, wherever he hid, wouldn't hear her. Being here, begging for attention from Greek gods, would get her kicked out, she was certain. But it appeared the gods weren't listening, anyway. She'd been crying and pleading for what felt like hours, but they hadn't said a word. Hadn't manifested or sent any signs.

She rose to her feet as another wave of tears threatened her eyes. Was that what humans sensed on a daily basis? Betrayal? Abandonment? *Fear?* She got it now. She understood this world, its poor and deprived people. How they lost all hope because *no one ever answered.*

"Guess what, guys? No one will answer me, either!" She growled, fists forming at her sides as she veered from the altar she kneeled before and walked towards the door.

But as her footsteps carried her away, a loud *thud* stopped her dead in her tracks. A thunderous bang, like actual thunder, without the accompanying lightning.

"It's not raining..." She gawked at the tainted windows, not seeing any droplets of water. "Is... a storm coming?"

The noise was distant—but as it occurred again, she recoiled, recognizing it. It *was* thunder, but not the natural kind. It was the tempestuous, overcharged, sizzling one she'd been acquainted with for centuries. And when a blinding flash of lightning followed, and heavy power and electrifying energy surrounded her, she knew.

No way... he came?

Had she succeeded? After all her ridiculous pleas, was he finally appearing to her?

"*Zeus?* Your Majesty, is that you?" Another overwhelming bang resonated near her, forcing her to her knees and facing the large, wooden door. It didn't open, but she stared at it, waiting.

Seconds later, he spoke. "*Aphrodite!*" His tone bellowed, toppling over chairs and benches, thunder rumbling inside the church. "You have the audacity to summon me *here?*"

She dared a peek at the windows—nothing was happening outside. No one had any clue the king of the skies was *there,* in New Orleans.

His electricity fizzled under her skin. He had *power*. Oh, how she envied him, how she wished for *her* abilities. How she'd love to be a goddess again. "Majesty, I had nowhere else to go, I—"

"—You are not to approach Eros yet. You found out what he's doing, yes, but you don't know *why*. Which means you're not ready for your powers, and you may not come home. Continue your mission."

The roaring timbre drummed in her ears, deafening her, but it disappeared as quickly as it had arrived, leaving Aphrodite moaning on the church floor.

"Zeus?" She whimpered, struggling to stabilize her limbs. "*Zeus!* How dare you do this to me? I'm older than you are! More powerful, if I want to be! You have *no* right!" Pounding on the tiled ground, she groaned, her tantrum like that of a child. "I don't know why Eros is doing this—but I doubt there's any way to find out! He's dangerous! I don't know why he's so mad, so furious, so *carnivorous!* Why won't you help me?"

Looking all around, frantic, panicked, she begged for Zeus to return.

A clap of thunder echoed inside the sanctuary once more, and she dropped her forehead to the floor, paralyzed.

Zeus' disembodied voice shattered windows, destroyed tables, cracked the marble altar at the far edge of the room. "*Figure it out!*"

The once calm church became a godly battlefield—and Aphrodite was responsible for the mess.

She had to get out, fast, before someone caught her and connected her with the disaster. The FBI wouldn't appreciate one of their employees at the scene of such a catastrophe. Gathering her wits, tears still streaming from her eyes, she ran.

* * *

"What a waste of time." Aphrodite slammed her hotel room door shut and ambled over to the bed. She slid her shoes off, stretched her legs, issuing silent thanks for having disposed of those dreadful heels.

They wouldn't help her. She'd figured it out, got more answers... and they *wouldn't help her.* It wasn't fair; everyone was against her, and she had no idea why.

She begged, she prayed; and it wasn't enough. And though safe in her hotel room, the images, so vivid, so recent, still racked her with shudders. Zeus refused to give her more resources but expected her to figure out why her son killed people... all the while *not* speaking to him.

Am I supposed to guess?

She no longer had that kind of energy. Her back smashed against the mattress as she huffed. Under-qualified, unimportant... so close to human, she sensed sobs swelling at her lash-line again.

How could Zeus imply humans had such instincts? They would have eradicated all crime in the world, if they did. Wars would no longer happen; politicians wouldn't be corrupt.

She sighed, pressing a hand to her forehead, and finding her skin burning, covered in sweat. Her clothes clung to her, and she missed her light tunics. Her comfortable bed with its plush mattress and delicate silks. For a moment, she found comfort in her recollections of home.

"I need a bath," she concluded, standing, preparing to undress.

A gentle knock on her door stopped her. She glanced at the clock—it was *late*. Who would visit at that hour? Another knock almost made her stumble backwards onto the bed.

Lukus' rushed tone echoed from the corridor. "Agnes, are you in there? Agnes, open up!"

Eyebrows furrowing, she crossed her arms. *Now* he wanted to talk? No... he came to yell at her, fire her.

Should I let him in? Or should I make him wait?

"What do you want?" She approached the door, peeking through the peephole.

Lukus waited behind the wooden barrier, his shoulders drooping. His hair, messier than usual, had lost its vibrant shine and his suit was ruffled.

"What on earth..." Her hand hovered near the doorknob, ready to let him in. Had he woken from another nap? Or did something else happen?

She saw him shrug. "Look, I'm sorry, okay? I was... a little harsh on you. Can I come in and explain myself? I've made discoveries too, and I want to share them with you."

So, he doesn't wish to get rid of me?

Curious, Aphrodite took a deep breath and unlocked the door. "I suppose."

Lukus strode in, closing the door behind him. He turned on his heels, his gaze cloudy as he gaped at her.

Aphrodite scrunched her nose. "So? What is it?"

If he had showed up to apologize, he had work to do. But did he plan to admit her supernatural theory was true? *Did* he figure something out?

He rubbed his chin. "I mean it, Agnes. I misjudged you. There was truth to your words, and so I... did what you suggested. I looked into the Greek myths."

Aphrodite's brows shot up towards the ceiling. "*Did* you now? So, you understand me, then? You see the supernatural link?"

She smiled on the inside, pleased he came to his senses. With this, he'd be able to support her mission to stop Eros. And if he *did* read the strict minimum about the myths, she'd be able to fill him in on the rest. On the truth—at least, what Zeus authorized her to reveal.

"No." Lukus winced. "*That* I can't agree with. But the Greek myths may still be the answer to who our murderer is, and what their motives are."

Aphrodite frowned as her heart sunk somewhere in her gut. If he didn't believe... why was he there? Hadn't she made herself clear?

Glancing at her darkening features, Lukus gave her a weak smile. "I'm sorry, Agnes, there's only so much I can accept. But... hear me out."

He had no clue what he dealt with—it *was* paranormal. Godly. His best bet would be accepting her claims and allowing her to help. Letting her words imprint in his human skull. Because otherwise, he was vulnerable. Lacking knowledge. What would Eros do with Lukus once he found him?

Because he will.

"Fine. Tell me."

He cleared his throat. "The killer is *inspired* by the Greek myths. They're obsessed, certain *they* are a Greek god. Allowed to hunt and kill for whatever motive they please."

Aphrodite's blood boiled. "Oh, agent Arvantis, you don't get it, you'll get yourself—"

He held his hand up to silence her before she could say *killed.* "I narrowed it down to one god who deals with soulmates. *Eros.*" Aphrodite suppressed a gasp. "Eros inspires this killer! I mean, you established the whole soulmate thing, so this makes sense, right? The culprit targets soulmates because it's pissed or jealous or something. *That's* my theory, no supernatural shit involved."

Aphrodite cringed. Though he was partially right, their killer was no copycat. No, they faced the real Eros. Her angry, brutal, passionate son who now held a grudge against soulmates.

And who'll target you next if you don't get on board with the facts so I can protect you!

She pinched the bridge of her nose, unsure how to address his triumphant conclusion. He had to hear the truth, but he'd be harder than ever to convince. "But what about the hearts? The cannibalism? How do you explain *those?* Is our killer *also* a cannibal?"

"I... haven't figured that part out yet." Lukus pulled a chair from the rickety desk in the corner and sat.

"You want to make sense of all this, I get it. But this theory... it can't work. It doesn't include the gruesome aftermath, the missing organs, the witness accounts." Aphrodite set her fists on her hips. "You're saying *every* witness on *every* case lied. Do you mean they're backing the killer? The murderer has that many connections? Think about it."

He put his head in his hands, setting his elbows on his thighs. "I'm not implying that, but... maybe they *were* all coaxed into helping? Maybe they had no choice, or we're dealing with more than one person. One does the killing, the other steals the hearts, and the witnesses make up a crazy story to lead the authorities astray! Don't you see it?" He lifted his chin and glared at her.

Her cheeks heated, unsure if anger or shame grew in her. *He* didn't see, and she couldn't prove it. She had no powers to use; and by revealing her true self, she'd jeopardize the mission.

Why can't you trust me?

"That is... absurd." Her temples throbbed as she dug her gaze into his, begging him to see the truth in her. "You claim to have all the experience, but you didn't think this through! I'm sorry, I'm sticking with my paranormal conclusions. Someone bigger and inhuman is responsible for this. My logic makes more sense, you have to admit."

She pivoted from him and marched to the window. But jolted around when he scoffed.

"*No*! What I said is the reality—a culprit obsessed with Eros, with an accomplice, and one hell of a network to get their crimes completed. I'm telling you; this is what we're going with and what I'll tell the boss." He stood, arching his back. Moments before he cowered; but her conviction only pushed him further.

A clock ticked in her. A deafening clicking, a buzzer, a gong echoing in her soul.

Time is running out!

She watched him, again praying to infuse her faith into him. Wishing he'd open his mind, search inside, understand the *real* Eros was there, provoking real cannibalism, real chaos. That she was a *real* goddess, and all he saw was *real* magic, real powers.

Don't settle for normal. Normal doesn't exist.

But she couldn't stop him. His stubbornness clouded his vision. He was convinced of her crazy, psychotic nature—and he was so sure that he didn't understand that *he* was the same.

Nodding at her silence, he moved to the door.

"*Screw it!*" She scurried over to bar his route. Her time ran out. Eros hunted his next victims for certain; if she didn't spill the beans, her chances of stopping him hovered below zero. "Wait."

He smirked, cocking his head, opening his mouth—

A cell phone rang, interrupting him. She didn't recognize the ringtone at first, but Lukus' insistent eyebrow raises showed *his* phone wasn't the culprit. It was hers.

She put her index finger in the air. "Please, *wait.*"

He sucked in a deep breath and tapped his foot. "Hurry."

Scrambling through her purse, she snatched the device before it stopped howling. "Hello?"

"Miss Agnes? This is the coroner's office, in New Orleans."

She stared at Lukus, pupils widening. "Yes, *yes,* thank you for calling me back."

The man on the other end choked up, his voice hesitant. "I... would like to meet with you and agent Arvantis. *Now,* if you're still in town." He gulped, the sound so loud it almost made the phone vibrate. "I uncovered significant evidence I can't explain, and... well, it's best I see you both in person to go over it."

Aphrodite didn't remove her gaze from Lukus. "We'll be right there." She hung up, dropping the phone back in her purse.

Lukus' nostrils flared as his foot tapped faster. "Oh, *we* will, you say?"

Aphrodite slid the purse strap over her shoulders. "Yes. That was the coroner's office, and this is urgent. We have to go."

A trace of anger swept across his face. "Why would they call—"

"—*because*." She slipped her shoes on. "Growl at me all you want; you'll thank me later. Now please, come with me to the coroner's office. He has something to show you, and it'll convince you I *am* right. The supernatural is involved in this case."

‖17. PSYCHOS & FANATICS‖
LUKUS

Discomfort crawled up Lukus' spine, settling in all his nerves and muscles. *Was* she clinically insane? Or a little too persuaded by her beliefs?

"You... called the coroner's office behind my back?" He sensed his face morphing into a frown as he watched her ready to leave the room. "What the hell are you instigating? What the hell are you *doing?*"

She didn't move, only glimpsing him with an innocence in her eyes that made him sick.

"You're... you're throwing your career down the drain because you're certain our killer *isn't* human? What is wrong with you?"

Agnes swallowed and, after muttering something under her breath, she crept up to him. "Just... please, come with me. Discover what the coroner found. If it's nothing, and you still don't believe me, *fine*. I'll give up, you can report me to the boss, have me fired. But don't judge me until... we've seen what needs to be seen."

His mind racing, Lukus anchored to the spot. He wanted to fire her *now*, for being so insubordinate... but he had waited for significant evidence from one of the coroners for weeks. His curiosity ate him on the inside; that, and the need to find out what went on.

He crossed his arms. "I..." His fury bubbled in his gut, wondering what she dared to tell the coroner in his name. And *how* she sent them orders without his stamp of approval. Was she higher on the FBI chain than the boss told him?

She clutched her purse, gaze darting about the area, fidgeting as she waited for his decision.

Growling, Lukus scratched his chin, containing his anger. "I guess... I have nothing to lose." Maybe he'd get another hunch as they talked to the coroner; and maybe they *had* something to work with, just not what she expected. "Fine, then." He released his arms and jolted around to open the door. "We'll figure out what he found, but after that I'm calling the boss to discuss your future as an FBI agent. He... may need to reassign you."

Despite his words, she smiled, slinking out of the room. "You'll be surprised." As she passed him, a light rose scent permeated the air as if flaking off her skin. "You might... visualize things differently."

Lukus blinked, his voice caught in his throat.

She's deranged.

* * *

The moon shined bright above them, and the raging parties in the surroundings died down, everyone getting too drunk to keep dancing and frolicking. Lamp-posts flickered with electricity, charging the air with a staticky energy that made Lukus uncomfortable.

Agnes kept quiet while they waited for their vehicle, and quieter still once inside. Not that Lukus *wanted* to make conversation—he preferred not to hear her speak again until they reached the morgue. And he preferred not to understand how her complicated, messed-up brain worked.

A few miles from the hotel, Lukus swerved to her, despite his desire to ignore her. "Agnes... what did you ask the coroner to look for?" His mouth wouldn't stop from forming sentences. "What did you tell him to do?"

The streetlights they drove by illuminated her face, revealing her glittering eyes and her lips parting, plump and delicious. Her skin, so smooth, appeared unreal. "You'll see."

Lukus caught himself staring and scoffed, angry that someone so beautiful and so talented could be so... weird.

She pulled her gaze from his, but he leaned forward, desperate to understand her thoughts. "You need to tell me what's going on. You're creeping me out. I don't know you, and don't trust you, and you're pushing your luck."

His coat jacket felt empty—and he realized he forgot his gun.

Probably should have grabbed that... just in case.

This excursion was a bad idea.

She finally flashed her shimmering glare towards him, freezing him. More lamp-light from outside splashed her cheeks with color. Something ominous yet wondrous drew around her, giving her a robotic, unreal vibe; and sending shivers down Lukus' back.

"*You'll see,* Lukus." Her tone came out lush, thick like honey, but direct. "Please be patient, things will explain themselves. You'll... understand."

Defeated and weirded out all at once, Lukus turned to his window, watching the buildings pass in a blur. Party favors littered the ground, wobbling people wandered the streets, causing a ruckus, yelling, some retching in dark alleyways.

He grimaced at the New Orleans sights. But would he not be safer out there, with *them?* He knew what their issues were. But Agnes? She puzzled him. He couldn't figure her out and trying gave him a migraine.

"You believe this stuff? The Greek myths? The gods? Is this why you're so persistent?" he asked, as the car turned left, down a wider, more popular street.

Agnes shifted in her seat. "I do, agent. Not many people do, nowadays, but I am one of the rare remaining."

"My family…" He swallowed. "My family is part of that *rare remaining* too."

She uncrossed her legs and shuffled again. "Well… your name betrays you; you *are* Greek. And if your family follows the ancient traditions… why don't you?"

Lukus removed his gaze from the busy sidewalks, returning to her. "Because I had a right to choose, and I chose *not* to believe in that bogus crap." He groaned. " I grew up here, in the

United States. A place where, like in Greece, everyone has different beliefs."

Why is she so old-fashioned and critical?

Agnes touched his hand, sending jolts through his spine, giving him unexplained urges. Desire surged through his veins, passion stirred in his belly, traveling lower, expanding farther into his groin. He closed his eyes—though not of his own will—and his thoughts stirred, fuzzing into things he never remembered imagining.

What the fuck? Did I fall asleep? Wake up, Lukus!

He saw himself jump on top of her, right there in the cab's backseat. His mouth covering hers, slipping her clothes off, piece by piece, trailing kisses down her exposed skin as she moaned. He pulled her close, sniffing her like an animal, clutching her near as if he had been deprived of physical contact for years. *Sexual* contact. His pulse quickened, his heart racing in his ribcage as his tongue twirled.

With a start, and a sudden surge of energy, he gasped and yanked his hand away. The images stopped. His eyes wrenched open to reveal he sat in his spot, unmoved, but breathless.

He hadn't fallen asleep. "What the *fuck*—" His heart, thumping, thrashing, cut off his voice. "What did you do?" He blinked, adjusting to the darkness in the vehicle, desperate to calm down.

Shame coursed through him as he fought the need to cram his fingers around her neck and jam her against the cushions to interrogate her.

"What?" Her timbre, so naïve, so velvety, dissuaded him from snatching her wrists and shaking her. Why, *why* did he have to be so attracted to her? Why did he spin out of control like that, just at her touch? Her strangeness repulsed him, her beliefs weirded him out, her psychotic nature put him on edge.

What the heck is happening to me?

He shook his head, wishing to dismiss all awkward feelings; and within seconds, his heart and pulse relaxed. He drew in a large breath, resuming his speech where he left off, hoping Agnes hadn't sensed the odd tension between them.

"I left my family because of their warped religion. I ditched them in New York *because* of how they persevered worshipping something that so few still do. Their multi-god beliefs were unreal, and I couldn't handle having them shoved in my face. I didn't want to be forced into something I couldn't assimilate with." The woman beside him didn't move, but he knew she was listening. "So I'm going to tell you what I told them, what I hoped would persuade them to pull out of their fantasy world; these *gods* you believe in? They're fictional. Myths. Real people *might* have inspired them, I'll give you that. I enjoyed listening to the tales as a kid, because they always had a lesson attached. But here, in the real world? As adults? No. And you're insane to think they have anything to do with this case!"

He hated to bash on someone's religion, but Agnes couldn't bring such claims into the case. There was no such thing as a cannibalistic, carnivorous god—but there was such a thing as a killing duo intrigued by fairy tales.

"You didn't want your family to over-indulge you, I get it. You moved away to pursue your dreams, have your beliefs. Well..." she craned her neck towards him, squinting, "... don't shut mine down until you know for sure."

The car slowed as they arrived at the morgue. Lukus prepared to reply, but Agnes exited before he could. He tossed money in the cab driver's hand and rushed after her, grumbling about her feisty, psycho nature. A Greek god obsessed rookie. Was he being punished? Was it some kind of joke? He was far from perfect, for sure, but why him?

What did I do to deserve this?

He followed her into the dark building, not bothering to reach for his badge—the late hour meant no employees would be working, and the back areas with all the bodies wouldn't be guarded.

As they glided down the halls, a faint light emanated from one of the rooms. Lukus peeked in to find a man, several decades older than him, hunched over two silver tables.

"Sir?" The man whirled around and nodded. "You called us?" To avoid frightening the coroner, Lukus found his badge and flashed it as he entered the room.

A metallic stench slid into his nostrils and, no matter how used to it, Lukus' forehead wrinkled. Agnes slipped in behind him, inclining her head in greeting.

"I'm sorry *she* made you work so late into the night," said Lukus, as the man wiped his hands and came up to them.

Morgues never left Lukus in a good mood. The reflective surface of all the cubbies stared at him, as if daring him to open each compartment, analyze the bodies, get his answers. But that wasn't his task.

"No, please, it's my job." As the coroner approached, Lukus noticed two large lumps on the silver tables, both covered with stained cloths.

The victims.

The coroner smelled of deodorizing spray and antibacterial wipes—almost worse than the layers of decay decorating the room.

"But thank *you* for coming in so late," said the coroner, holding a clamp in one hand and shaking his head. "I wouldn't have called... if I didn't think it necessary." The dim lights reflected his worried features, his bloodshot eyes, his sullen skin. He shook, his fingers struggling to keep hold of the medical instrument.

"Are you... okay?" Lukus took a step back. "You seem... on edge."

What would have a coroner so... petrified? People like him saw gruesome things on a daily basis. And yet this man, exhausted, terrified, appeared as though he had seen a ghost.

Freezing by the doorway, Lukus' eyes widened.

Is he nuts... like Agnes? Are they working together? Is this a trap?

A tug on his arm wrenched him from his thoughts. Agnes pulled him from the threshold. "He's tired," she whispered, not sparing a glance at Lukus, but gaping at the coroner instead. "Please, don't mind my partner. He's over-cautious." Lukus' jaw dropped. "Show us what you got."

Swallowing hard, the coroner pivoted and lifted the blanket covering the first body. He dragged it down to the waist, revealing the female victim's lifeless head, followed by her bare neck, shoulders, breasts, and stomach. The large hole in the chest was still blackened and burnt, almost as scary as it had been when they first saw it. Her pallid and deathly complexion made Lukus hesitant to get any closer. Though he was used to seeing bodies, he couldn't help the nausea swelling in his abdomen.

Agnes didn't flinch as she approached. "Okay..." She peered at the coroner. "*Show us.*"

Lukus' body tensed, filling with angst, anticipation, and a mountain of questions.

What does she expect to see? Why is she so confident?

The coroner dug the clamp into the chest, spreading the skin further apart. Grabbing another unknown instrument from the table, he pointed at the ribcage; he had detached several ribs and separated the cage from the spine and vertebrae for easier access. With a quick tug, he jolted the ribcage upwards, turned it sideways, and jutted his chin at it, urging the agents closer. "I found engravings on the body of the ribcage. Only the top part, at first."

Lukus kept his distance while peeping at the bone; but Agnes angled close, her lips parted as she focused on what the coroner tried to show them.

"But eventually, I noticed... they were *all* over. I have no idea what the words mean, but they look ancient. Like they were tattooed to the bones. I even tried to wipe them off but they're... permanent. *Engraved.*"

Lukus let his gaze wander on the area the coroner specified—and sure enough, he deciphered the encryptions traced along the internal part of the sternum, lining it from top to bottom. In shiny, black ink. The words, definitely foreign, imprinted on the surface as if a machine had stamped them there.

"What the..." Lukus tugged at his collar and cleared his throat. "You... didn't notice these during your initial autopsy?" The stench of the woman's rotting epidermis flared up through his nostrils, and he flinched, striding backwards. "Did she... have heart surgery? Maybe the doctor... did this?"

The coroner shrugged. Agnes tilted further forward, nearly sticking her head *into* the ribcage.

The more Lukus saw her intrigue intensifying, the more disgusted he became. He stopped himself from gagging. "Are we dealing with a medical professional who... tattoos his victims after they're dead?" It was sick. Sicker than the cannibalism, stranger than the removal of hearts.

But not impossible.

Agnes perked up, pulling away from the engravings. "It's ancient Greek."

Both the coroner and Lukus snapped their eyes to her. "How... how the fuck do you know that?" asked Lukus, wary of the strain in his tone, the scratch in his throat. "What... what are you hiding, Agnes?"

"I learned it when I lived in Greece. Part of my education. *I* didn't dismiss my family," she sneered, her comment meant to destabilize Lukus.

He backed farther away, too shaken to put her in her place. "Okay, fine, so... what do they say?" He folded his arms, realizing his biceps tightened and his skin had turned cold. "A signature? Is this a super smart, super-educated surgeon? Who... *what* could do this?"

The coroner covered the body and went to the second one. He removed the blanket and motioned Lukus forward to look inside the ribcage.

Though hesitant, Lukus slithered over—and choked at the eerily similar sight of engravings.

This is disgusting.

"I... I don't know what to say. I can't accept it, but this proof, this... it's disturbing." He returned to his spot feet away from the tables, massaging his temples.

Agnes wagged her finger in disapproval. "It's not a signature. It's a *name*. The other victim's name." Lukus' eyebrows shot up. "In code. Back then, the language didn't have those names,

202 | CARNIVOROUS CUPID

so it's a rough translation. And... it's followed by the word *soulmates.*"

The coroner remained still, and Lukus sensed his cheeks heating.

A sick Eros copycat. A doctor who met the victims, engraved the name of who he believed their soulmate was while in surgery, and later killed them, certain no one would ever look at the ribcages for proof. Gross satisfaction and twisted delight— he couldn't wait to put this sick creature behind bars.

"This supports *my* theory, not yours, Agnes. The insane murderer who wants to imitate Eros. You see? Your supernatural ideas are only inspiration."

She'd have to admit defeat now. She'd have to come clean, confess her over-the-top ideas, allow him to call the boss and have her removed from the case.

But instead, Agnes smiled, and twirled to the coroner. "Sir, in your expert opinion, how long would you say those engravings have been on the ribs?"

Lukus glared between them, huffing. "They died earlier today, so it would depend on when they had surgery, right? Anywhere from a few months to a few days?"

Without turning to Lukus, Agnes lifted her hand to halt him from saying anything else. "I'm speaking to the medical professional, Lukus."

Jaw dropping—for the millionth time that night—Lukus grunted, gawking at her. "How dare you—"

"—I... I can't explain it, agents." The coroner switched between Lukus and Agnes, chin quivering. "But... it seems they've been in there for a while, based on the bone structure and how deeply engraved they are. I'd say... well, I can't believe this but... they've been there since *birth*." He coughed, holding the base of his neck, twisting away from Lukus and Agnes as he stared at the ceiling. "I've never, *ever* seen anything like this. One hell of a psycho killer. To target these people since infancy? I didn't know that was possible."

Agnes snapped her head to Lukus, her glowing gaze making his skin crawl. "That's because it's not a human killer. It's a *god,* and this finally proves it."

‖18. ENGRAVED‖
APHRODITE

The truth—as much of it as she could reveal—now dangled before Lukus. Aphrodite stared at him, waiting, desperate to find out if her method succeeded. If her ploy worked. But his closed body language didn't help her decipher his thoughts. She had messed him up earlier, in the car. Not meaning to provoke such desire, she only wanted to change the subject, divert his attention. But she had no clue her attraction ability still swirled in her touch; and no clue it'd work so well on him. As the only power Zeus allowed her to keep... she didn't expect it to function at all.

The coroner, puzzled, glaring at her as if she had committed the murders herself, didn't help the situation. But she didn't care for him, insignificant as he was. She only needed Lukus on board.

"Lukus?" she dared, not moving from her spot.

Spinning to the coroner, Lukus scoffed. "Is this some *prank?* Are you in on this?"

The man raised his palms in surrender. "I'm only giving my expert opinion, agent. I did as I was asked, and I had no idea you weren't aware of this request." His voice trembled as he struggled to stand upright.

Aphrodite scrunched her eyebrows. "No one is teaming up against you or trying to fool you, Lukus. This is the truth. You're dealing with a god, not a human." She sensed her muscles tensing, but she had to keep her cool. "Who else would do such a thing? Don't you see the signs?"

The coroner backed away from the corpses, his features drowning in more confusion. "I... I can't... I mean, she..."

Praying he'd leave them to discuss the important matters, Aphrodite removed her gaze from the frail man.

Lukus shook his head. "Why... why did you do this, Agnes? Go to such lengths to show me this? And... how did you know there would be something to find in the first place?" The croak in his voice, the lightning flashing in his irises—he was mad.

She knew it would happen, but he *had* to see the truth now. To understand a human didn't do it. She had the proof, and his anger would dissipate once he cleared his mind. Once he listened.

"You... wouldn't have allowed it. But you'd never believe me if I didn't get real proof... so here it is. Aren't you happy? I solved your case, Lukus! I figured it out for you!" She waved her arms about the room, smiling, proud of her accomplishment.

Next, she had to go find Eros—

One step at a time, Aphrodite!

She couldn't reveal her identity yet, so she lowered her flailing arms and gaped at Lukus.

He strode backwards. "*Happy?*" He grunted, the sound guttural, almost animalistic. "My partner mysteriously knows there are ancient engravings inside dead victims, and she won't tell me how she found out! *And* she happens to read ancient Greek! How would that make me happy, Agnes?" He growled, hands forming fists at his sides. "Explain yourself!"

Recalling the moments from the taxi, she gulped. She had to brush his hand again, take his negative thoughts away. Calm him, focus his troubles elsewhere.

She slid forward, her fingertips twitching, itching to entwine with his. "Lukus..."

But he recoiled, panic drawing all over his face. "Don't touch me again! Who... who the hell *are* you?" He panted, his shoulders tensing as his fists tightened. "Pushing me into your theories... you're a freak! A dangerous psycho! I... I need to get away!"

Every ounce of his posture screamed disgust, and as he glanced between her and the bodies, his expression lit up—he was trying to establish a link. To blame her.

"Lukus, *no*—"

She'd never seen him like that. Usually so strong, hard-faced, never showing weakness; but now, facing the unwavering truth, he was weak, scared, unsure. Guilt riddled her as she watched him slide further and further into his shell, refusing to understand; refusing to let her lead him.

Oh, you poor, innocent thing. I'm so sorry.

"I'm *not* a freak. It... was a hunch, all right? The lore says Eros knows the soulmates by their matching engravings. I figured the best place to carve ancient Greek words would be near the heart—so the ribcage, right? Simple as that, Lukus. Please, don't fear *me*."

If he discovered *she* gave Eros his powers, he'd faint; but the truth behind the myth might convince him. Whatever eased him into the situation, urged him to trust her—she was willing to try.

His cheeks flushed as he lowered his chin. "How... can you be so sure it's *supernatural?*" When he pulled his head back up, a fire swirled in his irises. "Why are you so obsessed with this? Why can't you accept the logical explanation I've offered? It's insane, Agnes. You're crazy."

Wary she was failing to protect him, she did her best to control her tone, turning it soothing, soft. "You heard the coroner. Those engravings were there *long* before the murders. So, unless we're dealing with a surgeon who happened to operate on *both* the victims at birth, and who learned ancient Greek, *and* also has a penchant for eating hearts... you need to accept that supernatural is our only option."

The coroner nodded from his corner though trembling like a leaf.

Aphrodite smacked a hand over her forehead. She wasn't supposed to reveal herself, yet the human she posed as had terrified two others in the space of minutes.

How will I fix this? Turn it in my favor?

Lukus stood his ground, but the angst in his aura was almost blinding. Aphrodite wanted to reach out and calm him, but her touch would only send him over the edge. She had no control.

"I... I can't. It doesn't add up. Makes little sense. *Why? Who? Which god?*" His nostrils flared. "Eros? No way. What if it's a coincidence?"

"I don't believe in coincidences, Lukus, and neither should you." Her timbre raspier than expected, she gasped.

Shoot. Regain control, Aphrodite.

"Call the other coroners. Have them check the bodies if it's not too late. I bet... you'll find the same result."

The coroner squealed, re-immersing himself into the conversation. "A-actually, miss, I took the liberty of doing that."

Aphrodite and Lukus jerked their heads towards him. "What?" they said, in unison.

The man nodded so fast he almost lost his balance. "After what I found, I was so confused... I wanted to see if the other bodies had the same markings. I called the Las Vegas office, and the coroner over there put me on speaker and performed the revised autopsy while I listened. The... victims over there have the engravings."

Lukus ceased breathing, and Aphrodite smiled.

You're not as insignificant as I thought, Mister coroner.

She turned to Lukus, watching him wipe his forehead and his lips parting as his eyes widened. "I... we..."

That was it. The moment he *had* to see it. Aphrodite prayed, her desperate words clouding her brain; she prayed he came to his senses before Eros attacked him. And his soulmate if he had one. Because she was certain Eros spied on them. He ogled Lukus—he was his type—and prepared to pounce, to eat him, to murder him. Especially since Lukus was human *and* working with her.

He won't like that.

"See?" She clapped her hands. "I'll bet if you call the crime scenes before Las Vegas, you'll hear the same. Do it. Because... I mean, good luck finding a surgeon who operated on all fourteen victims for the same cause. This is *no* coincidence."

Fear brimming in the form of tears at his lash-line, and arms swaying beside him, Lukus cocked his head. "But... I'm sure they've incinerated or buried those bodies. It's too late." Visible shivers rushed from his shoulders to his calves.

"Try anyway. Call Seattle first, they may still have access. It's worth a shot."

The coroner escaped his corner and brushed past her. He scurried to the doorway, then twirled to motion for Lukus to accompany him. "I'll help, agent."

Aphrodite jutted her chin at him. "*Go!* Contact the offices and see what they're able to dig up." She maintained her smile as she snuck closer. She didn't mind having to get her hands dirty, to retrieve the corpses herself, extracting them from coffins. Because she'd do anything to prove her point, to save Eros' potential victims from having their hearts devoured. And their souls banned to Tartarus without explanation.

Lukus, snarling, jumped out of reach. "Okay, but *don't* touch me."

Blowing out her cheeks, Aphrodite stepped back, watching as Lukus followed the coroner out of the room. Alone, at last, she returned to the bodies. She lifted the covers and began her own analysis—an in-depth confirmation of godly touch. Peering at the burned chests, zooming closer to the engravings. Confirming it was indeed Eros' signature and the soulmate's name, and the word 'soulmate' encrusted beneath it all.

I'm glad I told them the truth, no matter how weird they think I am.

She grabbed a pair of gloves from a nearby counter, wrapping the uncomfortable material around her delicate skin. Unaffected by the gruesome nature of what she had to do, she dug into the hollow cavity of the first female body—checking for any other engravings. Any clues Eros might have left; anything to help understand his actions. Patting the empty spaces, inspecting each rib, she ensured she missed nothing.

She bowed her head in defeat. "No, he wouldn't want me to have it easy." She groaned. "And I bet he senses us, too. Always been a sharp kid that one..."

She swirled around, checking the doorway in case the coroner and Lukus came back. But she was still alone.

Sighing, she removed the gloves and let them drop. "All grown up, killing humans, leaving a trail of blood for mommy to follow, huh? What does he want? How can I stop him?"

She stared at her palms, at their boring human shape, their lack of luminosity—as a goddess, she glowed. But here, she lacked color, as if stuck in black and white.

She needed her powers. Lukus' negativity hampered her confidence, and his disregard for his origins weighed on her soul. Could she save him, too, while saving her son?

Fastening her hands, she took another deep breath and gaped at the ceiling. "Zeus," she whispered. "Zeus, *please*, return my powers. We've uncovered new evidence. I'll figure out Eros' motives at any moment now."

Her fingers clasped against each other, she squeezed her eyes shut. Zeus had to perceive her desperation, understand the danger—the peril Lukus was in.

Eros won't stop unless someone physically interferes. Me.

A sense of responsibility washed over her. Though she earlier refused to be the one to face him, she knew now. She had to catch Eros.

She dropped to her knees, clenching her hands so tight they ached. "Zeus, please. Appear, speak to me. I *need* my abilities. I'm powerless, and Eros is on a rampage, a real one. He's not playing games, he's attacking soulmates, and it's gory." She gulped down an acidic bile lingering at the top of her throat. "The human... he's in over his head and needs protection. *Real* protection. I can only provide that with my powers. *Please.*"

Her whispers turned louder than she wished, furious that Zeus ignored her, instead of showing up to scream at her in person—*again*. She imagined the gods and goddesses on their thrones, staring down at her, laughing, pointing, mocking her inability to follow orders, making fun of her incapacity to bring her own son to justice.

"Where's your thunder *now*, Zeus?" Her knees scraped against the tiled floor, her pants too thin to protect her skin. "Why won't you come to me here, in this place, huh? Why do you continue to treat me this way? Won't you at least give me a chance to confront him, to succeed in this mission? What have I done to offend you so?"

A loud *thump* echoed nearby, as if something had been thrown or had fallen to the ground. She jumped to her feet, opened her eyes, and searched for the source of the noise.

Twisting her head, she found Lukus in the doorway—his phone on the floor and a notepad dropping beside it, sending papers flying out of his grasp. His jaw tightened, his lips thinned, and every inch of him turned immobile, as if under a spell.

She racked her brain to remember the human expression for the intense emotions washing over her.

Oh, that's right.

"Shit!"

‖19. SUSPENSE & SUSPECTS‖
LUKUS

Her voice had echoed into the hallway, drawing him closer, making him curious about what she said when talking to herself. But he regretted it. Lukus found Agnes kneeling, hands clasped together, as if praying, staring at the ceiling and mumbling words that were far from prayers.

They were *summons.*

His body froze the instant she mentioned *Zeus.* When she told him to come to her, to appear. Why would she ask such a thing? And how could she assume he'd arrive and speak with her, anyway?

He doesn't exist. He's a myth!

Hands trembling more than he wanted them to, he picked up his phone, making sure the screen wasn't broken. He only found a few scratches, then glared at Agnes, who now stood straight and watched him, fear paralyzing her face and turning it paler than a cloud.

"I... uh... didn't know you came back." He saw her lower lip quiver.

His eyes narrowed. "Obviously." A nerve in his neck pulsated. "Is... this what you do when you're alone, Agnes? Call the Greek gods to you and expect them to... show up?" He snorted. "What the *fuck* was that about?"

He bent down to pick up the sheets he dropped—reports faxed by the Seattle office, confirming their discovery of inscriptions. It turned out, they had already found the marks and were preparing the report for Lukus, anyway. But now, seeing Agnes in such a state, her eyes wild, her hair almost whipping in a nonexistent wind, he had no desire to share his findings with her. The coincidence had become too creepy for him to handle. She was psycho, for real—he didn't want to fire her, he needed her locked up.

Agnes gulped and threw her palms behind her, lowering her chin. "I... uh... do that when I panic, okay?" She shuffled her feet, her flats tracing a line back and forth on the ground. "I talk to Zeus, like other believers talk to God. I'm sure they ask Him to show up for them too, right? I'm... not *that* weird." She flushed and, out of nowhere, her irises changed colors—going from an electric purple to a deep night sky blue.

He tilted backwards. Sure, some people's eyes shifted; but like *that*? So quickly?

Who is she? What is she?

"Talk?" He scoffed, crossing his arms over his breastbone, still clutching the papers. "You call that *talking?* You were yelling at him like you've met him before. Like you were family. Asking for... *powers?* What kind of freak are you, huh? You think you have powers? Seriously?" He released an arm to shove his phone in his jacket pocket.

He had discovered a lot of fanatics in his time, but this... he'd never witnessed. She was a lunatic, and he had no clue why the boss hadn't checked for something like this before sending her on a dangerous case.

Agnes attempted to approach him, but he backed away and shook his head. "Oh no, don't come near me. If what you have is *contagious,* I don't want it. What I *do* want is an explanation, and a solid one. *Now!*" Though his voice boomed around the room, the fear he sensed within bubbled in his gut. Criminals, mass murderers, conspiracy theorists... they were all *nothing* compared to the crazy woman before him.

I don't understand.

"What did the other offices say, Lukus?" she asked, her features relaxing, her pupils going from blue to dark green.

He wanted to rub his eyes, squint at her, lean in closer—it was too unreal. Was she wearing special contacts? Testing him, changing the colors on purpose to draw him in?

Or was it all some sick joke?

Is someone filming me?

The angst in his belly transformed to rage. Deception. A heavy need to get the truth and seek vengeance on whoever thought any of this was funny. If he laughed at the situation, would Agnes laugh with him? Come pat him on the back, high-five him for figuring out the ruse, reveal the locations of the hidden cameras likely waiting for his reaction?

The boss—did he send her to test him? To make certain he knew what he was doing?

The murders aren't even real, are they?

"Earth to Lukus, can you hear me?" Agnes snapped her fingers. "What did they say?"

Returning to reality, deciding to play along with her, he glanced down at his papers, now crunched in his palms. "Seattle... confirmed their victims have the same markings. We caught them as they were about to transport the bodies... and they were already analyzing, trying to debunk the engravings. So, they... faxed over a report, and they'll be sending pictures soon too. The coroner waits for those as we speak."

Agnes smiled. He watched her, waiting for her to tell him he passed, he didn't cede to her paranormal paranoia; he used his logic. Maybe it'd get him promoted; or transferred to a less gruesome department.

But Agnes only continued to smile, standing tall, her chest puffed out. "Great. And those pictures will be identical to here, Lukus. So... please, *open your mind.* Stop following reason, look outside the box, tune in to your intuition... I promise you; real results will appear. You'll find the real killer if you listen to me!"

She slid over so fast he had no time to skip away from her touch. Her hand grazed his, fizzling energy up his nerves, shooting up to his brain and controlling his thoughts. Like in the cab, earlier. With one stroke, she provoked him. He had no command over his mouth and couldn't yell out for help.

Stop this, Agnes!

His internal protests were in vain. His mind, jelly-like, uncontrollable, morphed to reveal flashes of his fingertips reaching for her face. Pulling her near, planting his lips on hers, slipping his tongue around hers as the background faded, transforming into... his hotel room.

What the...

Their clothes in a line, leading to the bed. A mess of sheets, pillows, and blankets littered the mattress—and behind those, he and Agnes groaned, grunted. Their bodies molded, blended, moved together and ground like a perfectly oiled machine, over and over. Surfing waves of pleasure and desire, panting in unison.

No! Enough!

He jerked his hand from hers and shoved her off him. She stumbled across the room, heaving as she hunched over.

"I thought I told you *not* to fucking touch me again!" He brushed off his pants, and Agnes attempted to keep her balance. "What the hell was that?"

Though she kept her head down, he heard her whimper. "Lukus, I—"

"—no, *stop* with the excuses!" The papers once in his grasp had fallen again. "I want the truth! Who the fuck are you, and how do you know the things you do? And *how* did you control me like that?"

Agnes tilted her head side to side, fixating on her shoes. "I... can't tell you who I am. But I *have* told you the truth." She let out a semblance of a snort. "You're dealing with a god. Eros. He's your killer... and I can't tell you how these facts come to me, they just... do." She craned her neck up, revealing her rosy cheeks and sparkling eyes. "Have I not come through? Fed your curiosity with those engravings, made you realize I might be right? You can't deny it, and neither can your body."

Not an ounce of sympathy coursed in his veins as her pained voice ran through his skull. "And you don't think you seem *suspicious?* Showing up as my new partner, pretending to be clueless, then having all the answers and being so knowledgeable about all the Greek gods? And you *suddenly* assume one of them is responsible for this carnage? How does that make sense to you? Tell me... tell me why I shouldn't arrest you *right now!*"

He flinched, recalling he had left his handcuffs at the hotel. And his gun.

Shit. I bet she knows that.

His shoulders dropped as his gaze darted around the area, desperate for an escape. It was a trap, and ambush, and he should have guessed it. He let her fool him, confuse him, *control him.*

"I've been sure a god was liable for this from the *beginning*, Lukus. But I couldn't barge in on your case and say that without proof. I had to put you through all this to *show* you. These engravings... they mean everything." Though every inch of him screamed to run, he kept his focus on her as she paced to the bodies and pointed at them. "Eros is Cupid, did you learn that? They're the same. He shoots arrows at destined soulmates to push them towards each other, to fall in love. *That* is his role amongst the Greek gods." She traced her fingers along the breasts of the first victim.

Lukus swallowed hard, still unable to pull himself from the sight. By now his gut warned him *she* had more involvement in the murders than he anticipated. Her unexplained abilities, her absurd knowledge... he never believed in witchcraft, but her aura reeked of it.

She's... been the culprit this whole time, hasn't she?

"But are you familiar with how he decides who is whose soulmate? How he recognizes them and figures out who to target?"

She stopped, pointing at one of the marks on the second victim's ribcage. "*These.* They're on each human at birth. Though some don't have soulmates, but I'm unsure why." Her steps cautious, she returned to Lukus, but stopped halfway, keeping her distance.

Had she grabbed a weapon before she left? What did she hide in her trench-coat?

He cracked his knuckles, prepared to fight for his life. Prepared to put into action all his skills, his training as an FBI agent. He lowered to a crouch-like state, waiting for Agnes to launch herself at him; but she didn't.

"Each marking tells Eros who to shoot, and when. Tells him which soulmates belong together. Only it seems lately, he's been using his arrows for a different purpose. These markings help him target soulmates, yes, but... *not* to make them fall in love."

Keeping his legs bent and his body low, Lukus glowered at her. *Her.* The psycho killer, for sure. The one who believed in myths so heavily she became Eros. Found a ruse to discover these soulmates and their engravings and murder them. Though how... was a bigger mystery that he feared he'd never get an answer to. She was right about one thing; he had to open his mind, to alter his beliefs a little... to frame and catch *her.*

She circled around Lukus, but didn't look at him. "He's mad. Making soulmates eat each other's hearts and by default, *kill* each other. That's what you're investigating. An *angry* god. And I am the only one who can help you with this, but you have to start trusting me. I can't protect you from him if you don't."

Lukus' eyebrows rose. "Protect me?" From having kept quiet, his voice had turned raspy. "From what? Am I... a target?"

Maybe she was an accomplice and took a liking to him; explaining why she hadn't killed him yet. Or... because he didn't have an online dating profile, she assumed he didn't have a soulmate, so she had no way to trap him, dispose of him like the others.

Peering at her as she moved, sliding like a snake, Lukus licked his lips. "What do I have to do with anything? Why are you telling me all this? I never saw it in the myths I read about, so how do *you* know about it?"

Had the coroner returned from his office yet? Did he lurk in the corridor, overhearing the entire conversation? Maybe he was calling the cops at that instant. Or perhaps he escaped, saved his skin, hurried to tell everyone what happened. That Lukus' insane partner had caused all the madness.

Agnes halted right in front of him. "Stop suspecting me. I am *not* the criminal. Do you think I'd commit such brutal acts? Provoke humans to eat and execute each other? Start chaos in an entire country?" She huffed. "Oh, I've done bad things, but *never* something so tragic. No, as I've said, your culprit is Eros. And he will come for you if you don't quit being so stubborn."

Stuck in his spot, Agnes' glare keeping him rooted to the floor, Lukus groaned. "How can I *not?* You... know too much. No matter how illogical. It... adds up." His heart raced in his chest, ready to burst. "Eros... that's who I figured the killer used as inspiration. And you... have too much information on him. Things... my mother never told me in her stories. Things I didn't see in the books... I don't believe in gods but you... *you* have a part in all this!"

Surprising him, Agnes chuckled. A feminine, flowery sound he never expected a murderer to have. "It's difficult, Lukus, especially for you. As you told me earlier, you ran from all this insanity. Escaped your family, seeing their religion as unreal. But it's *not.* All of it is true. I can't tell you why or give you proof, but it *is.*" A slight sweetness in her tone made him shiver and cringe all at once.

With a deep exhale, he tugged himself from her hypnotizing eyes. "That's my problem. I *can't*, no matter how much you drill into my head. You may have found these engravings, but I still don't know how. And until I do, until you come clean, I *will* suspect you, and consider you insane. I can't picture some imagined god on the loose killing people because he's throwing a little tantrum."

In those moments, Agnes' features morphed. Her pupils switched to a bright blue, her lips thinned, her skin paled. Without warning, streams of tears erupted and spiraled down her cheeks, dripping to the floor as heavy as fountains.

He had seen women cry, but Agnes looked far from normal as salty water trickled down her cheekbones and jaw in waves.

"I... can't... *do* anything," she wailed.

Unsure how to react to a murderous psycho having a mental breakdown, his brows lifted. "I, uh..."

"He is killing... humans... and he's *not*... supposed to!" She wiped her face, but that only caused more tears to burst out. "I can't stop him... Lukus... my son, he's *violent*... scary...

dangerous. Help me..." She dropped to her knees, hiding her expression with her dampened hands.

Her son?

"Wait, you... you said he... this assassin, the one you think is Eros... he's your kin?" Confusion burned his brain, messing with his senses.

Who is Eros' mom?

"My son... slaying innocent... humans." She shivered, her tone unrecognizable. Soft but broken, delicate but powerful.

Fuck.

"Eros' mom... is Aphrodite." He arched his back, looking at the woman at his feet, her tears spilling out like overflowing bowls of water. "Agnes... are you saying... you're Aphrodite?"

Agnes' neck jolted up, her tears disappearing, and her usual suave and seductive tone returning. "Hello, Lukus. It's nice to meet you."

‖20. HUMAN EMOTIONS‖
APHRODITE

She had no choice. As her tears swelled up again, she struggled to contain them. Wondering why she hadn't better prepared—did human women carry tissues?—she drew in a breath, aware she had cried enough for a lifetime. She stared at Lukus, waiting for a reaction, hoping he would understand the depth of the situation. The engravings, the proof other victims had them, pouring out her heart and soul—it had to work. She shivered, conscious of how much trouble she was in. Doing what Zeus asked her not to—reveal her identity. And in the process, she'd spilled secrets about Eros' skills, his goals, how he does his job.

I'll be punished for this.

Lukus covered his face with his hands.

If only she had her powers. She'd be able to smooth him into it, ease his pain, help him understand the truth without shocking him. Maybe even fiddle with his mind, give him a gentle push towards trusting her.

He hunched over, his back moving up and down; as if he struggled to breathe or... was crying.

Oh dear... what have I done to him?

She peeped at her trembling hands and gulped. Lukus had every right to call her a *freak*, no matter how hurtful it was to hear it. Because she couldn't blame him.

She made a move to approach, but he uncovered his face, causing her to gasp. His eyes, red and swollen, letting tears streak down his face, had never been so intense.

"Lukus, I..." Regret filled her as she gawked at his expression, worry sneaking its way into her abdomen. He seemed so afraid, so overwhelmed with finding out her real identity, so shocked to the core at the goddess who stood before him.

But when she understood the truth behind his reddened eyes and sudden tears... her guilt dissipated. He wasn't crying; he was *laughing*.

"Oh... my... gosh, Agnes!" He exploded. Saliva spat out as he sputtered. "You... *you* think..." Laughter gushed from him like a broken faucet. With each squeak he made, his giggling amplified, and his body shook harder.

Growling in offense, she watched him mock her. The sadness she contained moments before drained as he wiped his forehead.

"You... you think you're *Aphrodite?* The goddess of love and desire? You actually do, don't you? You fucking *freak!*" He released more obnoxious giggles, his face redder than a juicy tomato.

But Aphrodite's human body didn't accept his jabs. "No need for tones, Lukus." Though she wanted to slap him, she refrained; as they were now, he overpowered her. "You have a tough time believing in these things, but it's the truth. How else do you explain my behavior? My knowledge?"

If he didn't respect her, and fast, she would punish him once her powers returned. Regardless of Zeus' wishes—she wouldn't have this inferior creature insult her.

No one speaks like that to Aphrodite.

Lukus shook his head, still laughing, though he seemed to control himself a little. "I explain it by calling you a *freak.* Obsessed with your religion and those myths, and that explains your knowledge. And your behavior? Well... you're nuts, that's all."

This man before her no longer held all the desire and yearning he did when first meeting her. He lost all those sensations amid her revelation. Even if she tried to touch him, he'd recoil, brush her off, refuse her control. The little power she had... wouldn't serve for anything anymore.

She frowned. "My name isn't and never has been *Agnes*. I am *Aphrodite,* so please address me as such from now on."

Her fingers tingled with a pulsating energy she didn't recognize. Violent anger? She didn't want to hurt him, no; she only wished he'd stop belittling her. Unleashing her fury on him would be reckless; physically, without her abilities, she wouldn't damage him much... though her mortal frame appeared to disagree. A part of her wanted to rip Lukus apart, piece by piece, expose his internal organs; and yet another hoped for acceptance, for a chance to forgive his transgressions.

I hate being a mortal! And a female, above all else!

Too many confusing emotions washed over her at once. Fear, fury, an eerie lust for his angry self, disgust at that lust... As a deity, she embraced all rage and hunger, let it flow; she threw things against walls and had illegal adventures with Ares to calm down. But what did humans do? Bottle it all up and wait to detonate, like now?

This is terrible.

Lukus scoffed. "I will call you insane, that's what! And a *criminal*. And the cops!" He slid backwards. "You think you can get away with all this by posing as a goddess? Trying to make me believe you? I'm the most hardcore skeptic you'll ever meet, so don't bother. It's over. I caught you, whatever or whoever you are. Better to surrender." He patted his suit jacket, in search of something.

A tiny ounce of hope rose in her. He didn't have his gun or handcuffs, she was certain; a win for her. So, unless he chose to beat her up, he had no means to harm her.

Keep talking, find a way to sway him!

Lukus peeked at his phone as he got it out. His fingertips hovered over the screen, hesitant. The ounce of hope vanished. She had to prevent him from calling the police. They'd believe *him*. Lock her up, keep her detained—what good would she be stuck inside a prison cell?

"No, Lukus, *please*," she begged, her voice breaking up. "Please, let me prove it to you. Let me explain. Give me a chance to show you who I am." The emotions in her amplified, and she had a hard time keeping her balance, ready to overflow.

Humanity was uncomfortable. Unable to control her sobbing, her will to break everything in sight, her deception at each word leaving Lukus' mouth, she sensed her fists clenching. Did all women feel like that every day? And was it worse when in love?

Is this what Eros and I cause?

She straightened herself as she puffed out short breaths, praying for focus. Her goddess urges were *worse* than her human ones. For now, she had to prevent Lukus from acting irrationally; locking her up would be suicide.

Fingers still floating above the phone keypad, he squinted at her. "Why should I give you a chance? To give you time to formulate a plan to assassinate *me* too? No. You won't do that. I don't aim to get my heart eaten, thank you. This ends *today*." Finally, he allowed the pads of his thumbs to type on the screen.

Crap.

Punishment would come from the gods; she wouldn't have punishment from Lukus, too. She dove towards him and smacked the phone out of his hands as she landed on top of him. The device flew out of reach, and Lukus' face reddened in anger.

"How *dare* you—"

It was the physical contact Aphrodite needed. She snatched his palms and concentrated, forcing her desirable energy on him, pushing him to see the images from earlier. The want, the need, the attraction; he'd obey if too lustful towards her. But she barely got to the part where he ripped her clothes off in his mind before he shoved her off him, sending her falling onto her rear. He jumped to his feet with ease and glimpsed around the room in search of his phone.

Aphrodite prayed she had sent it far enough to keep him distracted.

She lifted her upper body from the cold floor to better see him. "Lukus, *stop!* Please!"

He jolted around, marched to her and stopped, lifting his foot right over her chest. Threatening to constrict her breathing, to end her complaints.

"No, please, don't..." She squeaked as the sole of his shoe got closer. "*Quit it!* I'm the only one who can stop this! Save you! *Believe* me!" She winced. "Didn't you grasp my power when I held your hands? Who else but the goddess of love and beauty would provoke such desire? Reach so deep inside you and pull out your true thoughts?" Bringing her palms up to cover her face, she prepared for him to press his shoe over her torso and squish the breaths from her lungs.

"A *witch*, maybe? Voodoo, or some shit." His voice rumbled like an earthquake; cruel and breathless.

Aphrodite gulped, sensing his foot against her breasts. "But you... you don't... believe in the supernatural, so you—"

"—I don't believe in *bullshit.*" She lowered her hands to see him snicker, his features turning dark, almost evil. "Witchcraft... well, I've dealt with folks who dabbled in it and though I don't get it, others do. Their conviction makes it *seem* real." He then growled, narrowing his gaze. "Don't test me, Agnes."

She had never been so vulnerable, so ungod-like, so weak.

Whenever you want to help me, Zeus, feel free! I betrayed you and don't deserve it, but you're about to lose the human version of me! Don't you care?

Grimacing at her begging thoughts, she dared to glower right back at Lukus. "I'm not a witch, come on! Let's not get violent, that solves nothing!"

The shoe pushed down harder and the corners of her vision began to blur. She sensed every inch of the leathery sole shoving into her diaphragm, causing her to wheeze. "Lukus..." She choked, coughing, and closed her eyes as she sensed her life force drain; and yet he pushed, harder, heavier, uncaring of her desperation.

And suddenly, she could breathe again.

She wrenched her eyelids apart to see him pulling away. "*You* started with the violence." He stepped backwards as Aphrodite hacked out her lungs, grabbing at her throat. She was relieved, but in agony. "And now you want to *talk*?" Lukus sneered and pivoted towards the door.

Hissing in pain, Aphrodite hauled herself up and brushed the dust off her pants. "I never meant for things to veer out of control."

He swerved sideways, casting her a side-glance worthy of Hades himself. "Make up your mind, *freak*."

"Don't call me that." She readjusted her clothes, tugging down on her shirt, images of her death sending goosebumps all over her flesh. Never had she been so close to Tartarus.

He watched her, his gaze showing intrigue at the bare skin of her neck—but he snorted as he peered at the ceiling instead. "Then what the fuck am I supposed to call you? You said your name wasn't Agnes, and I refuse to call you something you're *not*. Looks like we're at an impasse unless you somehow prove me wrong."

Lungs expanding with difficulty as she continued to regain her senses, Aphrodite shifted her weight. "I can't show you powers if that's what you're requesting. I only have my lust and passion. That's... all Zeus left me with."

Lukus rolled his eyes. "Uh huh."

"Dismiss me all you want, but it's true, Lukus. He's a twisted king, but my son is *worse*. I was sent down here to intercept him, but also deprived of my powers. To be undercover, but... I blew it."

And she was on her own, with no support system, no help. At least Lukus had *her* whenever he decided to get on board.

He pinched the bridge of his nose. "So, all you can do is make me want to have sex with you? I've met regular women who did that without the flashy visions. I can explain your *power* away from lack of sleep and stress of this case." He slid his fingers over to massage his temple instead. "Sure, I'm attracted to you, but those images *came* to me on their own. I'm not convinced or impressed. I need more than that if you want me to accept your insanity."

He scoped the room.

He's looking for his cell-phone.

She waved to get his attention. "My godly form can be too harmful to humans, that's why I am here as someone else. To blend in. And I *was* summoning Zeus. You caught me, red-handed. But only to beg him to give me my powers! I realized I can't confront my son without them. Eros is vengeful, angry, bloodthirsty—and as a human, I have no way to make him stop murdering innocent soulmates. I don't even know why he's doing it. That's what the gods wanted me to find out, but I'm too afraid to approach him as I am. And you should be too."

He already heard so much, she had no qualms revealing everything, including her fears. If he saw a goddess of her standing feared Eros... he'd see the danger. Walk away until she got her powers back, at least.

Be smart about this.

Eyes widening, Lukus plunged sideways. "You're *full of shit!*" When he rose, he held his phone, a victorious smile spreading across his mouth. "So, I'm gonna go get a drink, erase this crap from my brain. You didn't try to kill me, so... I'll let this slide." He put the phone into his jacket pocket. "But you're off the case, I'll tell the boss. You'll never be an FBI agent with ideas like that. Go back to... wherever you came from. Before I change my mind, and have you arrested for tampering with my case." He took a few strides backwards. "I can get you to burn for *witchcraft*. I... never want to see you again, got it?"

Before Aphrodite could retaliate, beg, pray—he whisked around and disappeared, doors slamming in the distance behind him.

Alone again, Aphrodite dropped to her knees. She let the tears come, no strength remaining to stop them. *"Zeus..."* She sniffled. "Do you see what you've done? What your idiocy caused? Your special protégé will die! Eros *will* target him! And since I have no power, I can't stop it!"

Pools of salty water formed beneath her. She had taunted the gods—so she'd likely die soon, too. Along with Lukus, the fierce non-believer.

‖ 21. REVENGE IS SWEET ‖
EROS

The strong energy in the vicinity was painfully obvious. The sizzling static, the heavy, charged atmosphere—all signified a powerful presence.

Eros loomed in the shadows near the morgue, observing the dark doors, awaiting their opening. His heart throbbed with trepidation, nervousness, fear, happiness—all ranges of emotions entangled in him.

I'm so glad I stayed.

As he prepared to depart for a new town—he thought somewhere in Texas—he sensed a conflict raging in New Orleans. A familiar sensation he had encountered before; an energy that flitted under his skin and made his muscles twitch. It didn't take him long to identify it as an argument between a human... and a god.

A rare occurrence, yes; but Eros had no trouble recognizing such godly anger, as he'd come across it in his youth—with all the horrible things his mother made him do for the Olympians—and would never forget the way it scarred him.

The feeling grew in intensity the closer he got to the spot where he tracked it—the coroner's office.

Only one god lingered in the city, he knew.

Mother.

So, it was her and the human FBI agent, it had to be. His mother's rage trickled under his skin as he sniffed the atmosphere, stationed near the morgue, silently waiting for the results.

The strength of the argument permeated the air—whatever their disagreement, it was unsolvable, and he wished he could hear the details. Pleasure ran down his spine, tingling his limbs.

Mommy's got a lot of emotions!

Her soul was confused, crying, screaming. Never had Eros pictured the mighty Aphrodite as one to break down so easily.

As he chuckled, he grunted, reverting to a frown almost at once.

Why hadn't she killed the human yet? She didn't need him. She was more powerful than him. More powerful than anyone. Yes, Lukus was handsome—but useless.

Eros breathed in the light ambrosia scent still weaving in and out of his aura, tasted its sweetness on his tongue, its delicate nectar coursing through his veins.

"Thank you, Anteros." His brother had risked his immortality to revive him, and Eros planned to reward him when the time came.

Now, his power levels exploded, amplified, engorged. His fingers prickled with delight, his heart beating fast at the idea of shooting more deadly arrows and destroying more humans.

More chaos to provoke, more cannibalism to enforce, more carnivorous murders to come.

He envisioned the gruesome crime scenes he left behind. The decaying corpses, the thick puddles of blood, the pieces of eaten flesh. The overwhelming stench of death, the horrified witnesses, the chunks of hearts surrounding the dead bodies.

He smiled, reveling in his brutal methods. Pleased with his torture, his manner of pushing humans to absolute disgust and despair.

But he still had to deal with Aphrodite. Make her admit her crime, confess the truth. *She* started it all though Eros didn't plan on torturing only her. But with his renewed strength, he no longer feared confronting her.

Gaping at the doors, unsure who he hoped to see escape, he crossed his arms. *Someone* would storm out at any moment. They were both furious, he could tell; a hint of mortal irritation peppered Aphrodite's immense fury. Lukus was *also* mad. But surely she would incapacitate him, murder him, and be the first to leave the premises.

Eros grinned, wondering how she'd do it. Aphrodite's methods were far and wide, and her grueling temper only rendered Eros' plots easier to pull off.

But why did she work with Lukus, anyway? She found Eros—she *had* to have sensed him near.

Come get me, Mother!

The air, heavy with intrigue, hot with alcohol and lust, made Eros sigh, unwind, relax. The lack of people nearby eerily soothed him, and he enjoyed the momentary silence, basking in the glow of his accomplishments.

Aphrodite was furious, and it pleased him. The angrier she got, the bigger the chances she'd confess what she did. He knew she slipped up when infuriated; got sloppy, too full of rage to care to cover up her mistakes.

And she's getting sloppy already, I can tell.

He rubbed his hands together. Sure, it wouldn't be simple. Aphrodite *was* an Olympian goddess, part of the twelve elite. She had much more power than him, but he had knowledge she didn't. And extra ambrosia he was certain she had no access to, too busy playing around with the useless human.

He perked up, a sudden epiphany shooting delightful tremors up and down his arms. "Wait... has Mommy dearest taken a *love* interest in Lukus? Changed her mind, given up on her despicable husband? And on *Daddy?*" He licked his lips. "This might get more interesting the further I dig."

His eyebrows raised, and a tantalizing wave of pleasure took over him, almost paralyzing. Because he knew now how to weaken her; through her feelings for the mortal.

She will be easier to disarm... easier to hurt.

He could barely tolerate the delectable thoughts pouring into his brain, dancing about in his skull.

She'd barter, try to persuade him she's innocent—he knew her better than anyone. *She* molded him into the murderous creature he was now. And under other circumstances... she'd be proud of all he'd done.

Disturbing memories of her crept in and ruined his positivity.

"No, Mother, get out!"

He'd weaken her, remove her immortality, for what she did.

"Taking my Psyche... you weren't supposed to. If you harmed her... Aphrodite, you will *die*."

He had no qualms about killing his mother, and he didn't care how much strength it would take. If it had to be done, he'd be the one to do it.

The morgue doors busted open, pulling him from his trance. A figure stormed out, its dark suit and clump of raven hair signifying it was *Lukus* exiting—not Aphrodite, as expected.

Odd.

Lukus rushed off, paused at the street, looked left and right, then crossed between two cars before hurdling over towards one of the bars across the way.

"Really odd. He's alive... and leaving?" Eros cocked his head. "She released him?" He snorted, struggling to contain his laughter. "Oh, she cares for him more than I anticipated."

He studied Lukus' confident strides, his clenching fists, the fumes escaping the top of his beautiful mane of hair.

"Oh... he's *thirsty.* Pissed." Lukus stormed on, oblivious as always. "He'll get drunk. This benefits me."

He snickered as the careless and inattentive FBI agent meandered into the bar, not a thought for the killer on the loose. And his stance, so irritated, so purposeful, reached Eros and vibrated in his core, turning him on.

Excitement. Anger. Lukus, the perfect target; the one that would attract his mother and force her to fight. She'd sacrifice her immortality to protect him, for certain.

Love all around—but love doesn't always win, does it?

‖22. PROTECT, OR SAVE?‖
APHRODITE

The shadows lurking in the hotel room frightened Aphrodite more than they should have, projecting her fears on the walls, forcing her to face them.

"I'm a goddess, dammit!" She growled, nostrils flaring as she gaped at the forms slithering about in the dark. "Things like this don't scare me! I'm more powerful!"

The ride from the coroner's office had been brief, silent, and lonely. Even the cab driver didn't interrupt her quiet, and mumbled when they arrived to wake her from her dream-like state, her nightmarish situation.

Lukus had left her on her own. Not that she blamed him; but she worried at the thought of him locked in his hotel room, smoking like a chimney, drinking from a bottle of cheap liquor. Seeking isolation from her assumptions and protection from the difficult truth.

And at this point, she found herself on the verge of giving up on him, as he had given up on her. He only saw her as a psycho, and he'd never aid her as needed; but maybe she *didn't* need him. Maybe his isolation *was* his protection. Maybe she had no choice.

When leaving the morgue, she realized the coroner had disappeared. She prayed he was too spooked to share what he witnessed and would stay out of the way until she took care of Eros.

But her instincts refused to believe in anything positive. She'd observed enough humans to understand this one would be no exception. He would likely prepare a novel on all he saw and overheard; if he hadn't already called the police and reported her to Lukus' bosses. Had he contacted reporters, too? Leaking information out into the world as she sat on her hotel bed, powerless, vulnerable?

She had blown her cover *so* badly to stop Eros—she had sacrificed so much to get an ally and instead had made enemies.

Once I retrieve my powers, I must erase the coroner's memory.

The shadows danced as she closed her eyes and hummed, reminiscing a tune from her days in Cyprus aimlessly wandering, unsure who she was. The more she sang, the drunker she felt; as if she had ingested too much ambrosia liquor, causing her head to spin and spin, to feed on the fear wallowing in her gut. The harmony didn't bring her the peace she had hoped for. She was lost then and lost now; it all happened again, but this time... no one would save her.

Thrusting her eyelids open, she sat up to glare at the walls. "I... am... *not* afraid!" She arched her back, cracked her knuckles, confronting the beings floating in her room—imaginary or not. "Because I always make it out. I always survive. There is always a loophole... and I will find it."

She stood and crossed her arms tight across her breastbone as she peered at the ceiling, a desperate sigh escaping her lips. She was only alive thanks to the gods, no matter how much she hated to admit it. And she needed their help again, now, like all those years ago.

As she released her arms, an eerie stench slid into the air; anger, fury, rage. It snuck under her door, weaving around her, enveloping her insides. The pungent odor forced her face into a frown as she sniffed, hoping to recognize it—but her powers weren't active. She couldn't identify the culprit.

But she could still smell the intensity; whoever it was felt such wrath, such morbid feelings that she sensed her knees buckle as she erupted into shudders. Who would be so *angry?*

"Lukus? Does he harbor that much spite?"

Freezing on the spot, she focused on the scent again, praying to get a whiff of who it came from. But it wasn't Lukus; it wasn't *human.* Her shivers amplified, her breaths slower, fewer, her heart banging in her chest.

Eros.

He was near, lingering in New Orleans. Prowling for victims, hungry for blood.

"I'm not safe. No one is..."

Ignoring the overwhelming shadows, she dropped to her knees. At the end of her rope, reminded of her powerless state, she felt the pull to the edge. And though she'd attempted this desperate plea one time too many since she became mortal, this time was different. Eros was *there.*

"Zeus, almighty one! Please help me. Come to me, listen to my words, assist me in this task. I'm failing! *Please!*" She squeezed her palms together, blinking back tears, determined to control the urge to sob until her eyes dried out.

A soft wind escaped from the cracks of the closed window, moving through the stained curtains, whistling around the room, raising hairs on Aphrodite's mortal body.

Are the shadows playing tricks?

"He's here, Zeus, in New Orleans. Please come and guide me or give me the strength to confront him. Return my powers so I may save your humans. So I may save Lukus. You wanted him alive, no? I can't guarantee that without my abilities."

The breeze picked up speed, zooming in so fast it came close to knocking her over. It ripped the curtains from their hinges and threatened to break the glass panes.

No... he's coming to me.

Slowly, a ghostly shape formed in front of her. Colorless, see-through, but bright. A tunic covered the lower portion of its body, and as the rest appeared, she noticed a long, fluffy beard and matching mustache covering pinched lips, narrowed irises so sharp she lost her breath, and curls flying like the sails of a ship.

The wind roared, faint sounds of thunder echoed in the distance outside—and Zeus' irritated self floated before her, arms crossed as he squinted. "Aphrodite, I grow tired of your incessant beckoning and begging. It's beneath you. Yes, you're human, and you can't help it, but it's *exhausting*." His voice tumbled in dangerous waves in her skull, resonating with a sickening crash in her heart.

His face showed more rage than she had prepared for. "Sir, I—"

"—I've chosen to appear, but I will disappear just as quickly if you say you still haven't figured out what motivates Eros' erratic behavior."

His glowing pupils fixated her, peeling every layer of her soul. In regular form alone, he was terrifying—but ghost-like Zeus brought bile to her mouth.

"Sir, I... I can't approach him *without* my powers. And without approaching him, I can't find a motive. It's impossible to investigate this as a human, don't you understand?" She gulped, wary of her rising tone. "This is why I'm so annoying. You... *made* me this way. Fix me, so that I may fix our problem."

Zeus grumbled, the muscles in his biceps pulsating. "Then you didn't think deeply enough. You didn't search within, remind yourself of your son's feelings, actions, past behaviors. Didn't make connections to any other gods, interrogated no one of importance." He leaned his chin a little closer. "You figured out he targets soulmates, bravo. But *why?* Until you have this information, I can't allow you to be at full power. You'd kill him, like I would if I were the one pursuing him. Did you not listen to anything I told you?"

The wind blew on and on, now sending objects flying, spinning, crashing into each other.

Aphrodite bowed as a pillow narrowly missed her and darted into the wall instead.

"I *have* thought and listened, and I've come up with nothing! He's angry, but I have no idea why!" She kept her head—and voice—low, but shame washed over her. She barely knew her own son, who built a life, a business that she stayed out of.

I learned my lesson when I tried to meddle with Psyche many centuries ago.

"Oh... *wait.*" Lifting her chin, allowing Zeus' terrifying gaze to pierce her, she winced. "*Psyche!*" She snapped her fingers. "*That's* who I need to talk to! She'll tell me why her husband has gone mad. Let me speak with her!"

Zeus, solemn, tilted backward, his form hovering a few inches above ground. "I'll consider it. She may have answers, but I want you to dig deeper first." He huffed. "I'm disappointed in you. You did everything I asked you not to. Used your appealing energy *and* revealed your identity to Lukus. Truth be told, you... don't deserve my help."

Her punishment would be next. She prayed he'd remove her from the case, lock her up, take her away from Earth and its confusing humans and difficult emotions. She wanted her powers, her apartments, her tranquility.

I changed my mind—I don't want to know why my son went crazy.

"You'll continue to think hard about the reasons, and you will *not* confront your son. You may have blown your cover with the human, but I still need you to protect and watch over him from a distance. If Eros caught him... we must hope he gets out of the situation alone."

Aphrodite's heart stopped. "I... don't think I understand, Majesty." Why would he leave the mortal to die in Eros' claws? "You want me to defend him, but... not save him?" She dared to stare into Zeus' eyes one last time.

He lowered to her level, his forehead a mere inch away, which sent her falling backwards. "That's correct. Follow orders, Aphrodite, and *stop* questioning them. Do not summon me again unless it's for real. If I hear your obnoxious crying again, I will send lightning *and* thunder, and you're not strong enough to save yourself from those in your human form."

Without warning, he shot through her, splashing a tingling breeze over her cheeks. She turned in time to see his blurry figure mold into the wall and disappear.

The wind stopped. A hairbrush, on its way to smack her in the back of the head, dropped. All tension drizzled from her in the form of tears, streaming out like waterfalls. Louder and louder she wailed, fearing her deadly, crazy son. Fearing he'd go for Lukus because he sensed her near him, knew they were a team. And then he'd come for her.

Mortal as I am... he'll finish me.

"But why?" She hiccupped, spittle flying from her mouth. "Why are you so mad? Why won't you tell me? You hear me, you do, don't you? You insolent child of mine! Are you resentful towards *me?* The gods? *All* of us? Show yourself! Speak to me!"

Someone yelled in the corridor though she didn't decipher the words—meaning her screams woke the building.

Quiet, Aphrodite!

Wiping the streaks of water from her cheekbones and chin, she forced herself to her feet. She had to go, get out, get away. If Eros targeted her, everyone in the hotel might be at risk. She had to protect the innocent—starting with Lukus.

Wobbly, she marched to her purse and dug out the hand-carved, heart-shaped locked box. Staring at it, her pulse sped up.

Also safely stored in her bag was her gun, in a protective case. Thanking the heavens American women carried oversized purses, she blew out her cheeks, clicking the lock open, revealing the contents of the package.

The tranquilizing bullets.

"Thank goodness Ares showed me how to use these things..." Her breaths shot out of her nose in quick puffs as she found the gun and loaded each delicate bullet inside. She then stuffed the weapon in her pocket—but knew she had to hide it better.

After a minute of frantic looking around at her belongings, she spotted a suit jacket that matched her pants, and slipped it on—finding that it concealed her pistol.

Ares taught her well. She felt prepared. But glancing at the door, she worried Lukus wasn't. It wouldn't be easy to convince him to leave, especially after all that transpired at the coroner's office. But she had to try.

She exited her room, walked several doors down, and knocked on the one she knew to be Lukus'. But after several pounds, no shuffling, voices, or even grumbles echoed on the other side. Not a single sign of life.

"Is he drinking downstairs?" She knocked a few more times before admitting defeat.

The bar near the lobby was disgusting, she remembered... but Lukus had been desperate for a drink. With any luck, she'd catch him before he got *too* drunk.

She slid down the grimy steps, no patience to wait for the elevator. And as she busted into the bar, discovering it empty but for the bartender, she gasped.

The man looked up and smirked, his hungry gaze on her curves. "Fancy a glass, sweet cheeks?"

Aphrodite nearly choked. "Have you seen my partner today?"

The bartender shrugged. "Not since he left with you, earlier. And then I saw you come back, but not him. You guys have a little spat?" He leaned over the counter, licking his lips.

"Wanna chat with me about it? You know what they say about bartenders."

Aphrodite gagged. "Please have the front desk alert me when he returns, okay? We got separated, and this is important."

Her stomach bubbling with disgust, she turned on her heels and returned to the lobby.

"Lukus... where *are* you?"

She had been certain he'd come back here to drink, or at least to change. But could he be out there, still?

With Eros on the loose? Oh no.

She ran out of the hotel entrance and dialed numbers on her phone. Praying he was safe. Her limbs stopped when his line went straight to voicemail.

"He turned it off?" She stomped, uncaring who noticed. "Shit, shit, *shit!*"

She ordered a cab to pick her up at once. Panting, horrifying thoughts clouding her brain, she grimaced. The pain in her belly grew—an ache she'd never experienced, a twisting knot she'd never imagined.

"Please... be alive. Please, gods, let me be wrong! Don't... make me use this gun on my son!"

‖ 23. FIREBALL ‖
LUKUS

The cold liquid warmed his throat as it traveled down, heating his angry soul, calming his throbbing temples. It soothed him in ways nothing else could—except maybe sex.

"What a fucking lunatic," he grumbled under his breath, motioning for the bartender to bring him another shot.

Disgusted—he had no other words to describe his emotions. He had pictured himself naked with her. Sorcery or not, the images had been in him all along. He found her attractive, so the flashes must have come from his actual desires; but how did she draw them out? And how did she turn out to be so insane?

He twitched in his chair, uneasy. The bar was empty; it was three AM, and all the party goers had given up for the night, deserting public spaces to retreat to their houses, hotel rooms, or to wander the streets drunkenly.

But not him—an alcoholic like him reveled in the late night and early morning silence, guzzling liquor until his brain fizzled and all disgust welling in his gut became liquid. No one ever questioned his drinking habits, despite his job; but he wouldn't complain.

Eyes widening at the fresh shot before him, he rubbed his hands. The bartender, though uptight at first, was quiet, and didn't seem to mind serving drink after drink; Lukus tipped him well.

"Alcohol... my *best* friend," he slurred, swishing the liquid in the small glass. It didn't talk back, didn't make up theories about Greek gods, didn't seduce and trick him. And it didn't pretend to be something it wasn't. It surprised him she *hadn't* stormed in with more crazy hypotheses yet.

Downing the shot with ease, he contemplated another one at the idea of her barging in and disturbing his peace.

A sixth one, for the heck of it?

He had a blended drink nearby, ordered to use as a chaser; but the shots had been too tantalizing to stop. He had chosen a bar across from the coroner's office; but if she *was* a goddess like she claimed, wouldn't she have smelled him, or something? Tracked him? She didn't show up, and though he had stopped looking at the time after a few drinks, he guessed she'd probably not come back.

"Ha, her *bullshit* got the best of her." He chuckled, spitting out a few droplets of whiskey as he did. And then chuckled harder at the fact that he was alone, and no one would witness him drink like a slob.

He relaxed his shoulders, taking a quick swig of the mixed liquor to help the whiskey go down. *"Phony."* The bartender had wandered off to the other side of the room, and Lukus spoke to himself, too intoxicated to bother keeping quiet. "I don't want to see her crazy fucking face again. No matter how... hot... she is."

The TV above the bar showed reruns of some reality show Lukus never watched. A woman behaved erratically, screaming and crying, and he chuckled again, reminded of Agnes moments before. "That's her," he snorted. He recalled her lamenting, begging him to believe her, and that Eros was her son, responsible for all the chaos. "Ha! She's an *actress!"*

The flashbacks of the scene made him shudder. Something bad happened to her, for sure. To push her through such trauma and prompt such things in her brain. He'd feel sorry for her if she wasn't so sickeningly weird.

He glanced at his wallet, on the bar beside his booze. A shiny piece of his badge slid out, sparkling in the overhead lights.

He was a *good* agent. How did he deserve such a psychotic partner? How did he get set up with that mad bitch?

He chugged the rest of his brew, the sudden sweetness of it surprising him after the bitter shots of whiskey. What made her lose her mind? Perhaps she *did* have a son, and she lost him somehow. Or worse; she had a son who was a criminal, for real. Just not Eros.

He perked up so fast he almost knocked over his glass. "Is... that it?" He squinted at the counter, at the crumbs of pretzels and peanuts drowning in the remnants of alcohol left behind by other patrons. "The culprit... is her son? She's... working with him? And she's snatching the hearts... she's the *witchcraft* part of the case... messing with fancy ass explosives, yeah? Confusing all the witnesses?"

His boss would pat him on the back, reward him with a raise, congratulate him on solving such a complicated case. He imagined his Washington DC apartment transforming into a house, a mansion—with a pool, a tennis court he'd never use, a massive home theater. Surrounded by a harem of beautiful women, all clapping, swirling around him in admiration.

Catching two culprits at once—the ultimate accomplishment. Agnes—or whatever the hell her name was—would lead him straight to her son, the real murderer; and then he'd slap handcuffs on her, too.

Her insanity might yet help this case!

The bartender placed another mixed drink in front of him, and Lukus gulped some of it down as a patron entered the bar, taking up a stool nearby, ordering a refreshment. But Lukus was too stuck in his little world to care that someone disrupted his loneliness.

"Should have arrested her when she started *wailing...*" He chortled, finishing his shot. "Claiming to be *Aphrodite,* ha! My ass! If she thinks I'm cooperating... she'll bring me to her criminal son, right? Ha, yes, then I'll get everything."

The bartender, rolling his eyes, meandered away to prepare the new man's refreshment; and Lukus sighed, letting the alcohol poison his mind further and further. She didn't seem old enough to have an adult son, but if she dabbled in the witchy stuff, who knew? Lukus wanted to high-five himself, and as he considered doing it, he sighted the other patron from the corner of his eye.

"Whoa, where did you come from?" he asked, his speech slurring as he squinted at the stranger, seated on the stool beside him.

"Rough night?" The newcomer approached his glass to Lukus', as if wanting to clink their drinks. He didn't wait for Lukus to answer before groaning. "*Ugh,* what am I saying, of course it's a rough night... fuck it all! To being single and *lonely!*"

After a second of hesitation—and a smidge of embarrassment for mumbling to himself in the presence of this new person—Lukus snatched his mixed drink and collided it with the man's, sloshing liquid all over his pants.

"*Yeah!* Single!" He chugged half the beverage. "And to solving murder cases!"

He did it; he figured it out. Sure, it involved Wicca crap he didn't want to believe in, but he'd come across it before. And he preferred to believe in *that* than in mythological gods.

"Murder cases?" The stranger did a double take. "Whoa, wait a minute, are you that dude working on the cannibalism case?" His locks of blond hair covered his eyes, and as he shook the strands from his face, he almost fell backwards. Glazed, cheeks red, he was drunk; but harmless, according to Lukus and his instincts. An air of youth and innocence weaved around him. He wouldn't bother Lukus much longer.

Probably just got dumped or something.

"You got me!" Lukus hiccupped, swishing his liquid as he peered at the young fellow. "Not for long though. I'm finding more answers here than I did *anywhere* else." A gut feeling told him to keep quiet, not reveal details; but his alcohol brain had no control. "I'm super close to solving the whole damn thing. Fucking sick of discovering blood everywhere, you know? Sick of the cannibalism crap, it's *disgusting.*" He waved at the bartender for another round.

The stranger's expression changed. Though he appeared intrigued seconds before, his cheekbones started to turn green and his cheeks puffed up.

Oh shit, is he gonna vomit?

The man gagged, once, twice, three times. He raised a hand, hunching down for a moment, heaving. He wheezed, and Lukus panicked; but before he could reach out to stabilize the guy, he whipped his neck up, let out a giant belch, and grinned goofily. "Phew, that was close."

He couldn't be over twenty-one, a newbie in handling liquor. And there was Lukus, thrusting his work and its intensity in his face.

I should tone it down.

"Sorry man, I'm not supposed to share details. Didn't mean to spook ya," he apologized.

The stranger's grin widened. "Nah, don't worry about it!" He blew out a long breath, eyes shutting halfway as he tried to set his elbow on the counter. But he missed, and his bicep smacked into the surface instead, causing him to chortle. Lukus would have laughed, too; but he knew the effects of alcohol better than anyone. "*I* should be apologizing. You're over here unwinding and enjoying your time and I'm bugging you. I shouldn't interrupt." The dude stood, struggling to keep his balance.

Overcome with pity, Lukus poked his hand out and stopped him. "You're fine. It's *fine*. I don't mind the company."

As long as it's not that psycho partner of mine.

The boy smirked and dropped back onto the barstool as the bartender delivered their shots. Lukus wasn't sure what he ordered, but neither complained as they drank up, fire coursing through their bodies.

Fire.

Fireball.

The stranger took a sip of his mixed liquor. "Hey, wait a minute." He swerved to Lukus, leaning in close—so close his toxic breath made Lukus' nostrils flare. "Didn't you have a partner? I saw another one of you on the TV. A pretty lady? Busty, long hair, didn't really look like an FBI agent? Dang, she was *hot.*"

Lukus blinked a few times, his vision blurry. "Oh boy, too much whiskey." He had to leave soon, find the Agnes witch lady. But even the words slurred in his skull, proving he was in no state to work the case. "The lady? Oh, my partner. Yeah, uh... she's weird. I totally ditched her."

Psycho bitch accomplice of the murderer!

He was so close to spilling out his thoughts that he clapped a hand over his mouth, hiccupping again as the Fireball flavor lingered on his tongue.

The stranger giggled. "*Chicks,* man, I tell you. All the same. All fucked up. Oh shit, oops, 'scuse my language." He choked, a few drops of his beverage zooming out and splattering onto the counter. "It's true, though."

"Man, don't worry." Lukus angled sideways and cupped a hand around his mouth. "I think chicks are fucked up too."

They clinked glasses again, alcohol spilling in their laps and all over the counter. The bartender watched them and their banter, his patience likely running thin.

Lukus' thoughts still whirled out of control. Chicks who lied about their identity, infiltrated the FBI, posed as agents, led you to the killer to be the next victim. Rage burned inside, fusing with the whiskey drowning in his abdomen.

The stranger slammed his drink on the counter and turned to Lukus. "*Dude.* You said you were solving the case, right?" Lukus nodded. "Dude. *Dude*, you can catch the killer tonight. I... fuck, I shoulda said this but I'm so frigging smashed I forgot."

Lukus set his cup down. "Cough it up, bud, what d'you see?"

Gulping, the kid squinted. "I *totally* saw some guy leading a couple down this weird ass alleyway." Lukus frowned, and the man waved his palms, frantic. "Whoa, *whoa*, that sounds bad, but listen. I was leaving the nightclub, right? The one a few blocks from here, down by the river. There's an abandoned warehouse down there, shady spot but the drinks are cheap and shit."

Lukus snapped at him to hurry.

"Okay, *okay,* well the couple looked out of it, like, dazed or something, maybe drugged? And a really weird guy followed them towards that warehouse. I guarantee it, man. Creepy shit, right?"

Lukus froze. "You're sure?" He scratched his chin. "What did the creepy guy look like? Any firearms?" He struggled to keep calm as his heartbeat screeched in his ears.

It was too good to be true, but... could he catch him? Catch *them?*

The kid's shoulders lifted. "I dunno. It sounds too easy, but for real, man. The guy wore black? I think? Looked like he was wearing *all* leather. No weapons, I think. Just a backpack. I was trashed, way more than now, man. But I know what I saw, I do. My vision's still good when I'm wasted."

Lukus jumped from his seat, wobbling on his heels to regain his balance, and reached for his wallet, throwing several twenties on the counter. "Call the cops. Tell them to meet me at the warehouse, okay? Lukus Arvantis is my name, and I'm an agent of the *FBI*." Covering his slurred speech was harder than normal.

I'm too intoxicated for this.

He looked at the young man, considering bringing him along, but decided one drunk person was more than enough.

Should I call Agnes?

"Fuck no, Lukus, she's the accomplice," he grumbled to himself. "Probably already there, that bitch. Didn't come looking for me... can't wait, I have to go now!"

Hesitant, he gawked at the kid, who descended from his stool. Lukus saw two of him, even three, before squeezing his eyes shut. He patted his pockets, front and back, and groaned.

"No weapons, *fuck*... I can fight. Stop it with my bare hands, wouldn't be the first time."

The man appeared in his peripheral. "Yo, you good? I can come with, give you backup!" He raised his fists, taking a swipe at the air. But he was so unstable on his feet that he nearly toppled over the barstool.

Lukus' sense of direction would be foggy; having the kid take him to the place shouldn't be a problem. "I, uh..." But despite his intoxication, his reason took over. "No, bud, thanks for the info but, you stay here. Talk to the police for me, okay?"

He waved at him and soon stumbled outside, marching past the other bar, heading for the river.

"Warehouse... by the water, right?" He walked, but it was more of a drunken wobble.

He got closer to the river's edge but had no clue which direction to go from there.

"Think, Lukus. Fuck."

He pulled out his phone, fighting against gravity to stand still, and fumbled to turn it on and pull up the maps application to see his location. With difficulty he zoomed in, and though his vision was still blurred, he figured out which way the warehouse would be.

"Left, go left."

He turned left, following the river, and passed what he believed to be the nightclub the stranger described. Decrepit, beat up, with debris all over the front portion of the ground, and even a few sleeping bodies by the door—though he had no clue if they *were* bodies, or just piles of trash. The place was closed, and definitely the dump the kid in the bar mentioned.

"Shitty... is it even a *real* nightclub? Looks deserted." He shrugged off any bad vibes and ambulated onward. "Hurry, Lukus... kids in danger..."

The faster he walked, the blurrier his senses. He barely saw ahead of him, but his legs kept going, unable to stop. He had to find them, save them, stop the criminal. Arrest pretty Agnes and win it all.

"Abandoned warehouse... so cliché," he moaned, sniffing the air, stuffing his hands in his pockets. "Smells like a trap. Smells *wrong*." He groaned again when remembering he had no weapons, no way to defend himself. "I'm fucked." He stumbled another step forward. "But... they're fucked too if I don't go, right? Cliché abandoned warehouse... it's my job. Gotta go... stop the psycho carnivorous killer."

‖24. WHERE IS LUKUS?‖
APHRODITE

Lights shined inside the cab, blinding her. Not the lights from Olympus—the sun pouring beams into her marble-floored room, or the moon blanketing the palace in an arctic blue glow. *These* lights were fizzling frauds fueled with electricity. Hurtful to her eyes and unappealing.

Yet Aphrodite stuck her face to the window, desperate to use the fake light to glimpse Lukus' handsome figure, stumbling drunk, or strolling with confidence, his anger fueling him, leading him away.

But she feared she may see the frightful Eros, which prompted her to shudder. She had to find them both; but locating Lukus first would be preferable. She had no clue where he would've gone for a drink, especially since he hadn't returned to the hotel. Would that shabby bartender lie?

No, he's desperate for attention.

She shrugged, the image of the crude man making her cringe. Humans lied often, but she had no time to dwell on it. Lukus was out there, drinking his rage, and she had to protect him.

Vulnerable, full of alcohol, hunched over a table somewhere; she didn't know his liquor tolerance, but he *was* unarmed.

In danger.

She urged the cab driver to take her to the coroner's office—she'd start there and look around for clues of Lukus' whereabouts.

"You're looking for your partner, right?" asked the man, streets away from the desired location.

Aphrodite nodded.

The man turned his head here and there before proceeding past a stop sign. "There are two bars across the street from where I'm dropping you off. Might wanna look in there. Most law officers hang around in them. Not that I blame em, I'd probably need a refreshment after seeing dead bodies too."

Aphrodite gulped.

Well, it's a start.

"Thanks for your help, I think I'll do just that."

She had no idea where to go, anyway. So, though most humans lied, some were observant, helpful. She'd have to remember that.

The car screeched to a halt by the morgue, and Aphrodite looked out her window to the right, noticing two tavern-style bars with large, wooden doors, and separated by an ominous alleyway.

Eros' favorite murder location so far—near alleyways.

I'd better investigate that before I even bother going inside.

She paid the driver, thanked him, and exited the car into the night air. She breathed in, appreciating the smell—she hadn't noticed how close they were to the water when they first came to the coroner's office. Too preoccupied with her mission to show Lukus the engravings.

Inhaling the breezy, fishy scent, she let it relax her mind, allowing her to better gather her thoughts.

Was Zeus right? She should have thought harder, reviewed evidence, taken her time before throwing her identity at Lukus. They were in this mess because of her.

She marched straight for the alley, anxious and shaking, not looking forward to what she may find. Did Eros lurk there still, waiting for her? Would it be a trap? He'd sense her mortality; he wouldn't hesitate to take her out if it allowed him to keep murdering.

The gun in her pocket bumped against her upper thigh and, though not reassured, she sighed. The weapon wouldn't kill him, no matter how tempting it would be after all he did.

Again, Zeus was the voice of reason; with her powers she'd have been too ruthless. Regardless that he was family, she'd slay Eros for disrupting the universal balance.

The balance we strive so hard to maintain.

She snuck into the dark pathway lined with dumpsters, piles of rubble and trash, and possibly a few bodies. She rushed over to check the large lumps, only to find they were more heaps of waste, covered by garbage bags. A horrible stench filled her nostrils. Not a decaying body, just rotting food.

Eros killed no one here—only debris and leftovers going bad, mixed in with spilled booze, and vomit.

I need to get away from this disaster.

She returned to the street and picked the bar to her right first, opening the door to find a dim, empty room with a small counter, a few tables and chairs, and a beat-up pool table near the back.

"Can I help you, miss? I was just closing," said a woman, appearing on the other side of the counter.

Aphrodite walked up and on instinct, showed her FBI badge, remembering Lukus' instructions from the crime scenes. "I'm searching for my partner. Male, about six foot two, messy black hair, striking blue eyes. Handsome, charming, maybe got a little too drunk... did he come in here tonight?"

The bartender wiped her hands on her apron and shook her head. "No, no one like that. I would have remembered a nice-looking dude in a crowd of morons like the one *I* had this evening. Sorry, miss. Did you try next door?"

Aphrodite looked at the wall behind the counter. "I started here, so I guess I'll do that next. Thank you for your time." She meandered outside, rubbing her biceps as a chill coursed through her. If Lukus wasn't in the second bar, she'd be screwed. She glanced at the door of the bar she exited. Did the lady lie?

"Should I go back in... and insist? How did the officers do it in the movies I watched?" She shrugged. "Ugh, I can't waste time."

Lukus may already lay in a pool of blood, his heart gone, his soul on its way to the Underworld. She lost any sensation in her limbs for a moment at the image. Eros eating the thumping organ, cackling in pleasure. Did Lukus have a soulmate? She didn't think to ask Zeus and didn't recall Lukus ever mentioning a wife or girlfriend.

She emerged into the second location. It resembled the first but appeared to have recently contained more life. A TV above the bar area showed graphic images of a fight, and a male bartender watched, quietly encouraging an actor on the screen.

Aphrodite cleared her throat, and the man jumped around, his hand smacking onto his torso. "*Shit.*" He panted, before flashing a smile. "Probably shouldn't watch scary movies in the middle of the night when all the customers are gone."

Aphrodite's eyebrows furrowed. "Indeed."

"How can I help you?" He waved her closer. "We're not closed, I can fix you something if you'd like." He was the polar opposite from the bartender at the hotel, and it warmed Aphrodite's icy heart for a second. His genuine offer tempted her, but she was here on business.

"I'd love to, but unfortunately I'm working," she started, approaching. The bar was eerily similar to the one next door, yet with a more frequented feel, a friendlier vibe. The lights weren't as dim, and though the set-up was the same—tables, seats, and a pool table—something was different.

Odd.

The bartender shrugged. "Okay, so what can I do for you then?" He appeared nicer than the lady from moments before, and Aphrodite hoped she'd get more information from him.

"I'm looking for my partner," she said, showing her badge. "I'm not sure if he was here, but we were recently at the morgue, and the last time we spoke he claimed he needed a drink."

She sat on one of the stools, another odd sensation creeping up and down her spine. Tingly spikes, flashes of light, a pulling discomfort.

A hunch? Did something happen here?

Her godly intuition had left when Zeus removed her powers, and yet something told her to interrogate the bartender, to be thorough; to not miss the evidence here.

"He's probably about six foot two, messy black hair, striking blue eyes. Really *looks* like an FBI agent, you know? Hard to miss. Yet I missed him and have no idea where he went. We were at the coroner's office one moment, and the next..." She drifted off, worry invading her soul.

He was dead. She was too late. She bet he never made it into either bar because Eros waited outside. And she'd been too busy with her proof, trying to show Lukus who she was and didn't sense Eros in the surroundings.

He was here. And he felt me. And now he's taking it out on Lukus to get to me.

She gasped. Eros' anger directed at *her*, for sure.

The bartender hunched over the counter. "Oh yeah, he was here. Stumbled in all pissed, a little rude at first, too. Said he had a spat with his partner."

Aphrodite jerked her head up. Did the *bartender* hurt Lukus? Was he working with Eros? Her eyes narrowed.

Are YOU Eros, in disguise?

It explained the peculiar tingles still shooting up and down her back; her extremities going numb.

Oh Lukus, I'm so sorry.

"He ordered a mixed drink, like a Long Island Iced Tea but stronger. Didn't want to give it to him initially, but then he flashed that FBI badge and honestly, I was scared to refuse. He wasn't happy," said the bartender, reaching under the counter for a glass. He filled it with a brown, bubbly liquid and gulped a few sips before setting the cup down.

The man puzzled her. His aura was blurry, troublesome to read.

"We... we had a spat, but... well, I realize how stupid we both were. His life might be in danger. The criminal we're hunting is still on the loose, and I believe it may target *him*. I need to figure out where he scampered off to, as soon as possible."

Whoever this barkeep was, she prayed it wasn't Eros. Surely, he'd have attacked her by now, powerless as she was, right? She didn't want to trust the man, but he remained her only lead.

"He kept ordering shots, and he got himself pretty shit-faced, if you ask me. Talking to himself, kept muttering stuff about the paranormal and witches and goddesses... I left him alone, though. I was close to calling the cops, or an ambulance, but..." He trailed off, looking at the stool beside Aphrodite's.

"But *what*? Tell me. Where is my partner? You know, don't you?" Her hand slipped down near her pocket, prepared to grab her gun.

The bartender gulped. "I don't. But I know where he was headed." He rubbed the back of his neck. "Another guy came in, gave him a tip about potential victims. Said something about the cannibalism murders and how he saw a couple, and a weird man, going towards the abandoned warehouse down by the river. Your partner didn't think twice and took off." He took a few more swigs of his drink.

Aphrodite wanted to reach over the counter, grab his collar and shake him. "And you didn't *stop* him?" She brought a clenched fist to her mouth. "You said he was *drunk,* and you let him wander off? He's *unarmed*, you jerk. If he did head down there to investigate, he probably got himself killed, his heart eaten... oh dear, I could arrest you *right now* for endangering an agent!"

Hopefully, I didn't just make that up.

Her eyelids on fire, her heart pounding—she decided she hated this man. Did he let it happen on purpose, collaborating with Eros? Or because he was a self-centered moron?

"Hey now, I didn't do anything! You wanted *me* to stop him? *Angry* as he was, like, super pissed? I won't get in the middle of that. He would have punched me and broke my nose or something. Plus, that other guy totally egged him on. You should get mad at *him*." He backed away from the counter.

Aphrodite stopped breathing. Yes, Lukus turned violent when annoyed, she remembered. "Was the other guy drunk too? Do you know where *he* went?"

The man shrugged, his features paling. "Honestly I... actually, I have no idea. After your partner left, the guy... he sorta... well either he disappeared, or I don't remember him leaving at all."

A chill ran down Aphrodite's spine. "And what did you say this other guy looked like? Get as specific as you can if you remember." Jolts of electricity pinched her skin.

The bartender held his chin. "Blondish hair, but I couldn't tell the length, he had a hoodie on. Hard to see his eyes, but they weren't blue or green... probably a light brown. *Amber,* maybe? Scruffy, wearing a black leather coat. Had a big backpack with him, looked heavy. Long. Not your average bag. Come to think of it, he was kinda... ugh, you'll never believe this, but he was *glowing.* Like some angelic aura surrounded him. Wow, why am I only now remembering this?"

Aphrodite stood up. Her heartbeat echoed so loud in her ears, she feared she'd turn deaf. "Close your bar, *now.* Go home, lock your doors. Stay inside. Don't speak with anyone."

The bartender tilted his head, but Aphrodite was halfway out the door before he could ask her what she meant.

"Lukus, don't die yet. I'll find you. Please... be alive when I do."

‖25. HUNGRY‖
LUKUS

Thump, thump, thump.

Lukus' eyelids struggled to move, forcing him to remain in darkness. The constant, uncontrolled twitching didn't help, but he had no way to stop it, eyes instinctively wanting to open. He had no clue where he was, or how he had arrived.

The thumping continued, halting his thoughts from processing. What *was* it? His head throbbing? An agonizing pain shot to his temples—confirming his suspicions. A pain he had never experienced, a twinge that made him wince; and somehow, he sensed it would only get worse.

Had he smacked into a door? Fallen onto his skull and possibly cracked it? Let a giant piano smash his brain, like in a cartoon?

Fuck, am I even alive right now?

He attempted to open his eyes again, lifting his eyebrows, pulling with more force. The small slits parted, but he couldn't see much. Everything was blurry, as if trapped in a dense fog. Like a swamp. There *were* many swamps in the state; maybe he fell into the river and floated farther than planned. But, with a slow sigh, he realized his clothing wasn't damp, and no 'bathed in fishy water' stench lingered in his nose.

Guessing game time. Why did he drink so much?

Through his barely-opened eyelids, he noticed how close the ground was. From this angle, he could tell he wasn't standing, but seated, his legs sprawled out in front of him, his body limp, somewhat numb. He hit his scalp *much* harder than he thought but didn't remember it. Did he fall?

Am I that drunk?

He moved his right arm up and reached for his face, touching around for any bruises or blood. Anything that would show what he did to be in such a state. The last thing he recalled was approaching the warehouse... but nothing else. The images in his skull scrambled like an old, broken television, unable to adjust its clarity no matter how much he moved the antennas for a sharper picture. Where was he, and how did he get there?

He blinked repeatedly, hoping his vision would come back. A few tears slithered down his cheeks as he squinted hard, then wrenched his lids apart, yet still seeing nothing. He sensed little to no airflow, and around him loomed a deafening and creepy silence that only intensified his throbbing head. He wasn't outside anymore, for certain. Nor was he in the bar. Though only a vague assumption, it helped trigger his memory; he had stumbled beside the river, passed the decrepit nightclub, and hobbled closer to the warehouse.

The warehouse.

Was he *in* it?

He had to be, and had bumped his head on something while sneaking in. Or fainted, out of intoxication. If not both. His right arm hurt the longer he held it up, but he had to rub his eyes. Gentle, then firm, adamant to retrieve his vision. To confirm his hunch.

He'd never passed out, and never been *that* drunk, either. Always a heavyweight drinker, he knew five shots of whiskey and a Long Island Iced Tea wouldn't get him this woozy. Weak. Drowsy and forgetful.

His eyesight cleared only a little, but a heavy obscurity engulfed him instead—and a terrifying realization hit him hard in the face, making his skin turn cold.

Was I drugged?

His heart thrummed, faster and faster, and his head spun, threatening to send him into a pit of blackness again, pushing him to faint. He didn't remember getting in, sitting down, meeting anyone; drugged would make sense, but who? How? *When?*

Shapes formed in front of him. Cracked, wooden beams up above; rusty and metallic pillars holding up the ceiling; creaky stairs to the side, leading somewhere unknown; stained concrete floors beneath him, shining in the light—

The light?

He peered around for the source and found a large window, high up, letting in a slither of moonlight.

His pulse raced. How much time had passed? How long had he been sitting there, drugged, dazed? He breathed in and out, hoping to calm his nerves; panicking in such a situation would be suicidal.

Who did this?

He lifted his left arm to scratch his temple—and started when he found his hair matted. Stuck to his forehead and skull, sweat drizzling down the side of his face. There was no denying the truth now—the killer found him. His stiff fingers and even stiffer back seemed to confirm it. Drugs? Alcohol? Drawing him to the warehouse?

Not so supernatural after all, are you?

He exhaled and put both hands on the floor to push himself up. He heaved, arm muscles tensing and bulging, but he lifted an inch up before dropping down with a resonating *thud*. His legs, limp, lifeless, refused to bend, and his feet refused to help him up. Help him out. The drugs lingered in his system still.

Lukus, you dumbass, you should have grabbed your gun!

Years of training, and he still wasn't prepared for all outcomes. He failed as an FBI agent in more ways than ever.

"Oh yes, you should have remembered your weapon, boy." A voice. A male. Deep, threatening. "Not that it would have saved you." It came from somewhere ahead of him, hidden in the shadows.

Lukus shuddered, a striking pain hitting his spine, immobilizing him further. He recognized the tone; familiar, as if he had spoken to him before.

He tried to move, but it only sent more spirals of suffering up his arms and shoved his shoulders down. He held in the scream stuck in his throat, unwilling to show his terror.

The coroner, maybe? He had heard the voice *recently*.

"Oh, you poor, *stupid* human. Guess again."

Lukus repressed a chill.

Human? Why is he saying that?

He froze, listening for footsteps—but all that happened was the echo in his cranium from his hammering head. Who else had he spoken to that night? He pinched his lips, concentrating. Then gasped.

The bartender? He had access to his drinks. He spoke with him. And the voice was masculine, which ruled out Agnes.

"No, but you're correct on *one* thing. Agnes isn't here." The man's words thundered through the space, hitting Lukus hard in the chest.

A rustle of clothes jolted his chin up to look before him, but he still saw nothing.

"You do know her name is Aphrodite, right?" The man chuckled. "It's true. She's a *goddess.*"

The noise got closer, yet whenever Lukus peered in its direction he noticed nobody. His ears clogged, as if he was underwater. Drowning. Dying.

The bartender. All this time—posing as someone who served drinks, but then drugged the victims and led them off to city streets or dingy alleyways to wait for his accomplice to arrive and take the hearts out. That was how they did it—it was all staged.

Not as sly as you think, culprit.

A chilling cackle reverberated in the warehouse. "Poor Lukus. You really *are* a skeptic, aren't you? Unable to believe the truth even when it's right in front of you. Well... you're wrong again, unfortunately." Creeping nearer, his timbre deepening, darkening, the fellow continued to taunt.

Lukus wanted to run, but his legs wouldn't cooperate, as if they no longer connected to his brain.

"The bartender was just a bartender, nothing more." The mystery being grunted. "Though he *was* most useful. But he didn't hurt you lot of moronic humans." He had to be only feet away now, to the right of Lukus' limp body.

'Humans'? How is he any different?

He gulped down a glob of bile forming in his esophagus. A rubbing material sound approached. Nails on a chalkboard, scratchy; leathery. The killer came closer and closer, and Lukus sensed his nerves twitching out of control, begging him to escape, to stay alive. He again attempted to stand, but no body parts heeded his desire. He couldn't move.

What kind of drug immobilized his entire lower extremities? Hospital strength and illegal, surely. Or... *was* it witchcraft, after all—but this guy was the wizard, and not Agnes?

"W-who... are you?" Lukus' voice came out raspy, his mouth dry and cottony. "And how... do you know what I'm thinking? My name?" He swallowed more bile. "What do you want with me?"

The man cackled again; his harsh hoarseness echoed inside the warehouse, paralyzing Lukus' thoughts.

"You'll believe in witchcraft yet not in gods and goddesses? You're a curious one, Lukus." His laughter ceased. "*Aphrodite* isn't a witch, and neither am I. You know who I am, deep down. You've been told, you've *read* about me, so go ahead. *Guess.*" The footsteps became louder than the pounding in Lukus' head, and again he regretted not having his gun. Such a sad waste of an agent, forgetting his only weapon while investigating the most dangerous case of his career. If he somehow survived, he'd lose his job. Or receive a demotion.

I'm an embarrassment, no matter what.

"What do you want?" he said, hoping to live long enough to see what the murderer looked like. If paranormal crap existed, he wanted to at least visualize the dude; to discover if he appeared like the drawings in books.

The figure slid onto a patch of concrete illuminated by the moonlight pouring through the windows. Lukus gasped the moment he sighted him. "*You?*" He nearly choked on his spit. "But you... you said..."

The hooded, blond man now loomed two feet away, pointing an arrow right at Lukus' chest. *Smirking.*

"I thought you were helping me!" Lukus' extremities shivered, his insides bubbled. His heart skipped beats and his mind raced. The little brat—pretending to be drunk, to lead him toward the culprit. That kid was the criminal all along? The cliché trapped him. Each moment spent unraveling the truth only worsened his shame; he almost hoped he wouldn't survive. He wouldn't be able to tolerate the humiliation.

"They all call me a brat." The boy, his eyes glowing, sneered. "All the other gods. A *spoiled* brat with fluffy wings and a fancy set of arrows. An array of cool powers, a hot mom, a bloodthirsty, war-hungry dad. They gave me an easy job, right?

Make people fall in love. But you know what? *Screw* love. If I can't have it, neither can any of you." He pulled back on the string, his arrow pointed, prepared to strike.

As his entire life flashed before him—yet another cliché he couldn't escape—Lukus fought for air, as if oxygen leaked from his lungs. He prayed to someone, something, to not die, not like this. He prayed the bartender called the cops, who would show up at any minute, and save him.

Believe in logic!

He had to get up. He had to try.

The young god, his leather pants rubbing as he shifted his position, snorted. "No, you can't. I've won. Stop fidgeting so I can shoot this damn arrow into your heart, *human.*" His hood slid an inch down, revealing some of his youthful, smooth skin. "I'm not a brat, don't you see? They all had it wrong. I'm Eros, god of love and desire, and right now, your *worst* nightmare."

Lukus' mind went blank. A white screen appeared, scenes playing with children laughing, parents screaming, cars honking in the distance. A little boy shooting a toy gun, hiding in his room, crying. A teenager wrestling in a schoolyard, cheered on by other students, blood dripping from his knuckles, a smile on his face. A man packing his bags as a mother watched him leave, powerless to stop him from pursuing his dreams—and a father ignoring him, unable to praise his decision. A uniformed man in an empty office, holding a badge and a gun. And a beautiful, strawberry-blonde in a tight green dress, with matching green eyes, waiting in a hotel lobby, her face bright, glowing, *perfect*.

No. Agnes, Aphrodite, *whatever her name,* wouldn't ruin the flashbacks of his final moments. And yet the woman lingered in his thoughts, waving at him as she giggled, her perfect hair bouncing, her voice pure happiness.

But he wanted her out. Even now, prepared to die, he wouldn't let a filthy, lying piece of crap like her cloud his dying thoughts. She didn't belong there.

Get out, Agnes! Get your sorry self out of my—

The pain knocked him in the chest first, as the arrow plunged through his skin, sinking straight into his heart. Tearing through every artery, every vein, splashing his shirt with blood, drenching him in crimson stickiness. Then came the metallic scent as it filled his nostrils. And the agony intensified as the arrow disintegrated *inside* him, melting into every cavity in his body, molding into his heart—*becoming* it. A warm liquid squished inside, mingling with his bloodstream, blending in, modifying every structure in his frame, every cell in every organ, every neuron in his brain.

What the...

He froze, suspended in time. He no longer thought for himself; his cells remote-controlled, operated by someone else as he watched them work from a distance.

He expected death; to never again see his family or friends, to never again work as an FBI agent or have the chance to meet beautiful women and eat delicious food. Wasting his last moments of clear vision on the man who shot him, he had no strength to utter a single word to beg for mercy.

And he wanted to open his mouth, but the will had left him. He had no say in any of his actions.

But to his utter shock, instead of closing his eyes for good, forever falling in an endless black pit, his body powered up. Muscles bulged, expanded, swelled with a toxic energy he'd never experienced before. His torso puffed up and out, his buttocks tightened, his shoulders heightened, full of an unknown force fueling him inside and out. His head stopped hurting. Any blood shed by his wound disappeared, erasing from his shirt, his palms, the concrete floor.

Lukus' knees bent, and the soles of his shoes pressed to the ground. He rose, mechanical, robotic, his eyesight adjusted. He sniffed the air, once, twice, three times—

I smell her.

His nostrils widened, gathering every human scent for miles. But *she* was all he cared about. So good, so perfect, so *near.* He tensed, knuckles cracking, rolling his shoulders, twisting his neck back and forth. Her flesh, her blood, her heart—all provoked a burning desire within. With each step she took, her scent tempted him more, brought drool to bubble at the corners of his mouth.

"Lukus, come." Eros snapped at him, waving him closer.

Lukus battled to obey, captivated by all he smelled, all he heard with his new powers.

"Lukus!"

He walked, zombie-like and controlled, until he stopped beside the fellow who pierced his soul. Heeding his words like a dog called by its master.

Eros *was* his master.

The god patted his back. "There, there, human." Lukus cast a glance upon the leather-clad man, whimpering on the inside. "You're hungry, aren't you?"

Lukus licked his lips, stomach growling, knotting, *desperate.*

So starving.

His favorite human's scent stuck in his nose. He yearned for her, for her flesh. And she came to him, now. Aphrodite—his soulmate.

Let me eat your heart.

‖26. ZOMBIE SOULMATES‖
EROS

Under other circumstances, Eros would care what happened to Lukus. But not today; today he was a pawn in a game much bigger than he realized.

Eros watched the shift in the man's behavior as the makeshift virus progressed—limbs strengthening, face paling, contorting, showing the pain he felt within without ever knowing. Lukus' heart yearned for Aphrodite. Yearned for her to be close, for her meat to be available.

Eros' magical concoction was fascinating. The arrows, so potent—and more so when they affected someone in love with a goddess.

An experiment I'm glad I attempted.

His eyes creased as he smiled, witnessing the struggle in Lukus' mind, able to read every thought as if they were his own. In Eros' case, mind-reading was a power that only worked on humans, and some weakened, lesser gods—though Eros hoped to develop it to one day get into the almighty Zeus' brain. He wouldn't complain; even in its weaker form, the ability brought him delight. To know what Lukus thought came in handy.

He flinched, remembering the limitations of his abilities. Reading Aphrodite's mind was out of the question, but he hoped she'd be weak enough to strike, regardless.

Lukus sniffed the air, his body stiffening. He disappeared into the shadows of the warehouse, hiding, waiting.

Eros froze, also sniffing the area. "Ah... she's close. Approaching. Knows where we are, but... is hesitant? I sense that." He cocked his head. "And... something else, too. Something is *missing*. But... what is it?"

He stilled his breathing, his extremities, closed his eyes— and grinned. The desperation, the lack of strength bubbling inside his mother meant she was weaker.

How? Has she been out of ambrosia for too long?

He ambled closer to the entrance, his smirk turning hateful, vengeful, pulling higher up his face as he scrunched his nose. Victory was mere moments away, and a glee he hadn't sensed in a while, filled his insides. Aphrodite... smelled different. Something was off, not the same as usual. Not as powerful. Not as frightening—

"Oh!" Eros gasped and clapped a hand over his mouth. "She's... *human?"* His eyes nearly bulged out of their sockets. "Well, I'll be damned. She made this almost too easy." His bow slid from his palms, but he caught it before it hit the ground. "So, I make an exception, I shoot someone who doesn't have a soulmate—that's *you* Lukus—I play with fate, since you are in love with my mother, deep down, and *now...* twist of all twists, my mother isn't a deity anymore? Stripped of her powers? She's *human?"* If at all possible, his smile expanded, stretching his lips so far, a regular person's jaw would split. "Oh dear, this gets more exciting by the second. Like she's delivered to us on a *golden* platter, friend."

Trepidation and anticipation flowed through him faster than his own blood. The ambrosia he consumed earlier left a sweet, tart taste on his tongue, and he licked his lips. He would execute his mother tonight. Violent images of juicy crimson liquid, pieces of flesh, hearts devoured, screams echoing in hallways—his joy amplified, exploded, drowned him in such satisfaction he could barely keep himself level.

302 | CARNIVOROUS CUPID

She was no longer a goddess, no longer protected by her immortality. He had no clue who made her mortal, but his gratitude would forever be in their favor.

From the bottom of my rotten, angry heart.

"Oh Lukus, you poor soul. In love with an imposter," he said, searching for Lukus in the dark. He found him lurking near the high range windows, grunting like a thirsty zombie, internally begging for Aphrodite to arrive. "It's *too* cute. The old me would have eaten this up and wrote a book about it. A handsome, supernatural skeptic who falls for a goddess who is no longer immortal, but he doesn't know it. And the *best* part?" He squealed. "She didn't *make* you fall in love, because she has *no* powers! You did this on your own, didn't you, Lukus? You fell for her, and you didn't even realize it. She had no control over you and yet you still chose to give her your heart."

Lukus grumbled and groaned, only focused on the windows he couldn't see out of. He paced in front of them, like a dysfunctional robot.

Eros observed with pleasure. "And now, poor Mommy will come to your rescue because she doesn't understand she cares for you too. Oh, and she *hates* loving humans, she does. Last time that happened... oh, poor Adonis. Mother's luck with human men has been horrific. She's better off carrying on her affair with Father, to be honest, but no... she can't help herself, can she? She has to *meddle.*"

Lukus either ignored him or wasn't paying attention; Eros spoke to himself as his newest victim only seemed to care for the approaching Aphrodite and the tender chunks of skin that layered her.

"And she'll arrive, powerless, no inkling what awaits her. I'll shoot her with these magnificent arrows too... And if she wasn't in love with you before, Lukus, she *will* be. In love with a human... and she'll be conscious, she'll feel it at the deepest part of her core. These arrows..." He lifted one of the wooden pieces, staring at its bloody tip. "... are different. They provoke cannibalism, yes, but they also have an interesting effect on gods. They'll make Mother unable to control her emotions, but fully aware of them. *Twisted*, right?"

Lukus grunted in response.

"She's so close... and still so hesitant. Walking, now. Afraid. Ha!" He lowered the arrow. "Mother's scared of *me?* Oh, this keeps getting better." As Lukus whined, Eros switched to a muffled tone, unwilling for his mother to hear. "Desperate, and in love, she'll have no choice but to let you *eat* her. Sink your teeth into her skin, my friend, feast on her godly body, *enjoy* it."

The pictures aroused him, and he struggled to keep his happiness contained.

"I'll remind her what got her here. Her behavior with me. Her favorite son, yet she tortured me most. *Me!* The innocent child who went around fulfilling her dirty business while she cozied up with my father!" He sneered. "And then she disobeys Zeus and harms my love, my one and only, and takes her? *No.* I won't stand by and watch as she destroys my world. But I won't let the gods get away with this either..." He looked up at the ceiling, as if peering at the sky. "I'll punish them too. My Psyche is gone, my daughter is gone too, and they did nothing to stop Aphrodite from plotting it. They're *all* guilty, and hopefully they'll learn when they find Mother dead. Otherwise... they'll die too."

Lukus' trance continued as he rushed away from the windows and hovered near the doors, concealed in the darkness. Eros still heard his thoughts—he wanted to *surprise* her.

Eros clapped, seeking Lukus' attention. "Patience, little puppet. I speak with her first. Words that'll weaken her more, make her all *ripe* and juicy for you. Ready and willing to sacrifice her heart. *Patience...* though I love the idea of you jumping on her."

Lukus shimmied about, arms flailing like a dog's tail. His hunger grew; Eros prayed Aphrodite hurried, before Lukus turned his desire... towards him.

These arrows are unpredictable, and I can't risk that.

He shifted to the opposite end of the large room, putting space between himself and Lukus just in case. He had to be at his best when she arrived; right there, bow at the ready, prepared to plunge her into the same messed-up obscurity as Lukus.

He couldn't wait to watch them consume each other. His lips curved up, and he stretched, eager to express his hatred. His disappointment at her taking away Psyche and Hedone.

Today, he'd kill his mortal mother. For good.

‖ 27. WEAK MORTAL ‖
APHRODITE

Please don't die, Lukus.

Because Zeus would kill her if he died.

Aphrodite's breaths rushed, turning harsh and hurried; but her footsteps were slow, hesitant, shaky. And every ounce of hesitation amplified as she approached the abandoned warehouse. That's where the bartender said he was. The out of place, dreary building, obviously a trap and possibly haunted.

Why would Lukus take off on a whim like that? Didn't he call for back-up if he planned to encounter the murderer? He acted so recklessly—and it was her fault. She pushed him to drink, got him wrapped up in her family drama.

She sighed, letting the disappointment cloud her thoughts. Shocked at his lack of good judgment. Did he not realize the one who sent him here *was* the assassin? She shuddered at the description the bartender gave her—the precise moment she figured out who Lukus had spoken to, though unaware, skeptic as he was.

Damn you, Eros.

He had observed them, more than she expected. Knew more than she anticipated. Meaning she and Lukus were in more peril than she planned.

Dragging herself closer to the dilapidated building, the scent of water nearby almost drawing her away, enticing her to quit everything and jump in for a swim, she shrugged.

Closing her eyes, she stopped walking, sucked in the sweet, foreign yet welcoming smell, letting it entice, attract, push her to reminisce of earlier years when she was careless, free, happy. When she never had to worry. Oh, how she missed her original home.

A small breeze captivated her senses, yanking her from her mission—and her eyelids pried apart as she shook her head. "No, Aphrodite. Powers or not, you have no choice. You must stop him. You must *not* be selfish. Humans are more important. You can rest when you're done."

And yet, a tug in her gut reminded her she was disobeying. She prayed for Zeus' forgiveness, his understanding of why she took this risk. Why she had to confront her son without having uncovered his motives; a sacrifice she had to make to save them all.

She drew a deep breath, raising her gaze to the sky as it slowly shifted from a midnight blue to a light, faded orange. "You wanted me to protect Lukus, and this is the only way. I can't leave him to rot in there with Eros. I *can't* leave him to die. Eros won't hesitate, and so... neither should I."

Hopefully, the gods heard her. But hopefully they wouldn't stop her before she reached him. Hopefully they gave her sufficient time to listen to his excuses and reasons.

She took a few more steps, dizzy, dazzled by the sudden surge of godly energy in the vicinity. The overwhelming pull at her core told her Eros was definitely close.

Sensing a god as a human was something she never thought she'd endure. And it felt different from Zeus' spiritual appearance. This was Eros, in the flesh, overpowered and insane.

She raised her eyebrows, scanning the steel walls of the warehouse in front of her. Sniffing, begging to analyze any other presences...

Lukus was there. In the building, hidden in its shambles.

Oh, poor thing...

She wanted to barge in, rescue him and leave, get far from New Orleans and never look back. But she had simple human reflexes, now. Slow, powerless, armed only with a minimum of knowledge and a gun with tranquilizing bullets she wasn't even certain would work.

Eros would snatch her from Lukus and kill them both. And human as she was, she *could* die. Eros would take advantage of that. His anger, billowing out into the early morning air, fizzling under Aphrodite's skin, made that clear. Never in her entire existence had she been so close to death. Born immortal, she always had strength. And even when Zeus threatened her, deep down, she didn't fear him. He wouldn't remove her life force—he *needed* her—but Eros... was a different story.

I'm in more danger than I've ever been.

She gulped, reluctant to sacrifice herself. There had to be another way.

Eros lured her to her death, and she shuddered, picturing the little boy she raised. The caring, happy child who hugged her, loved her. The teenager who begged for a job with a purpose. *Why* would he want to kill his mother? Why would her demise bring him such satisfaction? And what did Lukus have to do with it all?

She dared another small stride towards the entrance. Massive windows lurked above her, and big double doors towered before her.

Death. Sacrifice. She had no choice. This was what it would take to save him, to save other humans. She had to give up immortality and let Eros kill her.

Will that interrupt him from killing more?

"Is that what you want, son?" Her coat jacket swayed in the gentle breeze, banging against her hip. Reminding her of the gun, the bullets, her only chance to immobilize Eros if only for a moment.

She recalled her lessons with Ares, the terminology he used to educate her, the proper way to hold the weapon, and the appropriate posture to maintain while shooting. She counted the cartridges in her head and gulped again. Her window would be tiny, she knew; but if she tranquilized him, called for the gods, brought him up to Olympus for further interrogation... she'd succeed. And she'd be *alive.*

Once more, she glanced up at the sky. "I'm going in, Zeus, and unless you physically stop me, you may never be able to rescue me." Her voice, low and panicked, roused fear in her belly. "Please, save Lukus. Save me, if you can, but first, save my *son*—if he deserves it. If you hear this, forgive me for once more disobeying you, but I had no alternative. *Your* precious world is at stake, and I'm only protecting it as I see fit."

She inhaled one last time, and put her hand on the large, wooden door.

Darkness engulfed her. Dust slid into her nostrils, followed by a pungent rust scent and the stench of blood. And something else she couldn't identify, especially with the area cowering in obscurity.

Swallowing hard, she arched her back. "Eros, show yourself!" But no matter her desire to sound strong, she came across a weakened mortal, a powerless deity. She had to try harder; he'd only laugh once he discovered her lack of strength.

Caressing the space where her gun rested, she let the door close behind her and straightened up, fixing her face. She wouldn't show an ounce of fear—mortal or not, she *was* a goddess. Aphrodite.

I can overpower my son and save the humans, right?

"Wrong, Mother. Always wrong." She froze as her son's sleek, milky tone wafted over to her. He shattered the silence, prompting Aphrodite to wish she'd stayed outside. "So weak, so powerless. And soon, *heartless.*"

She squinted, finding a small stretch of brightness appearing in the farthest part of the building. Of course, he read her thoughts. Her immortality no longer concealed her, no shield, no barrier.

A figure walked into the makeshift spotlight, holding a bow, raising it right at her. Dozens of feet separated them, but she sensed the tip against her skin, nonetheless; tasted its bitterness on her tongue.

Eros, the emotionless, overpowered son, had arrived. "Hello, Mother. So nice of you to join us." A hood concealed his face, but he tilted his chin up, a tiny smirk wiping across his mouth.

A few strands of golden hair escaped, and his eyes shimmered in their amber shade, illuminating the entire distance between them. Black leather covered his legs, his torso, part of his neck; and high, ebony boots rose to his knees, shiny and stained.

A murderer.

Aphrodite frowned. This wasn't her son, it couldn't be.

"Oh, but it *is* me, Mother. Your one and only Eros. The one you birthed and raised. All me. Don't you *recognize* what you made?" He spun on his heels, showcasing himself. "You wanted to find me, did you not? Well, here I am!"

He peeled back the string of the bow, prepared to shoot at her.

But he had to know he couldn't hurt her, not with those. Immortal or not, his arrows wouldn't affect her. She *created* them, after all; they would do nothing to her heart.

Or so, she tried to believe.

She pried her lips apart to speak—but Eros notched the arrow further. "Ah, you are correct; but these are *not* my usual arrows. My regular weapon cannot harm you, yes. But *this?*" He chuckled, chilling Aphrodite to the bone. "Haven't you noticed the difference? Did you think my normal arrows would make humans eat each other? Tsk tsk. Your error will be the end of you."

He let go of the string, his smirk widening.

The arrow raced forward with precision, aimed at Aphrodite's heart. She had merely seconds to realize it was coming, and she dodged sideways as it grazed her arm, ripping her shirt.

She winced, though no blood splattered out—just a scratch.

But it was enough to prove Eros' intentions.

He's going to destroy me!

She regained her balance, praying for agility. Catching her breath, she reached for the gun in her pocket, but Eros was too quick—he fired another arrow, forcing her to crouch to avoid it.

He had to sense her weapon; meaning he wouldn't let her get the pistol out in time to shoot him. If she couldn't tranquilize him... how was she supposed to confront and stop him?

"I can read your thoughts, mommy dearest!" He scoffed, still standing in his patch of light. "You're armed? That's *cute!*" He loaded the bow with another arrow, the action paralyzing Aphrodite as she crawled behind a set of pillars.

Her breaths became coarse, deep, her heart thumping loud.

Too loud.

"You may try to confront me, but you can't stop me! You *poor* little mortal, I'm so sorry for you!"

Aphrodite sucked in more air to remain quiet, stealthy. If he missed again, he'd keep shooting. Maybe he'd run out of arrows, and she'd waste enough time to save Lukus—if she managed to locate him.

Eros' raspy laugh barked around the room. "I don't care if I miss! I have all the time in the world, so do your best!" His heels *clicked* on the concrete floor. He was on the move. "My arrows are infinite, and you won't find Lukus. We can go at this for all eternity if that's your choice, but you won't live forever. *I* will."

She squished herself against the pillar, sensing his approach, sweat forming on her forehead. Should she try hand to hand combat? Or would he drive the arrow straight through her?

Or does he have yet another trick up his sleeve?

She panted, unsure how to steady her heartbeats. At this point, she'd have to run—and she hoped she had enough stamina.

Eros guffawed, his paces close.

Aphrodite hunched behind the pillar. "Your arrows can't hurt me! You're *bluffing*."

Where *was* Lukus? Had Eros already killed him?

Eros snuck up to her and shifted into view, causing her to gasp. His bow at his side, no longer pointed at her, he squinted at her trembling frame. "Oh, Aphrodite." The strip of light followed him like a spotlight.

This wasn't her child. She'd never seen him that way—evil, *murderous.*

He dropped his bow and crossed his arms. "Maybe my arrows can't kill you. Maybe you're right, and I'm unable to murder you. But... *he* isn't."

Aphrodite's brows shot up, but before she had a chance to let out a single squeak, something violently shoved her sideways, away from the pillar, smashing her onto the cold ground.

Tackled by this unknown—and *growling*—force, she whimpered, glued down, desperate to push this strong being off her. But she was too weak, too *mortal*; and the creature weighed down on her, crushing her, driving her to lie on her back.

She thought of Cerberus lookalikes; of guard dogs controlled by Eros. But this being smooshed her so, she had no way of witnessing its full appearance. And she barely had the strength to turn her head sideways to find Eros marching around her, his face twisted, his lips wide and glistening, his amber irises glowing.

"Oh Mother, this is better than a guard dog. A robot, a *zombie* that obeys my commands. My arrows have various effects, you see."

She watched him move, her chest so heavy she felt her insides constricting. "Eros—" The being pushed down harder, cutting her off.

Eros stopped circling her and snorted. "I am eager to see what my arrows do to you, but first, I want to discover what *this* creature has in mind."

The weight lifted for a split second, as if it shifted atop her. She cringed, unsure what type of monstrosity Eros had summoned, created, controlled to harm her. Something from the Underworld? Replicating a monster from stories from Hades?

Grunting, Eros kneeled, snapping at the being. "Dig in, my pet. *Lukus*."

Eyes bulging, ice flowing through her veins, Aphrodite slid her head back to face the thing pinning her to the ground.

No way, no way.

But as the being slithered backwards, setting his chin just above her breasts, tilting his gaze up—she saw him. His bright blue eyes, wide and excited. His teeth, gleaming, bared and salivating at her like a wolf ready to tear into its prey. Wild inky curls matted with blood framed his hollow features, scarred like some rabid beast had torn into his skin.

"Lukus..."

He growled louder, and before she had the opportunity to beg him not to, to plead for both their lives, he sank his teeth into her right arm, gnawing away at her flesh.

‖28. ALL YOU CAN EAT‖
EROS

"Take your time. Leave her heart for last, Lukus, do you hear me? Start with her arm and slowly work your way up."

Eros' whispered commands at Lukus, seconds before Aphrodite erupted into the warehouse, played on repeat in his skull.

Now he watched Lukus devour his mother's arm, hunger spreading in the air like a putrid disease. But one Eros liked. She deserved it—and he deserved his revenge. And it was only the beginning of her suffering; he couldn't wait to see the rest of his plot unfold.

Sprawled on the concrete, Aphrodite moaned, shoving against Lukus in a failed attempt to push him, pry his teeth from her skin; but Lukus' overpowering strength kept her down. The magic in Eros' blood arrows made him thicker than a titanium wall; fighting was pointless.

Aphrodite was stuck, no choice but to be eaten alive.

And I get to enjoy the show.

How he wished he had a snack of his own to munch on while witnessing the once in a lifetime event. The grand Aphrodite chowed on by a human—so disgustingly poetic. She struggled, tears swelling in her eyes, glistening on her pale skin. Eros had never seen her so frail, so innocent, vulnerable. He smiled as her voice made its way through her chapping lips.

"W-why Eros? *Why?"* Her tone, soft but broken, shook with angst and fear.

All confidence lost, falling off her high horse—Eros loved every second.

He cackled, too happy for his own good. "Why did I shoot Lukus? Because he was *available*, Mother, why else?" He squinted at her, then at Lukus, enjoying his feast. "He offered himself to me *so* willingly. I mentioned this cliché, and he showed up, drugged and drunk, willing to fight something—*someone*—way out of his strength range. And not caring to lose his life in the process. Though he didn't quite figure out what he fought for yet." The monster he created loaded his lungs with fresh, exhilarating oxygen. "He has such love for you, I couldn't resist. I *had* to fire at him, to... complicate things."

Blood spilled down Aphrodite's arm, drizzling onto the floor while Lukus nibbled, tearing through her flesh with a satisfied grunt.

Soon, her speech would fizzle out.

She'd better take advantage of her last moments to confess her crimes.

To his surprise, she shook her head, salty liquid spiraling down her face and dripping into the growing puddles of blood. "No, Eros. *Why?*"

Her words made no sense; surely the panic filling her scrambled her thoughts, confusing her.

"Why *what?*" Eros' insides boiled. "Have I not explained enough?" He kneeled to get a closer view of the carnage, staying at a safe distance. "What more can I explain to you?" He jutted his chin at Lukus, not in the least repulsed by the squelching sounds his chewing made. "He doesn't have a soulmate; did you realize that?"

Aphrodite let out a weakened gasp, squeezing her eyelids shut. "Eros—"

"Ah, you *didn't* know." Eros' grin widened. *"*Well... isn't it strange the man without a destined mate investigated *me*, the god who controls love? And you were drawn to him? Isn't it intriguing?" He didn't expect a reply, but his mother squirmed about, hoping to say something. "It was to me, I'll admit. So... I shot him, to see what would happen... and the more I got into his head, the more I realized deep down, he loved *you,* though I already suspected it."

Lukus dug deeper into her arm. Taking his time, causing Aphrodite intense suffering.

Eros' pulse quickened with pleasure as he witnessed the effect his blood arrows had on someone without a lifetime mate; someone who had no engravings on his ribcage.

"*Eros,*" she whispered, her voice starting to give out. "*Why?* Tell me *why.*" She reached out with her free arm, frail, struggling to lift it.

And though Eros kneeled far from her, he recoiled. How could she think he'd have pity on her soul? He would spare not an ounce of sympathy for her. She shouldn't have wasted her ultimate moments hoping for forgiveness.

The fool.

Eros tilted his head, analyzing his mother's words—

"Oh," he said, understanding at last. She wanted to know why Lukus *ate* her, why he did this. "But... why do you ask? Have you not figured it out?" He nearly winced at the blood gushing from her wounds as Lukus inched upwards. "Don't pretend you're clueless as to why I'm punishing you. You remember what you did and should have realized I'd want revenge. Don't play the fool now. You're cornered! You'll die. Your best option is to confess, not waste time."

Mother or not, he hated her. She birthed him, taught him everything in life, gave him his weapons—but for what she did, she had to pay. The price was death, and no one would dare disagree with that.

Aphrodite whimpered as Lukus gnawed on her bone, blood splashing, pools thickening beneath her, drenching her clothes. Her wails bounced off the stone walls and her eyes flickered, preparing to close. She'd faint soon, yet she was still far from dead. Lukus hadn't dealt the ultimate blow yet. He had to eat her heart, seal her fate, make her vulnerable enough to die.

And she can't stop that—she's no longer immortal.

"I don't know, son... p-please." A hint of genuine confusion slithered into her tone.

An eerie sensation tingled through Eros' veins. A twinge he didn't enjoy—like a pang of guilt, an inch of regret. *"No."*

He wouldn't let her convince him. Though she never lied, he was certain she lied now. She was responsible for the mess, and he wouldn't change his mind. She'd pay.

The guilt dissipated almost as quickly as it had appeared. "You want to play dumb, huh?" He slid up to his full height. "You want me to say it loud? For Lukus to *hear* what you did? It won't change a thing. He won't stop eating you. He's already cursed, and you'll also be cursed soon, and then *dead!*"

Rage boiled in his belly, all the anger he held in ready to explode.

Aphrodite's small squeaks only infused him with more fury. "*Where* is Psyche?" He put his hands on his hips. "And Hedone? Where did you take them? What did you do to them?"

Lukus chomped, deeper, harder, eradicating every piece of flesh surrounding the main bones in Aphrodite's arm.

She let out a heart-wrenching, gut-breaking squeal. "Your wife? Your daughter? *Me?*" She went silent for a moment, Lukus' obnoxious chewing filling the quiet. "No." She'd turned so white she might have been a cloud.

Eros refrained from rubbing his palms together in satisfaction. She'd pass out soon; why did she waste her moments pretending? On the verge of death... shouldn't she be begging, pleading for her life?

"No?" His fists dug into his hip bones. "So, you're saying you *aren't* responsible for their disappearance? Their probable deaths?"

Aphrodite managed a slight nod.

Every organ in his abdomen and chest swelled with cruelty, anger. "*Bullshit*!" He dropped his hands but cracked his knuckles. "You never liked Psyche! Wanted her gone the moment Zeus made her immortal! And I'm sure my daughter tried to defend her, so you disposed of her, too. Where are they, huh?" He brought his clenched fists up, desperate to punch her face in, scar her perfect skin. "What did you do to them?"

He approached Aphrodite's limp body, glaring deep into her tear-filled eyes, noticing her arm—once flesh, now replaced by half-eaten bones, drowning in ponds of metallic crimson liquid. It was a scene straight out of a gory horror movie; something that would usually render Eros nauseous. But an evil joy warmed his soul, keeping him from wanting to be sick.

Aphrodite gasped as Lukus reached farther up, shredding into her biceps. "No, son. N-not me. I didn't... I *wouldn't*... Zeus' orders, I wouldn't... d-disobey."

She wriggled about, desperate to push Lukus, but to no avail. Eros' monster wouldn't move.

"Stop lying!" Eros backed away, an acidic flavor bubbling at the top of his throat. "Confess! Die with a lighter heart! My wife disappeared, with my daughter, and you hate them both. You can't tell me you had nothing to do with that! It's not pure coincidence! Someone took them from me; you! And you will *pay* for it!"

Aphrodite's eyes shifted—blinding white, matching her complexion, then back to emerald green. And he lost his breath when they became electric blue, then piercing violet, before finally settling on green again. She opened her mouth to speak, but no sound escaped. Lukus ate the life out of her. And her silence was all the proof Eros needed.

Goodbye.

‖29. LET'S BE TOGETHER‖
LUKUS

Eat. Eat. Eat.

Her meat, so good, so tender. So delicious.

Thank you, Master, for this gift.

Lukus tore through the soft, glistening skin, shredding muscles and tendons, ripping veins. Blood splattered, drizzling as it spilled, and splashed as it erupted. The thirstier and hungrier he became, the more of the crimson liquid he let escape and pour onto the ground.

Her heart would be next.

Aphrodite. Sweet goddess of love, tender and juicy, a perfect fruit ready for picking. So heavenly. Just ripe enough, and all his.

Thank you, Master.

She moaned as he dug deeper—signs of pleasure, of happiness, of pure enjoyment.

He was happy too. Her epidermis, so delectable, like a fresh-baked pumpkin pie. Her insides were juicier than a rare steak. Her body filled him with luxurious ecstasy, and his spirit swelled when she sighed, allowing him to tear into every inch.

He only wished to give her something in return.

Excitement fluttered inside as he forced his teeth harder into her muscle, slicing farther up her arm. The trek towards her heart would begin soon, but he had to wait. Eros ordered it.

Master said her body was wondrous, so velvety, so *strong*. Almost like poison—if he ate it too fast, he may not digest it properly. And would die before devouring the best part. So, first, he had to get his tongue used to her divine taste, before diving into the final piece.

His limbs tingled the more he ingested. Eros spoke, but Lukus couldn't make out the words, too busy enjoying his feast. And Aphrodite responded, her voice faint. They discussed something, and a fragment of Lukus wished to overhear, to take part... but he had a job to do. Had to obey Eros. Perhaps she thanked him. For uniting them, bringing them together. Her tone revealed happiness, of that he was sure.

Thank you, Master Eros.

He reunited them for the better, gifted him with this godly meal. So honored, Lukus would have smiled if his mouth wasn't full. Him, a mere mortal, allowed to devour such a pure creature—a once in a lifetime opportunity.

His teeth clanked against a bone. He licked it, ensuring he got *every* morsel before moving on to the next spot. He slurped up every drop, uncaring of his animalistic behavior—no piece of skin or bit of organ could go uneaten.

Such regret consumed him as he ate. Mad at himself for insulting her, not believing her, dismissing the truth, pushing her away. In the end, he was blessed; her chosen one, her soulmate. Blessed Eros shot him, permitted him to see his true feelings. He had no idea he felt this way; no idea the visions she provoked were his *actual* desires.

Eros woke his hunger, and now Lukus would wake *hers*.

So we can be together for all eternity, never separated.

His lungs squeezed, his pulse raced, speeding up the closer he got to Aphrodite's heart. Blood rushed through him, pumping his extremities with energy, giving him more life than ever. He had never been so hungry and yet so satisfied with each bite. A poisoned curse, for sure; but too pleasant to stop.

All skepticism from before had evaporated, replaced by admiration. He only yearned for food, flesh, blood. He was like a zombie, but with a functioning, thriving brain—though he wasn't completely in control.

No, Master Eros controlled it. Allowed him to think freely, accept his task without arguing. But to express his feelings with his *teeth*. To show Aphrodite how pleased he was to become a part of her. To have her body flowing through him, literally infusing him with power.

He chomped away, and Aphrodite groaned, squirming in pleasure beneath him.

Devotion. Pride. Blood. He looked up, finding her beautiful emerald eyes, watching as they changed; to purple, then deep blue, glimmering in the warehouse darkness. She was so magnificent, so radiant, so perfect.

Farther ahead was Eros—grinning, encouraging, proud.

Thank you.

Lukus' life had meaning, now. He would feed his hunger without shame or worry. He'd forever be in his Master's debt. Munching towards Aphrodite's shoulder, he hungered for more. A desperate thirst spiraled through him, a trepidation pushing him to chew faster, swallow more, digest quickly.

But Master's orders reminded him to slow down. Relax, enjoy the ride.

Soon, my love.

Soon, he'd make his way to her heart. He'd feast on it and offer up his own. She'd eat, binding them forever. Blood to blood, flesh to flesh. Heart to heart.

We will be one.

‖30. PUNISHMENT‖
APHRODITE

Stop, please, stop this.

Warm, gushing blood stained Aphrodite's shirt and jacket, dripping from Lukus fangs. Yes, *fangs*—Lukus was no longer human. The man she met days prior—the one she traveled with, laughed with, and lied to—left. Replaced by a murderous creature, a bloodthirsty demon. And transformed into this carnivorous monster by none other than her son. Triggered to fulfill her son's plans, however gruesome they were.

Her voice had fizzled out, but she still had enough life force to think.

Eros believed she captured Psyche? And Hedone?

Why would I do such things?

Zeus made Psyche immortal centuries ago, and Aphrodite barely spoke to her since then. And she'd never approached Hedone. So, what business would she have harming them?

She winced as Lukus nibbled on the skin pulling over her shoulder, thirsty for every inch. Her body was a piece of meat, her flesh available, easily plucked off for Eros' entertainment. She was food, no longer the immortal goddess she had once been. Luckily—or not, since it was all torture—she wouldn't die as fast as a human. She was mortal now, but still a deity on the inside. It would take a while for Lukus to... *finish* her.

She gasped, though the hushed sounds escaping her mouth were weak.

If he reached her heart, she'd perish just as quickly as the other victims. She'd be controlled, like them, no chance to stop the carnage. She'd fail.

Gaping at Lukus, she witnessed the zombie-like being he had become. His hair was no longer ebony, and instead drenched in a mixture of sweat and blood. And his eyes, once so pure, so crystalline, shifted to an unnatural and piercing cerulean, contrasting his red cheeks and sparkling white fangs. Though now, not so white—they were stained scarlet.

Possessed. Could he still think for himself? Was he still *in there*, somewhere?

She wanted to shake her head, but she had no strength. Lukus smooshed her against the cold concrete, and the loss of blood rendered most of her limbs numb.

Did she have a chance in talking this zombie out of his hunger? No longer mortal, no longer the man who refused to believe in the supernatural, wanting to lock her up—would this being respond to her? She wished for the old Lukus to return. The one who hated her. Sure, she'd be behind bars for her psychotic, god-loving tendencies... but he'd be safe. And she'd be alive.

But now, he believed. Absorbed, consumed by hunger, fueled by Eros' rage. Whatever Eros had tipped the arrows in had flipped a switch in Lukus' brain, turned him into Eros' obedient god-eating pet.

Am I able to stop this?

She glanced at the monstrous thing devouring her arm. "Lukus..." He peered at her, but didn't stop chomping. She cringed. "Lukus, *please.* Y-you don't... have to do this." Her throat, on fire, threatened her ability to speak. And without her voice, she was done. No powers, no energy, she only had her words to count on. She had to try, to get through to him before it was too late.

Lukus, eyes laced with a craving that made her shiver, continued his meal. All trace of humanity had escaped him; he was a robot who yearned to devour human flesh. In particular, Aphrodite's now *mortal* flesh.

He didn't understand her words. Couldn't comprehend her, with his bites and loud chewing—

Her head dropped to the side, giving her a good view of her son. Only Eros had control over Lukus. And Eros... wouldn't stop him. Too sure of her guilt, he'd rather watch her bleed, be devoured, than admit she *may* be innocent.

Eros stared at her. "That's correct, Mother. Don't waste your breath. There's no way to block him. So, unless you kill him, your little friend will eat you up whole." He snickered, looming nearby, holding his bow. "And you don't want to execute him, do you? You want him alive. Your adoptive daddy ordered it. So, you'd sacrifice yourself for this human, but not because Zeus wants you to... because you care for Lukus, just as he cares for you. Under other circumstances I'd say this was *cute*."

Aphrodite closed her eyes and inhaled, blood rushing to her wounds and flowing out like a crimson waterfall. The metallic stench caused her gut to churn as she bathed in the red lake beneath her, prepared to drown. To be engulfed below the floor, down a black hole, to arrive in Tartarus and be locked up with the Titans— and *other* godly monsters.

Bloody waves washed over her face, suffocating her, draining her last breaths.

But when she opened her eyes, she was still in the warehouse. Still drenched in her own blood, Lukus still grunting as he munched, Eros still pacing as he waited. Unbearable pain spread from her fingertips to her toes, and immobilized, she sensed her ribcage constricting. She couldn't lose her mind, not now. She had to stay conscious, force herself to stay alive as long as possible.

Then she felt them—her eyes, switching, glossing over, changing colors. She had no control, meaning for real, her time ran out. She needed help.

The Olympians...

She had to reach out, beg for guidance. In way over her head, only they could save her—and humanity.

She cleared her larynx, spitting up blood. "*Gods.* Zeus. H-help... I'm not worthy, but... my abilities... please, Eros... uncontrollable."

Eros stormed up to her, his footsteps banging on the ground, bouncing the back of her skull up and down. He kicked her uninjured arm and Lukus growled, howling as a wolf, digging into her clavicle.

The ache, searing, pinching, plunging, sent waves of dizziness to her senses. Any regular mortal would have been dead by now—but Aphrodite hung on to life by a thin thread as sharp jabs of pain attacked her.

Eros grumbled as he circled her lifeless form. *"Shut up, Aphrodite."* The soles of his shoes squeaked. "You think they'll come for you? That they'll help *you?* The one who disobeys, does whatever she pleases and kidnaps other mortals? No. They *won't.* They'll leave you to rot, eaten by the man who loves you, and then they'll watch as you devour him. As you partake in my horrific crimes as payment for what you did. And you know what? They'll never stop me. They can't!" He raised his hands in the air, triumphant. He thought he'd won.

Unstoppable, huh?

Her breaths deepened, harder, painful. Unable to react to her son's ego.

"They're stuck on their asses up there, so consumed with power and godliness they didn't detect my wife went missing over a month ago! *And* my poor, ignored daughter!" He screeched, prompting Aphrodite to wince—but her lips, chapped, torn, only worsened her agony. "Nor did they notice I abandoned my duties to go find them! No one cared, Mother, especially not you!"

Startled, Aphrodite opened her mouth, but her vocal chords were asleep, dying.

Psyche went missing a *month* ago? No one told Aphrodite anything. Nor did anyone say a thing about Eros leaving.

Terror ravaged her insides. He had to be lying; Zeus would have known if a god was missing, if someone abandoned their post. None of this would have gone uninvestigated.

She panicked, heart rate speeding up.

No, no, keep calm.

Begging the gods would put an end to it all. Eros was wrong; they *would* save her. They would come down here.

Eros' guttural chuckle pierced through her internal debate. "I love that you've developed a sense of humor *now*, as you're on the verge of death," he spat between giggles. "Your pleading is hilarious, as are your thoughts. Truly."

Aphrodite ignored him and focused every remaining ounce of her energy on her speech. "Zeus, I beg you. *Forgive...*

me. Let me... confront him. With my... p-powers." It took every fiber of her being to force her mouth to cooperate. The blood swirling on her tongue made her want to vomit, and her esophagus throbbed so bad she struggled to swallow.

Zeus wouldn't let her die. He didn't send her here for that; he sent her to figure out why Eros murdered humans. And she did; Eros found her guilty of kidnapping his wife and daughter, so he retaliated by killing charges, luring her into a trap to kill her.

I figured it out, Zeus.

She wished to scream to the Olympian mountains, to wake her brothers and sisters, to rouse Zeus and Hera from their thrones—but her fragile, decomposing body wouldn't allow it. "I was wrong... but now, I'm right. H-help me."

She noticed the crack in her vocal cords, the pinch in her throat. That was it. She gave it her all and prayed Zeus listened to her.

"You weak, unfortunate, *stupid* thing," grumbled Eros, his laughter fading. "Begging for your powers? So unlike you. You never beg for anything, let no one take anything from you. Like me. You were merciless, the biggest bitch in Olympus—yet here you are, a powerless mortal, a pathetic scrap of meat to my zombie pet." He snorted and spat on the ground near her. "If you're upset with *me*, remember this. You made me this way, Mother. Taught me not to let myself get stepped on, *especially* by you. Well, you overstepped. Taking the love of my life from me. I'm defending what's mine, as you should have when Zeus stripped you of your powers and sent you down here with me. Regardless of your crimes, you disappoint me. I expected a true fight."

With no voice to reply, she gawked at her son, tears clouding her vision. Yes, it was her fault. She created him, used him, hurt him—but she gave up her bad ways *centuries* ago. So why now, after all this time, did Eros punish her?

Lukus' unnatural weight shoved her down, his animalistic eating only worsening her trauma. She pried her lips apart. "I—" No other sound slid out.

Eros laughed. "Yes, Mother, *you*. You can't, you won't, you *shouldn't*. You're stuck, Lukus will eat your heart, and you'll eat his, dooming yourselves to a swift, bloody death even Hades himself can't revive you from. Visit the depths of Tartarus and, ha! You won't like it—trust me, I've been there recently, and it won't be up to your luxurious standards."

Aphrodite internally pleaded for mercy. He didn't have to do this. If he spared her, spared them all, came to his senses, he'd be forgiven.

I love you, still. You're my kin.

Eros snickered. "*No*. I will spare none until I get my wife back! Once you're dead, I'll taunt the gods until they reveal where you took her, or where you *buried* her! I assume you removed her immortality and butchered her as you've always wanted to, since she defied you all those ages ago. She was just a mortal!" An honest sadness crept into his tone, and for a moment, Aphrodite expected him to let his guard down. His fiery eyes and shaking fists proved her otherwise. "You punished her instead of educating her? Well, that's what I'm doing as revenge. Punishing you. Punishing *everyone*. With death."

The remaining droplets of her life clung to her soul, ready to slither from her essence. From her core. Lukus paused, as if sensing it; his pupils widened, his mouth expanded, his smile cruel and fearsome, stained with her blood.

No, Lukus, please.

"*Yes*, Lukus. It's time. Go ahead, feast on her heart. Then she'll feast on yours. You'll be as one."

Aphrodite poured her gaze into Lukus, wanting to appeal to him deep down.

No, please, don't do this.

She squinted, desperate to peel through the layers of his monstrous being, to reach his soul, to convince him to stop.

Don't eat my heart. Don't seal our fates. Hear me, listen to me.

Lukus whimpered like a dog waiting for a treat.

"He can't understand you, Mother. Don't bother!" Eros snapped at his pet. "Now! Eat her!"

You can overcome this. Save us both. Reach deep within, find the strength to defy Eros. Don't eat me. Don't doom yourself.

Lukus', like a puppy trying to comprehend its master, cocked his head side to side. Clueless, unfit to read Aphrodite's thoughts. She had only one option left. Suicidal and dangerous—but who cared, at that point? She was about to die, anyway. Maybe her actions would save others.

Concentrating that last drop of energy, of humanity, she squeezed her eyelids closed, parted her lips—and screamed. A piercing, nails on a chalkboard screech that even Eros had to crouch down for, covering his ears in agony.

"*Shut up!* Stop that! *Stop that!*"

But his wails only fizzled under her yelp. It was all she had left; all she could do. Her last weapon, her only hope— screaming until her lungs gave out. Her scream resonated in the abandoned building, echoing as it weaved between the wooden foundations, bounced off metallic pillars, and slammed into the walls, shaking them, rattling the ground.

If Zeus didn't catch it from the Olympian heavens, then he'd find her dead.

Briefly peeking at the ceiling, Eros stood up, dusting off his leather pants. "Impressive, Mother." He released a gut-wrenching cackle. "But I *doubt* he heard it. So... just accept your fate, and we'll make a deal. I'll make this... *quicker*, for you." He clapped as he meandered closer, again lifting his leg near Aphrodite's limp body, ready to kick her.

A blast of blinding light, a surge of energy, violently thrust him back a few feet, and though he wobbled, he kept his balance.

"What the—" The light grew in intensity, pouring into the room, illuminating every nook and cranny; even halting Lukus in his feasting.

Aphrodite recognized that light—and weak as she was, she recalled the vibrations it provoked in the very seams of her core. The pulsations it aroused in her veins.

Zeus.

On the brink of exhaustion, seconds from death, she smiled. Eros was mistaken.

Thank you.

The familiar brightness concentrated, hovering above her before shooting into her like a rushed breeze. It filled every cavity, replenishing the blood she lost. It fused with the flesh and muscles Lukus had eaten, slowly swelling inside, regrowing, re-birthing each member. Her epidermis glued back together, rebuilding her shoulder, biceps, and forearm.

Lukus watched in awe as Aphrodite became whole again.

She felt her fingers, gaining motion. Her hands shook, blood finally pumping through each fingertip, turning red and full of life. Inch by inch, the exposed areas of her arm covered up, healed, sealed from Lukus' claw-like teeth.

And another sensation crawled up inside her, blooming in her bosom, reaching her brain, firing her neurons—the thing she craved, desired, needed more than anything since her arrival on earth.

My powers!

An energy she hadn't felt in a while fizzled through her, bringing her to life. Her sweet abilities, her strength, her immortality. Her weakness faded down an invisible drain as every slither of her usual self replenished. Aphrodite, Olympian goddess—

"Wait, how do the humans say it?" she mumbled under her breath. She giggled. *"Ready to kick some ass."*

Rejuvenated, reborn, any trace of panic and pain dissipated. The human emotions that once invaded her mind frazzled, blew into millions of pieces and flew out, draining, replaced by her godly power and vibrant energy. So fueled by her returned confidence, she hadn't noticed Lukus' surprise, or heard Eros' screeching.

Fully healed, she shot up, unwillingly sending Lukus thrashing across the room, thumping on the pavement, smacking his head into a wall. He crumbled, inanimate, knocked out.

Agnes would have gasped, would have run to him—but Aphrodite had no time. At a distance, she heard his pulse, though it was weak. He was still alive; for now.

I'll deal with him later.

She turned her emotionless gaze to Eros. He was her only concern. And mommy *wasn't* pleased.

Eros removed his hands from his face, blinking at his mother's glowing skin, radiating power he had always envied her for.

She snarled at his form. "You disgrace me. Disappoint me. Dishonor me. *Disgust* me. Used your powers for evil because you assumed *I* did. You cruel, unworthy child!"

Her snarl widened as rage and anger grew in her gut. She sent her hands to her hips, glaring at her offspring, not an ounce of mercy remaining in her godly heart. The fight had only just begun, and as she growled, glowering at Eros who stared back with equal fury and disappointment, the atmosphere thickened with tension.

"Eros, god of love and desire, son of Aphrodite, betrayer of the gods, and murderer of innocent humans... you and I have a *lot* to talk about, don't we?"

‖ 31. POWER ‖
EROS

"What's there to talk about, Mother?" Body on edge, limbs shaking, Eros glared at her. "Your guilt? Your dishonesty, your conniving ways? The list goes on." He'd never had such power in his blood before. Such fury in his veins. The fight would be difficult, but he enjoyed a good challenge now and then.

I can still win if I use my wit.

Aphrodite took a step forward, shoes splashing in one of the scarlet puddles that didn't disappear when she regenerated. "We need to discuss your unforgivable mistakes, son. You're out of line. You're sick, and you need help because you jumped to conclusions without investigating!" He noticed her knuckles turning white as she pressed harder onto her hip bone. "If I've learned *anything* from my adventure as a mortal, it's that you need a proper investigation before making any drastic decisions!" Her strawberry-blonde hair flew behind her as her anger billowed through the building, manifesting as a strong, foreign wind.

He should have feared her, he knew; but he was too mad to back down. Too infuriated to retreat. He held his ground, but he sensed tension in his shoulders and spine. Did she expect him to cower? Run away? Did she not understand the trials he endured to get there, to confront her? The deals he had to make to avenge his wife?

Does she think I'll give up?

"And you assume I owe *you* an explanation?" He scoffed, and Aphrodite took another stride towards him. "That you may come down here and judge me? Punish me? You say that's what Zeus wanted?"

An idea sprung to life in his brain, prying his lips into a smile. He'd turn her against the gods. He'd use her, *then* kill her once he'd gotten the truth from her and all the other Olympians.

Ah, Mother, you inspire me with your cute little threats.

Another breeze shot through the walls behind him, whirling straight to Aphrodite; *his* anger. Powerful, wrathful, it contradicted her aura and collided with her Olympian energy, nearly knocking her backwards. She kept her balance, but rage flashed in her eyes.

"I may hate you, but *you're* a victim too, Mother. A casualty of Zeus' schemes. He manipulates you, and you obey without question." He waved dismissively. "Don't worry, I'll take care of him. He has acts to pay for, as you do. My blood arrows will help me get the answers I seek, with torture, and then death."

Aphrodite's irises flashed again before turning to a piercing scarlet shade, laced with violet and black. So bright, so poisonous Eros had no way to avoid their intensity from where he stood.

Her infuriated breeze amplified, gaining speed, pushing past his barriers and threatening to topple him over. Almost forcing him to bend the knee, accept her dominance over him.

Any other human—or god—would have obeyed, gave up; but Eros refused to let her tricks work on him. Exposing her true anger, revealing her eyes—that hadn't shifted this way since Adonis—was incredible, and only showed her weakness better.

The human.

Did she *really* care for him?

She snorted, her feet planted on the concrete. "You didn't trust your mother and ran off on your own to ruin the world Zeus swore to protect. That's an irresponsible, childish thing I might have expected from you as a baby, a youngling—but *now?* As a grown god? As a father? I'm upset." Her tone, softer, on the verge of crackling, proved her genuine disappointment.

Eros had no reply. He knew his attitude would displease most; he had no intention of changing it.

"You broke your vows, son." She dropped her hands, wiggling her fingers as if preparing to launch an attack. "You abandoned your post, and for what? To fight with *me*, the innocent one? To prove some twisted point that you're wrong about? You've lost your mind, Eros!" She strode a few steps forward to lessen the distance between them.

For the first time in weeks, Eros' throat dried up. His mind scrambled. Again, he had no decent comeback—his mother would outwit him if he didn't figure out a better plan, and quick. Had she regained her ability to read thoughts? Including his? He had expected her to be rusty, but perhaps... she was stronger than before.

Feigning a cough, brushing off his pants, adjusting his coat—he used any excuse to peer around, gauging the big doors, the large windows, the stairs. Trying to concoct an escape route in case she disarmed him, weakened him. Overpowered him. He wouldn't let her win, but he had to prepare for all eventualities. Regroup, regenerate, face her again later once he consumed more ambrosia.

"Innocent? *You?* Don't make me laugh." He stepped backwards. The doors to his right would be easy to run to if she attacked. Because she'd lunge for him, any minute. The resentment in her gaze was real. Angrier than during the Trojan war, more hateful than in the Adonis situation. And the more he thought about it, the more he realized—no, he'd never witnessed her so angry.

She's out for blood, but I'm not dying before I find Psyche.

"You're the least innocent of all the gods, Aphrodite. A lying, cheating, corrupt goddess who only thinks of herself. Admit it! All you care about is *you.*" She wouldn't and couldn't deny it. "What did Psyche do to you, huh? Aside from her offenses as a mortal, she did nothing to upset you. She apologized; don't you remember? Basically *begged* you to accept her! Not even to love her—just to tolerate her existence. Immortal and happy, minding her own business, with me. Why did you take her, Mother?"

Her stance menacing, Aphrodite inched closer. Her arms lifted, fingertips extended. Slowly, palms facing the ceiling, she drew more energy, the wind picking up the higher her hands traveled. Swirling, tornado-like, shattering glass windows and blasting the doors open, Aphrodite's strength had multiplied. But she had made Eros' escape easier, so focused on her abilities and displaying them before him, to scare him.

Maybe you're useful after all, Mother.

But as he pictured himself dashing out, the doors slammed shut. The air swirled, but around them only. Eros' hopes diminished.

He gulped, though he covered it with a throat-clearing noise. "You and the gods, always abusing me and my powers, making me do your dirty work, never concerned for *my* well-being. I'm finally pleased with my immortal life and you snatch away the one person who filled me with joy? Psyche was *all* I had, and our daughter was the fruit of that love. Yet you *had* to ruin it, didn't you?"

His words had no effect on her. Aphrodite continued her trek to him, though slow, her glowing eyes inspiring awe, angst, anticipation. She seemed closer by the second, and Eros' breath hitched.

Shit.

He had to keep talking. Surely *something* he said would stop her, deter her, distract her.

"You and the others, all too busy with your stupid vanities, aren't you? No one bothered to notice when one of us went missing. And no one bothered to investigate the deity who was clearly responsible for it!" Determined to express his emotions before she tried to rip him apart, he heard his voice turning weak.

She knew it all. She knew what she did. So why did she deny it, still? Did she only wish to silence him, make it look like an accident when the gods came to meet her? Did she plan this all along, to get away with Psyche's murder... then his?

Consumed by his racing ideas, he almost screamed when Aphrodite lunged, jumping up a few feet, and landed so close to him their noses touched. Her eyes were so bright they *bled*, her power so overwhelming it urged Eros to bow. She towered over him, a true goddess in her true form. Eros winced, squinting, fighting to resist her; but soon, her gaze alone made his knees wobble and his arms, their muscles once bulging under his leather jacket, became limp. Heavy, frail, he fell to his knees.

"No... *no*, confess! Tell me... the truth!" He tried to tip his chin up to look at her, but she forced his head down with her abilities. "Before you... execute me... tell me where... *where* is my

Psyche?" Again, he tugged, scrambling against her pull, desperate to peep at her as he begged for mercy. "Where... in Tartarus... is my wife?"

His chin slipped up, and her power released; but instead of shooting her fingers through his heart, she slapped him hard across the face, her handprint stinging on his cheek. He gawked at her, but not an ounce of emotion showed on her features.

"I did not kidnap your damn wife and child, Eros! Now *stop* accusing me of crimes I didn't do!" He blinked, and she lowered her palm. "*You* are the one in trouble, so stop plotting your flight and thinking I'll slaughter you, because I won't. I wouldn't murder my son!"

Eros, knees rubbing against the insides of his pants, hard against the concrete, cocked his head, a sly grin spreading across his lips. "You... *won't* kill me?"

He was wrong. She wouldn't torture him and dispose of him as if he were nothing. But now, thanks to her lapse in judgment, his plan took form.

His body re-energized, recovering from her slap as he took a moment to breathe. A moment where her powers didn't ground him. "Well, that's your biggest mistake. Because I *would* kill my mother."

‖ 32. THIS ENDS NOW ‖
APHRODITE

Eros' defiant gaze poured into Aphrodite's. The anger within her burned, racing through her insides. Rushing in her veins, disturbing her hopes of peace and calm.

Fire fueled her as she pressed her palms onto Eros' torso—and shoved him, hard. He fell with a loud *thump,* and the ground shook under him like a small earthquake, rattling the walls and threatening to break more windows.

She crossed her arms. "No. You will not kill another being, human or non. You're done. This hissy fit, this immature reaction stops *now."* She struggled to stop her voice from roaring. "You will end your torturous ways and return home to receive a proper punishment. To pay for your crimes."

She refused to murder him, but she'd teach him a lesson. She'd wait for him to explain himself, apologize. Because Zeus wouldn't tolerate his attitude as she did—he wouldn't hesitate.

Eros coughed, stabilizing his breathing. He then peeked up at her, a hint of his defiance returning. "I still have blood arrows, and they will *not* go to waste. Not after what I went through to get them in the first place." He choked a little as he got to his feet, fingertips grazing the red mark she'd left on his cheek.

She had slapped, she had pushed, she had yelled—and none of it moved him.

What will it take to stop him?

She remembered these arrows he mentioned. "Blood arrows?" She kept her gaze trained on him, analyzing his every move in case he tried something. "Is that how you got the power to turn humans into carnivorous monsters who eat each other's hearts and *die?* How in the world were you able to do that?" Her arm twitched, a phantom itch she'd never recover from. Thanks to Lukus. A twinge of pain twisted her gut, for just a second—where was Lukus? Was he okay?

She rocked her head side to side—no, she had to stop Eros. Lukus would wait. Her priority was to halt Eros and get him home. If Lukus was dead... she'd feel it. He was safer unconscious than awake.

Eros walked to a large lump on the ground Aphrodite assumed to be a bag. He reached inside and removed an arrow, golden and glimmering, its tip red and dripping with what appeared to be actual blood.

So, not just a name. His arrows were actually dipped in someone's—or *something's*—blood. She shuddered; this was unlike him. Terrifying. Who did he sacrifice to come up with such a demonic weapon?

Amber eyes glowing, he pivoted to her. "I traveled to the Underworld, Mother. Did you know that? When Psyche disappeared, I thought she was dead, so I snuck in, hoping to talk to good old Hades and bargain for her life. If you had anything to do with her disappearance... I assumed she'd be down there." He touched the point of the projectile with his index finger.

Fighting a gasp, Aphrodite's nostrils twitched. One couldn't *sneak into* the Underworld, all gods learned that. Every passage was guarded, payment due for those not supposed to be there. Only Hades granted true access. No one would have allowed a grieving, possibly psychotic god like Eros to trespass downstairs so easily.

Eros' crackling voice brought her back to his speech. "I didn't get far. I couldn't enlist a guide such as Hermes, or call on Hades, since both options would draw too much attention, cause too many questions. Instead... I took a wrong turn and... came face to face with Cerberus."

He released the arrow and pulled one of his sleeves up, revealing a large, glistening red scar indented in his arm. Deep, bright, painful and likely not healed.

Bile rose to Aphrodite's throat. Despite her rage, seeing her son wounded pinched at her heart. He fought with Cerberus—how? She taught him better than to taunt the guard-dog of Tartarus. He knew not to mess with *any* creature of the Underworld, to test monsters like those.

Eros shook his head as he replaced his sleeve. "Yes, Mother, of course." He picked up the arrow. "What was I thinking? What got into me? Wanting to overpower the dog of the Underworld, the guardian of the gates, the three-headed monster? What possessed me to do it? Well... *anger*."

Gesturing with his free hand, his other clenching around the arrow, he stepped forward. Aphrodite braced for impact, bending her knees in anticipation of his attack.

"I was *furious*. My wife disappeared, my daughter disappeared, and I trusted no one to help me find them. Distraught, I only saw negative outcomes. Horrible images flashed before me. Then... *she* arrived." He retrieved his bow from the floor, having dropped it during his exchange with Aphrodite.

"She?" She cringed, praying he didn't refer to who she thought. The only woman downstairs who had a lick of power, an ounce of authority.

Eros smiled. "Yes, *she*. Persephone. Your *best* friend." Aphrodite snorted, and he cackled. "Oh, excuse my sarcasm, it's too easy to taunt you with that name." He snickered. "Your enemy made Cerberus stop yapping, who knows how, and asked me why I was there. So, I explained my situation, my family being gone, and she was... cryptic. Stranger than usual. Said I'd need to fight and told me Cerberus' blood could *help* with that."

Eyes narrowing, energy pulsating in her fingertips, she fought a snarl.

You brat—you figured out using her name would trigger me.

Her fists tightened, but she refrained from letting violence warp her actions again. "Persephone has no control over Cerberus. Only Hades does." She glanced at her offspring, at his confidence, at his weapons—unsure if he told the truth. "Hermes informed us of this centuries ago. That... was not Persephone. She... she shares everything with Hades. And upstairs, he... told us nothing when we were all convened. Before Zeus sent me to earth.

And he... doesn't lie or plot. None... none of this makes sense, Eros."

The god only shrugged, as if not a single word Aphrodite said had reached his ears. "She helped me secure several vials of this precious red juice, and revealed when injected into a heart, it turned humans into cannibals, and gods into carnivores. She told me it would *weaken* a god like nothing else. Drains the ambrosia from their being. She assured me it would help me fight my battles when the time came. And *this* is the time, Mother. The battle she referenced." He lifted his bow and attached the arrow to the string with precision. So swift, Aphrodite barely noticed him doing it.

She slid backwards. She didn't want to fight, not like this. Not until he explained more, revealed the true source behind his arrows. She needed a better idea of whom to frame, of whom to kill for putting such ideas in his head.

She held her ground. "How did the humans not die immediately upon losing their hearts? Is that *also* part of the Cerberus blood trick?" She prepared to dodge her son's missiles, planting her feet, arching her spine.

None of it added up. Persephone didn't know these facts; Hades wouldn't allow it. None of the Olympians would.

This came from higher up, from someone or something more powerful. But who?

She watched the man in front of her, wishing for her innocent little boy to return, to run and jump in her arms, hug her, love her. Who corrupted that sweet child?

Eros relaxed his grip on the bow. "Excellent question. I wondered the same, at first. And it turns out it's because their souls were full of love, fueling them so much, for so long, that even once they removed their hearts, they had a few moments of life left. *Supernatural,* isn't it? Your buddy Lukus wouldn't have believed it, but us gods know better."

The snide tone he took, the proud posture—he wasn't himself, and neither was Persephone. Something bigger was at play; bigger than Psyche and Hedone disappearing. Something poisoned Eros, his mind, his actions.

Her nerves fidgeting, anticipating her son's desire to shoot her if she said the wrong thing, Aphrodite relaxed her stance—for a second. "Eros... son, *please,* come to your senses. What happened? Who did this to you? Why are you really killing innocent humans?"

He sneered and raised his bow. "How many times must I repeat myself? *You* stole Psyche and Hedone, *you* did this to me, and *that's* why I'm murdering mortals! For recognition. To aid with my revenge. Once I'm done with you, I'll move on to the other gods. They didn't notice, didn't realize Psyche didn't grace the halls of Olympus with her presence, didn't pay attention to anything but themselves! Don't worry, Mother, you won't be alone in the depths of Tartarus for long!"

He growled and took his aim—but Aphrodite growled right back.

This boy needs to learn his place.

She refused to move, refused to cower before his unnatural weapon. "I never held your wife in my heart, but I would *never* kidnap and assassinate her, Eros. Especially when Zeus made her immortal and married her to you. What business is it of mine to interfere in your love life? I learned that lesson thousands of years ago. Why would I disobey my king?"

Her senses tingled, fingers wiggling as a foreign numbness took over them.

There was more to it all. Eros wouldn't go crazy like this, not without provocation. And she'd never snatch his bride, not without reason.

My Eros would never accuse me this way.

She searched the confines of her mind, hoping for a divine answer, a revelation. To understand what pushed her offspring over the edge. Were he and Persephone taken by someone, or something else? Was his madness part of a bigger, more intricate plan? Were they dealing with someone unfamiliar? A new villain?

Eros cackled. "Stop lying! Stop claiming innocence when you have none! We discussed this, and I'm sick of repeating myself. You *hate* Zeus more than any other Olympian, you told me so! Of course, you'd defy him, and of course you'd steal Psyche to do so!"

Her blood boiled, her lungs swelled with furious oxygen, tightening her muscles and firing up her neurons. Her extremities still tingled, but she ignored them. "*Everyone* hates Zeus. But we obey him because he offers the protection of Olympus. An elite seat on his council. He offered you a wife, forgave our past transgressions, and *this* is how you repay him? I understand if you hate *me* for using you as a child, but I thought we moved past it, that you had grown up."

The concrete beneath her began to shake. A subtle tremble, a slight movement she didn't recognize.

That's... not me.

And as she sent a quick peek at her son—who seemed to have sensed the trembling also—she realized he hadn't caused it either. Her fingers twinged, infusing with power, strength, and cracks formed in the floor. A fresh gust escaped the slits and blew up through her hair, throwing Eros' hood back, revealing his messy mane and his shocked gaze.

"Mother?"

Something is coming.

Was it whatever turned Eros into this monster? The creature that *really* took Psyche and Hedone? Her senses flickered; the tingles became unbearable, and she winced.

It's arriving here to end me?

Eros frowned, his amber eyes speckled with evil. "You *lie.* You're doing this! Tricking me!" He snarled. "And you'll pay!" Without a care for the breeze billowing around them, swirling dangerously, he released the arrow towards her.

She ducked, dodging it in time, kneeling as the ground shook harder, ready to open up and engulf them both. Was it the Underworld? Did that explain why what she felt had such a foreign, unknown taste on her tongue? The twinging only accentuated, and Eros appeared to experience it too as he let go of his bow and backed away, glaring at her.

"Mother? Who did you summon? Is this how you killed Psyche?" The fear tainting his tone only proved he had no clue what happened. If someone used him for bigger plans, he knew nothing of it.

"I did not kill your wife, dammit!"

The warehouse filled with a sudden blinding light. Harsher than when Aphrodite's powers returned, stronger than when she shoved Eros. Thunder rolled in, lightning cracked, shattering every remaining glass window as the roof above caved in, forcing the daylight in at last—but not a single shingle or debris reached the floor. Every particle of the roof suspended in air.

A massive blast put both Aphrodite and Eros to their knees. More blasts shook the building's foundations, followed by multiple figures *popping* into the room. They were shadowy, blurry and foggy at first, but as they lined up beside Aphrodite, she knew. She *felt* them.

Eros crawled backwards, his face blank as a sheet, nearly turning green from the fear oozing out of him, the terror squeezing around his gut.

She breathed in, adjusting to the light. To the pure presences that loaded her with a new surge of energy, amplifying her powers, helping her regain courage.

Rising to her feet, she smiled. The gods listened. They were here.

"We heard everything." Zeus' booming voice filled the entire space, rumbling like a record-breaking storm. "Eros, descendant of Aphrodite and Ares, god of love and desire, keeper of soulmates and protector of hearts, what do you have to say in your defense?" Taller and more muscular than she remembered, the king of the gods marched towards Eros.

She brushed herself off, pleased they came to her rescue. And she sensed them *all*—the Olympian crew had showed up. Through the hazy light she found Dionysus, Apollo, and Artemis, their bows pointed at her son, their faces twisted in rage.

Near them were Athena and Hermes with swords in their clenched fists, dropped in fighting stances, gazes glaring. Hera and Demeter, farther back, sported oversized metallic shields, palms and fingertips at the ready to throw large balls of energy and power if attacked.

And at the front lines, Poseidon stood with his trident, and Hades with his scepter glaive, both encircling Zeus, prepared to defend their brother to the death. She then glimpsed Ares sneaking up on Eros, plotting to grab his son before any more blood spilled.

All were there—but where was her husband?

Eros stuttered, aware they outnumbered him. "I... *Psyche, she took Psyche!*" He pointed at Aphrodite, whimpering as Ares took him by surprise and pulled him up, holding his hands behind his back. Hephaestus appeared near Ares, carrying a contraption resembling a gun, aiming it at Eros. She grimaced at the sight— her husband and lover working together—but didn't move, waiting for orders from the king.

Zeus groaned. "This broken record gives me a migraine, Eros. Your mother repeatedly proclaimed her innocence, and you contradict her still? She hasn't laid a finger on Psyche, and neither have any of the Olympians. This delusion of yours ends *now.*" The threat in his tone shook her to the core.

She had to interfere, before Zeus struck Eros down, permanently scarring him. Eros wasn't in his right mind—he wanted to kill her, yes, but she wouldn't let him die.

Eros blurted out, fighting his father's hold. "But she's *missing!* Someone *took* her!"

"That's *enough!*" Zeus took off at lightning speed, a furious aura radiating behind in the spot he vacated.

Reflexes burning, bracing for his temper, Aphrodite rushed over to block Zeus before he physically harmed Eros. "No." Her breaths sped up. "No violence, Majesty. I doubt Eros is fully responsible... for all this. I apprehended him. *We* apprehended him. If you slay him now, we will never find out what, or *who*, motivated him to start this carnage."

As she barred the king from getting any closer to her son, a few gasps came from the line of Olympians. Ares cleared his throat, Hephaestus peered up at the dilapidated ceiling.

Before Zeus had a chance to scold her, she turned to Eros. "I didn't do it, I swear it on my homelands, on my immortal soul.

But we will find who did. The one responsible. Surrender yourself and calm down, so we may take over this investigation."

Silence reigned in the warehouse. None would speak up to agree with her; none would defy Zeus as openly as she had.

Zeus took a step back. "You are out of line, Aphrodite." He scratched his beard. "But... I agree." He glanced at Ares and Hephaestus. "Confine him in the dungeons until further notice."

Clutching Eros, Ares blinked and disappeared, followed by Hephaestus.

"I heard everything since the instant you entered the warehouse, Aphrodite." The king gaped at her, his expression hard to read. "So you think... this whole thing... might involve someone *else*? Another godly culprit?"

Uncomfortable, surrounded by an atmosphere of betrayal and questions, she scrunched her nose. "Yes, but... we shouldn't speak about it here. Let's... go home."

Zeus hesitated at first, his piercing eyes focused on her.

Believe me, Majesty. We are still not safe.

He nodded at her thoughts. "Fine." He whirled around, zoning in on Apollo and Artemis. "Clean up this mess. Wipe memories. Get the human to safety—cleanse him, too. He drank a lot of godly blood and ingested human flesh. It will infect his insides if not treated immediately. Then return to Olympus. We'll all convene in the throne room—we have much to discuss."

The twins bowed and, with a snap of their fingers, they were gone.

Aphrodite sniffed the air, desperate to sense the *one* mortal pulse in the entire area.

Lukus.

She couldn't smell him anymore. Apollo and Artemis had transported his poor, innocent soul away from her family chaos.

I'm so sorry.

Demeter and Hera clapped, their bodies covering in a thick mist as they whooshed up to Olympus. Poseidon thrummed his trident, causing a puddle of water to form under his feet, through which he evaporated. Dionysus and Athena twirled and shot up through the roof. Hermes exchanged a glance with Hades before winking at Aphrodite; and just like that, all were gone but she, Zeus, and the king of the Underworld.

Aphrodite spun to Hades, the lines around his eyes deeper than ever, his cheeks pale.

"Persephone..." she whispered.

"I know what you're thinking. Cerberus's blood, was I aware? Yes. But *she* wasn't. If she was involved in this... she won't remember. *Witchcraft*, brother." He exchanged a cryptic glance with Zeus before summoning a cloud of black smoke that transported him out of the warehouse.

Zeus pinched the bridge of his nose. "Witchcraft."

Aphrodite allowed her shoulders to droop, her muscles to relax, her limbs to lose tension. She removed the gun from her coat pocket and dropped it to the ground. It spun, pointing at her—and with a snap, she willed it out of existence.

She'd have no use for it now.

‖ 33. YOU'RE NOT IN LOVE ‖
LUKUS

Beep, beep. Beep, beep.

Loud ringing resonated in his head. His eyelids were heavy, and he wanted to open them, but massive weights rested on them, stopping them from moving. Numbness coated most of the area under his eyebrows, down to his chin.

Beep, beep. Beep, beep.

The beeping intensified, its volume increasing and causing severe aching in his temples. His limbs shivered, his extremities tingled. Pain radiated through him, waking him, dragging him out of what he believed was a peaceful dream-world.

BEEP, BEEP. BEEP, BEEP!

Lukus pried his eyelids apart. It was a struggle, as they stuck together; but he tugged with all his might and succeeded. Blinking, he gave his sight a moment to adjust. Lashes fluttering a few more times, he angled to the source of the noise—a machine. A *loud* machine. It was familiar, with wavelengths undulating on its screen, tubes attached to its peripheries, the beeps vibrating under his skin—

He was plugged into it. The beeps grew louder again, and he winced, the migraine turning harsher, agonizing.

"Fuck."

Was the medical appliance draining him? Or infusing him? He couldn't tell. Squinting, he peered around to figure out his surroundings.

Bare white walls, shiny charcoal floors, a fuzzy curtain-covered window off to one side and a large door to the other. A stale tray of food rested on a light-wood nightstand beside him.

I'm in a hospital?

He looked down, realizing he was in a bed, scratchy covers up to his lower torso. Arms uncovered and, as expected, needles in his veins. And though unsure how he arrived here, he somehow understood why. The pain in his muscles, the ache in his head, the agony in his organs—he *needed* care.

But how did he get in such a state?

He closed and opened his eyes several times before noticing the large door was ajar, revealing a corridor; other beeping noises seeped into his room from out there, along with muffled voices and footsteps. No one shared the space with him, and he wouldn't lie, he preferred the solitude.

Oddly, the place looked... familiar. Was it his hospital, in DC? Had he been in this specific area before, on these sheets, in this position?

BEEP, BEEP! BEEP, BEEP, BEEP!

As his heart raced, the machine picked up speed, screeching in his scalp. His brain throbbed, pushing against his cranium. He smacked his palms onto the side of his head, cringing, biting his lip to not yelp in agony.

Please, make the pounding stop!

No flowers or get-well cards decorated the space, he noticed, between violent thrashes inside his skull. He saw no trace of any visitors except for staff. No chairs by his mattress or kind faces welcoming him back. Not that he had many friends, but... if he had such a bad accident, wouldn't someone have called his family? His mother... she'd be there, panicked, helpful, loving.

He had to be dreaming. The machines, the pain, the place...

"Ouch!" Another sharp pang shot through his scalp, proving him wrong. No, he wasn't dreaming. It was all too real. He had a real injury, and a real, *severe* migraine. And the kicker? He had no idea how or why.

A rusty scent, a chemical stench, slithered into his nostrils. Cleaning products, pungent hand sanitizer, needles—he recoiled, nausea bubbling in his belly. He didn't like hospitals.

I need... water.

His stomach growled as he turned to the nightstand, gaze landing on the food. The lumps of what appeared to be potatoes, the steak that looked more like a rubber shoe sole, and then he found it—the glass of clear, life-saving liquid he so desperately craved. He reached for it and, despite the scratch in his larynx, he downed it all.

Licking his lips, he set the cup down. "I... need to get out of here."

The beeping, though quieter now, would only drive him to insanity. He had to call someone, speak to someone, understand what landed him here.

He shuddered as he sat up, not wanting to trigger the machine or alert anyone of his recovery. He wanted answers, but he had to compose himself first. Snorting, he peered under his covers—no way would he talk to doctors and nurses in a *hospital gown.* But where were his clothes? What *was* he wearing before all this, anyway?

Eyelashes fluttering, shoulders tensing, panic swelled in his gut. *Why* didn't he remember? He rubbed his eyes, shuffled his hair—messier than ever—seeking a bump, a bruise, something to explain the constant thumping. How long had he been out? Who got him there? He had no memory of losing consciousness.

All I recall is...

"Getting shot in the heart, and everything going dark, I assume?"

He froze. The sudden but soft, feminine voice shot through his veins like ice. Like velvet. He nearly jumped but remembered his tubes and instead took a deep breath as he sensed a figure approaching from his right. A figure that *wasn't* there seconds ago.

"No, no, this isn't right..." He gulped, wondering what was in the water he drank. Hallucinogens? Drugs? Medicine to put him to sleep?

The delicate, musical voice rang again. "I'm real, Lukus."

Shivers spiraled down his spine. He *knew* that tonality, that subtle accent, that melodious tone. He'd heard her before; but why—and *how*—did she get in his room?

"It's okay. You need not fear me," she said. Her steps rustled like leaves in a breeze.

Lukus swallowed hard as he craned his neck to see her. His breaths quickened at the splendor—the strawberry-blonde hair, flowing, shimmering as it slid down to her waist. Perfect, messy, sexy. Her professional attire had disappeared, replaced by a long golden tunic, draping around her goddess curves, hanging from one shoulder, slitted at her upper thigh, exposing her pearlescent legs. And her eyes—a heavenly mix of violet, blue, green, glittering like waves in the sea, splashing him with desire.

Shit.

Her skin glowed, basking him in light, showering him with pleasure. He had seen nothing like it—inhuman, captivating, impossible to turn away from. No, she was *not* human. Not Agnes, the psychotic FBI agent. Nor had she ever been.

A spell fogged his senses, a yearning urge pressing at the top of his groin. A vague image of déjà vu seeped into his head—a time when she hypnotized him.

Had she done it again? Touched his hand and provoked her witchcraft? He pinched himself, desperate to break the trance; but he only squealed, prompting the machine to go berserk again.

He tore away, gasping for air, struggling to relax. No, it couldn't be true. She couldn't be here, in this form, in her magnificence, as he lay in a ragged hospital gown covered by a flimsy sheet.

The lady chuckled. "Lukus, it is all true. Will you believe me *now?*" He caught her eye again, and his lungs squeezed as he once more became absorbed in her gaze, lost in her beauty. She regained her serious tone. "Can you pull the logic card on *any* of this? Can you prove all I've told you was a ploy for attention, a cry for help? Or do you see the truth, at last?"

She tiptoed closer, the silky material of her tunic rubbing against her skin, sending tingles to Lukus' fingers. "Agnes?" She shook her head, and he exhaled, narrowing his eyes, analyzing her. No, that wasn't her name. It never was.

So... what is it?

The drumming in his chest amplified, the beeping incessant... and yet it all faded as he gaped at her. As he drank in her gorgeous frame, as he wracked his skull for answers.

A deity. *The* deity.

He remembered. "No, you're *Aphrodite*. You really are. You, the gods... you exist? This is serious? I'm *not* dreaming?"

Despite the blinding light radiating from her skin, he spotted her smile. And still, he struggled to understand it. The gods, the supernatural... it was all made up. He hallucinated. He bashed his brains *real* good and paid the consequences now, with this eerie dream.

An odd discomfort spilled from her expression as she stopped, an inch from the bed. "How else do you explain what happened in the warehouse, Lukus? Do you remember any of it?"

Lukus wanted to shake his head, but the migraine prevented him from doing so.

She leaned nearer, her suntan lotion scent almost dizzying. "Do you know how you got here? Is any of this logical to you?"

The closer she got, the weaker he felt. Her presence overpowered him, caused his thoughts to scramble, his senses to mix up, his words to get lost. As if she took control of his mind. The longer he stared, the more his heart floated. Soared. His cheeks flushed, his pulse weakened, sweat formed on his forehead and drizzled down his cheekbones as he shuddered. Her aura encircled him, enticed him, *engulfed* him.

But she wasn't touching him, like before. She stood there, tranquil, breathing in and out, utterly unaware of the toxic effect she had on him.

Too strong.

She flinched and backed away. "Oh dear, I'm sorry. It's... my main power. I can no longer control it." She crossed her arms, as if concealing herself, ashamed. "When Zeus made me mortal, I had some command over it. It manifested by touching you, and I apologize for the discomfort it brought you. Now, with all my powers returned... there's no off switch. You must bear with me a little more." Her voice, a hymn slicing through the obnoxious beeping machine, set him at ease.

His focus wavered. Her glory washed away the little sanity he had, and he fought to hang on, to not plunge into the depths of her abilities. "I... um, the case... the killings... what happened?"

Aphrodite walked to the end of his bed—more like gliding, her steps like small indents on a cloud. "It's solved. Eros *was* the killer, as I mentioned. My fault, actually, though not for the reasons he believed. He was mad at *me*, and at the other gods. Blamed me for his wife's disappearance, and the others for not noticing she had disappeared. So, he took it out on Zeus' precious charges. Humans."

Lukus, energy draining, only blinked in response. Eros. His wife. Disappearances. He grimaced, unable to organize his ideas. Flashbacks of his investigation returned, only for visions of him kissing Aphrodite to cloud his thoughts.

Oh no, not again.

He saw himself releasing the clasp of her dress, letting it fall, sliding down her luminescent skin in slow motion. Then she climbed onto the bed, threw the covers off, hoisted herself atop him. Swaying her naked self back and forth, her mouth trailing sweet kisses starting at his neck, stopping on his breastbone, lingering near his belly button. Her fingertips wrapped around his hips as she moaned, and he moaned, and they moaned in unison—

"*Shit!* No!" His eyes closed, and the picture played on, but his mind wanted out. His soul begged for help, for the sensations to stop.

Aphrodite snapped her fingers—panting, he returned to reality.

"I... uh..."

"Again, my fault." She waved her hand. "I'm sorry, but I have to ask—are you able to recall what Eros told you in the warehouse? Anything he may have squeezed into your brain? Do you recall hearing anything at all?" As she lowered her palm, it accidentally brushed against his leg, jolting electricity through his nerves.

"Stop... go... I can't... *think...* "

She clapped. "Lukus, *focus!*" She glared at him, fists on her hips, cheeks reddening. "Push past the desire and search through your memories!"

As if something sucked him from his insides, sinking through his pores, the passion evaporated. New images popped in; a man, cloaked in black leather, locks of blond hair sticking out from under a hood, pointing an arrow at Lukus' heart, an evil grin on his face.

Eros?

The vision fizzled to show blood erupting from Lukus' chest, splashing, then zapping into nothingness. A sudden thirst for flesh, for hearts, for *Aphrodite.* He overheard discussions of soulmates, wives, children and powers—but wasn't able to process them, too adamant on eating her.

He gasped. Oh yeah, he remembered all right.

"He wanted to draw you near. He said I... he said I loved you, deep down." Eros' sickening laugh stuck in his mind, and he winced as he battled to erase it.

What did it mean? To love a goddess, to worship *the* goddess of love itself? His body tensed, but not from Aphrodite's presence. Eros shot him, he yearned for Aphrodite, so did that signify...

He inhaled so violently it hurt his lungs. "Are you my..." He forced his gaze into Aphrodite's. Nausea bloomed in his abdomen, and he filled with angst; was he *allowed* to stare a goddess in the eyes? "Are you my *soulmate?*" His voice cracked, like each of his extremities prepared to break, shatter into millions of pieces.

Aphrodite flashed a weak, sad smile. "No, Lukus." He deflated, though a nostalgic feeling lingered somewhere in his belly. "Gods like us don't have soulmates. Well, Eros and Psyche aside, or so Zeus claims. In any case, loving me would be your demise. Humans and I... we never work out. I was involved with one before, and... it didn't end well. It's too painful to discuss, to be honest. Lukus..." Her face turned serious again.

He couldn't move. What more did she have to reveal? They weren't meant to be, he embarrassed the crap out of himself—he got it.

You can leave now.

"Sweet man, I'm so sorry to do this to you. Eros informed me... you don't *have* a soulmate. Before we threw him in his cell, he... I'm unclear on why, but he wanted me to tell you. He doesn't understand it, but he said it happens every few centuries. You... aren't destined to be with *anyone*." True sorrow echoed in her timbre.

A pinch in his ribcage, a sharp tear in his spirit, ripping into his organs, shredding them to pieces—this pain differed from his physical wounds. Strong, impossible to define, hard to comprehend.

I have no soulmate.

Torn between sadness and a slight knowing, he went limp, falling against the plastic headboard. It explained why he never kept a stable relationship. Why the only woman he'd ever loved—what felt like eons ago—betrayed him. Why he only sought the company of temporary women, those wanting a one-night stand over adult commitment. It made sense... and yet, a bulge in his throat showed he *had* hoped, at some point. He had wanted love.

Aphrodite frowned, but still, Lukus' heaviness dissipated as he watched her. Her superb beauty, her confidence, her radiance—his heart revived, beating strong.

Eros was right—he cared for her. On the outside he despised every fiber of her being, but within, he had nothing but admiration for her. Absorbed in her, in her presence, her sublime self, he wondered... did he not have a soulmate *because* of her? Because he was meant to give himself to her?

Her eyebrows slid down. "Oh no, Lukus. Don't be fooled. You don't love me; you're under the spell of my powers. Only lust. Even *if* you loved me, we cannot be together. I'm married, I have a lover, and if I could have another, he'd have to be immortal."

Her strict comments did nothing to halt his imagination. Ogling her with hunger, though no longer wanting to devour her, he reveled in her anger. Her perfect features, her fury, her temper—all drew him nearer, enticed him. He *had* to have her. And if he couldn't be with her as a mortal... then he needed to become *immortal.*

"I helped you get to Eros, right?" Aphrodite nodded. "So, does that make me a hero? Does that grant me a chance at immortality?" He recalled the tales; the heroes, given access to Olympus, transformed into gods for their heroics.

A part of him screamed, shouted at him to wake up—*you can't be immortal, you dumbass!* But his deepening desire overpowered all other emotions.

His purpose was her.

Why else would I have met her?

To his surprise, Aphrodite chuckled. "You sly little human!" Her expression illuminated. "Yes, technically, rendering a service to the gods would give you immortality, however... it takes a lot more than what *you* did to receive that prize. And you didn't stop Eros: *I* did."

Lukus straightened up. There had to be another way. An eternal way.

If his life were threatened... would they save him for the help he provided? "What if... I die? Succumb to my wounds? *Then* am I eligible? Can I be immortal, be with you?" He sounded pathetic, for sure; but his speech wasn't his. His heart spoke, his soul yelped for recognition.

Aphrodite meandered close, pushing his body to grow tenser. In a soft, slow gesture she caressed his cheek. "You must understand. While you are destined for many things, being my immortal lover *isn't* one."

Holding back a sob, Lukus' chin dipped down. Again, his insides shattered—he had a long, lonely life ahead of him.

"I thank you for your help, truly." Her tone was distant, quiet. "For teaching me about humans, showing me how doubtful they are. How we, as gods, need to be more present, instill more faith in them."

Her outline lost intensity. Her beauty, fizzling in and out of focus, evaporated, and her smile, though, everlasting, sparkled before him.

No... she can't leave yet. I have so many questions.

"I'm destined for things? What do you mean?" He squirmed, desperate to get up, run after her, hold her back. But... his mobility decreased. He was stuck. "Please, tell me more!"

The goddess giggled; a breathtaking sound that made his heart skip a beat. "It's not up to me to explain it to you, Lukus." A whisper, a light breeze, a hum in the wind, she was farther and farther away.

His vision turned gray, dreary, dark. "No..." Her body became transparent, ghostlike. "Don't go, don't leave me."

His eyelids shut, plunging him into a deep sleep. He fought the unconsciousness, prayed to stay awake; but her voice, once more, tiptoed into his ears, easing him into dream-world. "Lukus..."

‖ 34. MEMORIES ‖
APHRODITE

Poor human.

Though no longer mortal, Aphrodite's thoughts still fizzled, running through her like before. Clouded in worry, in wishes—a list growing by the second. But her wishes would remain as such; ungranted, unheard. She had to obey.

So, she waited as Lukus slipped into unconsciousness, unaware of his surroundings. Alone in his hospital bed, full of doubts and questions that would soon fade to new memories— ones that weren't real. She hated to do it, but orders were orders.

As she admired the handsome man and his gentle breaths, she despised taking anything away from his mind. But she was in no position to disobey.

She had Artemis to thank for depositing him there, a hospital in Washington DC, his city of residence. She left little information for the staff, but luckily, they had all worked with Lukus Arvantis, FBI agent, before. A smart choice—for once, she agreed with the virgin goddess. And she sensed she'd continue to applaud Artemis. Aphrodite had a change of heart—and a change in attitude.

The hospital crew had a medical file for Lukus, likely from previous investigations. It explained the private accommodation, the special treatment, the isolation. And he deserved it.

Aphrodite smiled, recalling how she lurked in the shadows of his suite, waiting for him to wake... only to put him back to sleep. Against rules, she spoke with him one last time. To hear his deep, baritone voice, plunge her gaze into his blue pools of crystalline water and get lost. It took everything in her not to hug him, press him near, whisper sweet nothings in his ear. Comfort him, reassure him—maybe even kiss him, as a parting gift.

How she had prayed he could remember it all. All he learned, saw, felt. Remember her, their interactions, his emotions—only the *good* ones. They started out with hatred; but moments ago, she sensed his true sentiments, his affections. Past the desire and yearning, past the lust, he had feelings for her. And she had an urge to protect him, be near—but it scared her. She didn't understand it. She wished to provide him the answers he sought, but... she didn't have them. Her king rarely revealed *anything* until his sources were sure. She wouldn't lie to Lukus, pretend like she comprehended it all.

I'd rather you lose your memories than I feed you more lies.

He dipped into the final stages of sleep, blissful and unaware.

She closed the door, blocking the room from the corridor and any curious onlookers. After a few instants of observing him, reminiscing his words, his habits, she stole up to the beeping machine hooked to his arms and waved a hand to silence it; but didn't turn it off.

He's right—it's obnoxious.

No one would see her—she was invisible—and she thanked the heavens for it. Some of the staff had spotted her, and she couldn't take more risks. She lacked the power to wipe everyone's memory—and Zeus wanted no one to know she had been there. And alas, Zeus' decisions trumped all others. His world, his orders. He believed Lukus wasn't ready for the burden of truth; and Aphrodite agreed. She disobeyed her adoptive father enough in the past week; time for her to do what he commanded, regardless of her emotions.

She approached the human, a sad smile stretching on her face. "I'm sorry, Lukus. For putting you through such struggles, for lying, for not revealing all I know." Her lungs loaded with oxygen as she closed her eyes. "All in due time, my friend. All in due time."

His chest moved up, then down. His breaths, soft, comforting, reassured her. He was alive; she hadn't killed him when she threw him across the warehouse. Aside from a slight concussion, some internal bruises, and a bit of *intoxication* from "strange substances"—which no one would figure out were the muscles of her arm and a *lot* of godly blood—Lukus' wounds were minimal. Apollo had healed some of his wounds, but he would have to remain in the ward for a week or two, as a precaution.

"Please, though you won't remember me... I hope somewhere, deep in your soul, you forgive me." She whispered, praying no one outside the room heard her. "For all I've done and will probably do. I promise... I'll be a better goddess. More attentive, less selfish, more forgiving." She exhaled. "Starting with my son."

She placed her hands on Lukus' temples, massaging her fingers into his skin, sinking her nails into his head.

"I'm *so* sorry."

Her powers infiltrated his mind, like a golden toothpick poking in, seeping into his cranial nerves. Connected to him; she now saw his memories from the past few weeks, understood his thoughts. She met his hesitations, skepticism, doubt; and underneath it all, she encountered the yearning he called *love*. Powerful, overwhelming, poignant.

She cringed at the flashes of erratic behavior he imagined when she touched him. Shivering, regret swelled in her ribcage, ashamed at what her abilities caused him. Pained at how he suffered any time she was near. His imagination, stronger than any Aphrodite had ever found in a human, terrified her. Vivid visions; almost too palpable, even for her.

"This... is for the best." She dug deeper, wiggling her fingertips. "I will fix your pain. Take away the lust, the craziness. You don't deserve this burden. You'll be at peace... I promise."

She severed any ties between them, magically erasing herself from his brain. Like invisible shears, she cut out his visions of her, and of Eros, replacing all his recollections of the carnivorous case with an *ordinary,* standard murder arrest—images she had gathered from a mixture of American crime shows that she hoped he had never seen, and wouldn't recognize. She clouded the case in mystery—knowing him, he'd somehow push and guess it was all a ruse to conceal the truth. He was witty, and she wondered if her trick would keep his recollections at bay.

Hopefully long enough... to prepare him.

She focused, stretching her powers within his veins. "*These* memories are yours now, Lukus Arvantis." Her fingers pressed harder on his temples, sealing the magic, infusing him with her words. "You never met me, you never met Eros. You don't believe in the Greek gods. You recently worked a cannibalism case and solved it, though the circumstances were a little mysterious, unclear. But you won't question it. You injured yourself while apprehending the criminal, but you're alive, and the culprit is behind bars." Tears welled at her lower lash-line. "When you wake, all will be as it always was. You'll know nothing of soulmates and engravings. Nothing of gods and powers, of the looming dangers you encountered."

She extricated her fingertips and breathed in relief, happy the process was over. Her least favorite power, by far; though all deities had it, not all *liked* it.

As tears streamed down her face, she distanced herself from Lukus. "I am sorry, but your destiny means... you must remain clueless a little longer." She sniffled, wiping the salty liquid from her skin. "But there are *bigger* dangers out there. You being in the dark is preferable; our only way to look after you. Zeus... said you're valuable."

Aphrodite reached her arms up, heaving her feet from the ground.

"Until we meet again, oh destined one," she whispered as she spun on herself.

In a mist of sparkling pink smoke, she disappeared, the hospital room fading from view. For a moment suspended in the air, she floated in a cloud, invisible to all and on a different plane. She saw nothing, felt nothing, as if she had ceased existing. Instantaneous traveling—a strange ability. She had used it for centuries. Like teleporting, only time passed slower.

Traveling as a god is a longer process than one would expect.

Her eyesight adjusted on the large golden doors, glimmering high above the clouds. The porcelain steps leading her to where she belonged; the white marble palace in the sky. An ambrosia scent permeated the atmosphere. Music, melodious and enticing, swept out from behind the gates, attracting her forward. The small castle came into focus, and her thoughts returned to normal.

Eros waited in the dungeons, likely. Standing straight, prepared to push through the doors, to walk into the godly atmosphere, immerse herself into her tasks, she paused. Zeus allowed her to say goodbye, she knew. One last farewell, one last waste of time before the real work started. Real work that froze her intestines and chilled her to the core.

She stepped forward and breathed in. Home... but not alone. *Someone* else loomed the halls of Olympus. Someone hid in plain sight, plotting, planning destruction, tricking the gods.

She placed a hand on the doors and pushed.

Who took Psyche?

‖ 35. THE POTION ‖
EROS

The Olympian dungeons were no place for a god like Eros. A secret, a space in a large cave beneath the palace, concealed behind heavy, steel doors, reachable after a multitude of creaky stairs and eerie hallways. One couldn't *appear* in them or leave them; special enchantments prevented all forms of escape.

Eros had never been there—the dungeons, as far as it concerned him, were a myth. Undocumented in human books, never spoken of amongst the gods. Only Zeus, Poseidon, and Hades had access, along with Athena, occasionally. Dionysus and Aphrodite were once locked within, and both sworn to secrecy ever since.

Until today.

The magical metallic bars holding him captive now somehow calmed Eros, soothed his anger. He wasn't sure if actual magic lurked in the area; a spell that allowed him to clean his mind of the black clouds that took hold of his thoughts—or if whatever poison once looming inside had worn off.

Because someone had poisoned him, he had no doubt. And Persephone. And possibly his wife and daughter. The fog surrounding his memories had yet to clear. He only had flashes of brief images returning to him—but none made any sense. The ambrosia he consumed days prior still burned, keeping him strong, and yet... weakness wrapped around his limbs. He couldn't process what he had done. Killed so many people; so many innocent, loving, happy people. They didn't deserve their fate, it wasn't their time, and he forced them through it. In the most gruesome way possible.

Why am I alive? Why am I still immortal?

"Because you are the son of an immortal Olympian, Eros." A deep voice, breaking through the shadows near the dungeon door—a person he hadn't heard arrive. Had they reached the interrogation stage, or did he have an unexpected visitor?

"You do not deserve to die," said the tone, masculine, familiar.

Footsteps rushed towards him, followed by ripples of strawberry-blonde curls attacking the metal bars, soft hands reaching through to touch his. "It's me, son."

Her.

"And Hades. And... Athena," said Aphrodite, her bright ocean eyes now visible in the obscurity.

A torch ignited somewhere in the background. Athena's face came into view—solemn, hard to read, nodding to confirm her presence without a word.

And then the final figure, the one that spoke first, appeared. His long black cloak trailing along the floor, a staff in one hand. "Despite your actions, you were not alone in planning this," he said, features taut as he peered down at Eros.

Eros struggled to return the glance. Hades intimidated him; having him so close while unarmed and defenseless sent shivers down his spine.

Hades chuckled. "I'm not here to hurt you, child. I never would, not without reason. You're still needed, and loved, regardless of what you did. Apollo managed to subdue your violent urges—but we are not sure how long your bloodthirsty symptoms will remain dormant. We must hurry."

Though the strain in Hades' tone didn't reassure him, Eros exhaled. The interrogation would help. The questions might trigger his memory, force him to recall *what* or *who* brought him to this—locked in the Olympian dungeons and deprived of his powers.

Aphrodite stood, her flowing, golden tunic swaying with her every move. "So, you also believe *someone* did this?" She gaped at him as if reading through his skull. "What do you remember?"

Hesitant, overpowered by three gods who could insert themselves into his brain, Eros gulped. "I... I remember little." He rolled his shoulders, tension causing him to wince. "Whatever happened before... is a blur. I woke up one morning, Psyche was gone, I was full of rage—more than I would have usually been—and I... I took off. I hid, observed the gods in their daily habits, and... when I realized no one noticed Psyche's disappearance, I blamed you, Mother. Then I raced down the mountain to look for a way to sneak into Tartarus."

Athena lurked by the door, pacing, quiet. How Eros wished to hear her opinion, but behind the magical blockade, he perceived nothing. His abilities tamed, toned down, his soul available to read by all others. A chill spiraled down his limbs as he understood how vulnerable the prison rendered him.

Hades crossed his arms. "And how *did* you get in? Do you remember?" His eyes, almost darker than the black metal keeping Eros confined, flashed with curiosity.

Eros shrugged. "Not really. I searched in a rumored spot, and next... I was trailing one of the Underworld rivers in the dark as if I knew where I was going." Goosebumps covered his skin as all three deities watched him. "The memories seem to jog back and forth like that a lot."

Grumbling, Hades wrapped his fingertips tight around his staff. "And then you saw *my* wife? Was there anything... off about her?"

No one harmed Persephone—Hades protected her with his immortal life. So having to tell him his spouse was involved in all this...

He won't like it.

Eros swallowed, lumps forming in his throat. "If there was, I wouldn't have paid much attention to it consumed by rage as I was. I know she acted... out of the ordinary. Not totally surprised to see me, and not eager to dismiss me either. As though she... expected me."

Cloak swirling, Hades turned to Aphrodite. They said nothing, only exchanging a silent glare, passing words through their minds, secretive, careful.

What are they saying?

Seconds later, Hades swerved to Eros, his free hand sliding into a pocket of his robe. "I have a uh... an experimental procedure I'd like to try on you. To see if it'll help recover some of your memories."

Aphrodite took a step backward, wringing her hands, chin tipping up and down in agreement.

Her uncertainty sent waves of fear into Eros' gut. "An experiment? Have you... *experimented* it on anyone else yet?" His voice shook, and he had no way to stop it.

Hades released his firm grip on his staff. "No. But... it should help us, if only momentarily. In... theory."

Eros peeked at his mother. She nodded again, but an aura of angst floated around her. She kept her face tilted down, declining to connect her eyes with his.

Odd...

And Athena stayed away, pacing, listening.

"What aren't you telling me?" Eros approached his nose to the metallic blockade. "What is it?"

Hades extracted a small glass vial from the pocket. He held it up, revealing its transparent, slightly sparkling contents. "This is from the river Lethe. It's supposed to make one forget— but we hope, in your case, it does the opposite, since you already forgot."

Aphrodite slid closer and kneeled before her son. Eros dropped to be at eye level with her, though she continued to avoid him.

What is happening?

"Since you've lost your memory, we expect giving you a few drops of the river of forgetfulness might bring it back. Or at least... parts of it," said Hades, a raspiness to his timbre that Eros didn't like. The god of the Underworld wasn't sure.

Aphrodite revealed her eyes—emerald, darkened with concern, glistening with anticipation. But she quickly turned them to Hades, waiting for him to resume.

"Mnemosyne gave me the idea." He rolled the bottle between his thumb and index, angling it up, admiring its substance. "I consulted her on the matter; as a Titaness who has seen many things in her long lifespan, she is of great counsel. She suggested trying it, and... added a sample of her blood to the mix."

Titan blood?

No one trusted Titans, though a handful proved themselves useful. Mnemosyne had worked beside Hades for centuries, and *he* trusted her—but was this mixture a trap? Would it remind him of his deed? Or make his mind worse?

He bit his lip. Would it trigger his fury again? Send him into another crazy panic, a bloody frenzy? What if it made him hunt the gods and... he had no control? His heart raced, his lungs constricted, his senses dimmed as he felt faint—

"Son." Aphrodite reached through the barrier, squeezing her fingers between his. "This may be our only option."

He pressed his fingertips onto her knuckles. Tight, afraid. "Mother, I... I don't know if it's a good idea. What if it provokes me again?"

Hades tapped on the prison barrier with his staff. "Regardless, you can't leave this cell. Ask your mother—she tried."

Aphrodite rolled her eyes and huffed. "He's right."

Eros wouldn't agree yet; not until the shadow marching by the torch-lit entryway had her say. "Athena?" She stopped moving. "Your take on this?"

She was the wisest—if she had hesitation in her voice, he'd refuse the concoction.

She didn't come close but spun in their direction. He had difficulty seeing her expression, reading her body language. "Do it." She held something in her hand, but Eros couldn't determine what. "There are no other options. At worst, your carnivorous nature returns, but as Uncle said, you can't escape."

He peered at Aphrodite, then at his lap and his stained leather pants he hadn't changed out of. At the blood in the seams, the death on his skin, the stench of betrayal and cruelty.

Fine.

He let go of his mother, opened his palm, jutting his chin at Hades. "Give it, then."

Hades dropped the small flask through the prison bars and into his hand. "A couple drops, no more. Too much may be... lethal." He leaned away, but fixed his gaze on Eros.

Eros uncorked the glass bottle, exhaled, and brought it to his mouth. After a quick inhale, he tipped it, allowed three drops to slither onto his tongue, then handed the vial to Hades.

He nearly choked on the acidic, salty taste. "*Gross.*"

But no one said a word. They watched, hopeful, fearful, as the substance sank down into his belly. And they waited as he stood up, coughed, opened his mouth to speak—

Jolts of electricity ran through him in agonizing shockwaves. Images popped into his mind, slicing through his scalp—quick, messy, barely understandable.

"I... I..." Distraught by what he witnessed, he couldn't talk.

Aphrodite gasped and shoved her arms farther into the cell, but Eros recoiled from her touch.

Hades thrust his free arm out, halting her from pushing too hard on the bars. "Give him a moment." He nudged her. "I think... the elixir is taking effect."

Eros tried to register their comments. His vision turned blurry; a fog enveloped him. He no longer saw them, but something else; his past actions. Some of them ran before him, fast-forwarding like a tape, too quick for him to comprehend.

"Slow down. *Slow down!*" He'd never remember this all once the moment was over.

Everything he did since the morning of Psyche's disappearance flashed, fizzled into view; but too fast. *Too fast.*

Why couldn't he control his own recollections? He needed to *write* them down, before it was too late.

"Quill... paper..."

Athena sprang forward, slipping the requested items through the bars, as if prepared for him to demand them. Eros, though partially blind, snatched the quill and parchment. At once, he scribbled—in a trance, like receiving a prophecy. The gods froze as he jotted down all he visualized, but each sentence made little sense. The images made little sense.

Another pang sent him flying backwards. He smashed against the dungeon wall, like a violent breeze had shoved him into it. The reverie broke, Aphrodite and Athena wheezed, and Hades rushed to the cell door, as if ready to blast it open.

"Eros?"

He wasn't positive who spoke—the tones all mingled into one, morphing, distorted.

He rubbed the back of his head. "I'm... fine. I'm fine. It... it's over." He pried his eyelids apart, a stickiness making the motion difficult. "The potion wears off... quickly."

Aphrodite let out a relieved sigh. "Did either of you see what he saw?"

Hades relaxed his posture and moved from the dungeon gate. "No. I was... blocked from his mind the second he drank the potion."

"Me too." Athena bent down and gawked at Eros' scribbles. She squinted, scrunching her nose. "Can you explain... these? Since none of us were able to visualize what you endured."

Regaining his balance, he sauntered over to pick up the paper. Focusing his sight on the notes, he hoped to decipher his jumbled sentences and juxtaposed phrases.

Pieces came together. "I... was fine the night before she disappeared. But Psyche... wasn't." He swallowed. "Her behavior... strange, off. She ate next to nothing at dinner." His wife's sweet face showed in his mind. Her happy smiles, rosy cheeks. "The next morning, I woke... she wasn't in bed. Hadn't reported for her duties. When I went to ask Hedone... *she* was gone, too." Something burned beneath his skin. "Fury rose... and you know the rest."

The burn amplified, expanding into all his organs. Rage, powerful, vengeful—the emotions fueling him to hunt, torture, kill. The sensations that pushed him over the edge.

They were still there. The poison lived in him still.

He strode backwards, farther from the cage delimitations. "I... am not feeling well, guys. The anger... poison, spell, whatever it is... is still inside. Beneath the surface. I sense it. I'm... not cleansed, not yet." The flames spread to his extremities, heating his blood. "It is best if you... come back later."

Their presence only intensified the affliction; he had to make them leave, soon.

Aphrodite's jaw dropped. "Son?"

He heard Athena's discrete footsteps, fading from the area, getting closer to the exit. Hades put his forehead against the bars—unafraid and taunting.

Oh... he had better get out. Fast.

"One last thing," he said, as Eros growled. Both goddesses jumped, but Hades didn't flinch. "Did you eat or drink anything unusual that night? You, Psyche, your daughter?"

His anger simmered at Hades' defiance. He nodded, though an animalistic roar gurgled somewhere in his abdomen. "The ambrosia... tasted funny. A private dinner... only my wife, daughter, and I."

Hades pushed away from the metal. *"Funny."*

Athena returned, eyebrows rising. "What is it, Uncle?"

He kept his gaze trained on Eros. "I need to..."

Eros' guts churned and his spine crackled. He hunched over, nostrils flaring; as if a beast wanted to rip through his skin, ooze out of his body, dig its teeth into his family—

"Get *out,* all of you!"

You morons. Stupid, pathetic gods.

"Hurry, before I... hurt you."

Hades teetered backward, sneaking away from the enclosure at last, refusing to turn his back. "I must speak to Persephone." His voice frazzled, tuned in and out as he got near the exit. "If she can confirm this... if she takes the concoction and says the same... I may have a lead."

Eros' lungs filled with poisonous oxygen as he glowered at Hades' figure, slowly dissipating.

Hades' words muffled, but Eros heard enough. "Report this to my brother, will you? If I'm not back in time for the big meeting..."

The door closed, and Eros' last image was Athena, dumbfounded, and Aphrodite's eyes flickering to midnight blue. In the darkness again, the torch extinguished in all the hurry, only one thing remained—Eros' carnivorous rage. Reanimated, reignited, fueled by the potion. They'd never figure out the truth, he knew. And he'd never fully grasp the consequences of his actions, what led him to them.

The fury overpowers it all.

And the answers... were with Psyche.

‖36. NO ONE IS SAFE‖
APHRODITE

Her mind ached. Not just her brain or her head—the linings, the neurons, the nerves. Every fiber of her cranium pounded, filling with terrible outcomes, fear for her son, trepidation for the gods. If he were unleashed while infuriated...

"No, *no!*" She stomped her foot. "Gods do not worry like this!" She paced in her room, the marble tiles clicking beneath her heeled sandals.

"Darling, you *must* calm down." Ares, lounging on the seashell-shaped bed, arms sprawled out, legs crossed, stared at the ceiling. "Eros is safe."

Aphrodite jolted around. "You don't know that! That potion Hades gave him brought back the fury; I saw it!" Her knuckles tightened. "Those bars held me inside, but I'm unsure they'll stop the murderous monster he has become! *We* are not safe!"

Ares sat up, his chiseled arms bulging to hold his weight. "He won't escape, you must believe it. Uncle must have placed extra enchantments in the cell, if not the entire area, when he left."

Aphrodite's eyebrows rose. "I... I don't recall."

Ares patted the space next to him. "Father won't start the meeting until Uncle Hades returns, so try to unwind, okay? I haven't seen you in weeks, and I'd like to enjoy you."

He dared a smirk, but erased it the second Aphrodite's glare hit him, like a laser beam. And though she wanted to be mad, she couldn't when they connected. She had missed him.

She didn't always understand how the angriest of deities, the one who loved to fight and wage war, was the only one who soothed her, calmed her mind. He alone understood her—he alone cared. Despite their arguments, violent spats, temper tantrums, they were meant to be.

She smiled on the inside as she sat beside him—but declined to indulge in his presence. Too many possibilities clouded her thoughts, too many grueling situations that wouldn't leave her be. "But... his memories... they disturbed him... we must find out more."

"We *will*, my love, when the time is right." He rubbed her back. "But we must wait for reports first. Be sure he's at peace before we provoke him further." His fingertips caressed her jaw as he turned her to face him. "His fury will dissipate, and we will get answers. He's home now, and he can do no harm here. Trust in that. Trust in Father's wardings and Uncle's magic."

Shivers raced along her spine. Her extremities tingled, radiated with pulsing energy as her heart thrummed. Sensations *only* Ares provoked; emotions she hadn't felt in a while.

Their last hours together, before her earthly mission, were spent screaming, breaking pots, shoving against walls; then ripping off tunics, rolling around until they were bruised, sore, satiated. Their passionate rage always infused their lovemaking with ice and fire; she missed those moments while mortal, but...she no longer craved them. Since she'd come home she'd been unable to focus, or to get in the mood.

I'm too distraught.

She stood and resumed her paces.

Ares huffed and slid to the edge of the bed, putting his leg out to stop her—but when their gazes met, he shot up. "Whoa," he said, scurrying out of her way and towards the door. "Your eyes are red, love."

"Red?" She glimpsed herself in the mirror; sure enough, her irises had shifted to a devilish scarlet, and crimson lines dashed from her top to her bottom lash-lines.

My angry shade.

"Yes, and I know what that means… unless you want me to stay?" He froze by the doorframe, chest puffed out.

She pried herself away from her reflection and snarled. "No. Go. I can't have you distracting my thoughts, not now." She jutted her chin at the door. "It'll only get worse if you stand there looking at me like that."

He let out a weak chuckle as he grabbed the doorknob. "I'll… come get you for the meeting." He squeezed past the door and slammed it behind him.

She would have laughed under other circumstances. The high and mighty god of war was afraid of her, the goddess of love and beauty. But her aggravation forced her lips into a thin line, tilting downwards. She exhaled, releasing the tension. Ares didn't annoy her; she just didn't want him worrying about her. He didn't need to see her so… *human.* And of all things, she refused to let him read deep in her brain, to discover what she saw on repeat, banging inside her skull.

Lukus.

She feared for *his* safety, too. If Eros got out, he'd go straight for the FBI agent wrapped up in the middle of his rampage. And Lukus was special, Zeus said; surely, Eros knew it too.

She flipped to her mirror again. Her eyes flashed a violent violet shade; a step down from rageful red, but still showing how unsettled her soul was. Waves of strawberry-blonde locks spilled over her golden tunic, giving her the regality of a princess, a *queen*.

And yet, she didn't grin as she usually would upon admiring herself. The impatience and angst swelling in her gut made her disgusting. She had to relax, if only for the other gods. If they found her so riled up, they might grow suspicious. And since she had nothing to do with Eros' destruction, she had to ensure no one pointed fingers at her—ever again.

But he *was* safe. Harmless. His carnage over because she stopped him. She had much bigger things to worry about.

Glimpsing the jewelry box on her dresser, she tiptoed to it. She opened its intricate seashell top, revealing the pieces she had collected over the years. The items within, that once warmed her heart, now caused her to snicker.

Picking up one of the pearl necklaces, she remembered how she came by it.

At the expense of a human.

She let the necklace slip from her hands and fall to the ground—where it shattered. Pearls flew all over, rolling at her feet, under her bed, under the dresser. She sneered, touching a seashell clad band an old acquaintance offered her in exchange for her help in securing the heart of the woman he loved. *"Hmpf."* How materialistic had she been? How selfish and self-involved?

Once more, she frowned at her glowing appearance, at her extravagance. Then she threw the bracelet against the mirror. Both smashed, breaking into a mix of seashells and reflective shards, showering the drawers and scattering across the floor.

She didn't care to clean her mess. Instead, she considered all her jewels, recalling what she did to obtain each piece. If greed was her answer, she crushed them, stepped on them, cracked them in her palm, or tossed them across the suite in the hopes of them exploding, disintegrating into nothingness.

After a few necklaces and bracelets and a ring she struggled to pull apart, she realized blowing things up no longer worked to alleviate her troubles. She began igniting items, starting with a pair of earrings. She let them burn to a crisp, as the ashes dropped to the tiles, littering her once luxurious room.

A satisfied grin washed across her face.

She needed none of it, nothing that reminded her of how horrible a goddess she'd been all her life. Her despicable cruelty, the narcissistic ways in which she operated. She had fueled her son's rage, without realizing it. The blame for his behavior rested on her shoulders. She'd accept the punishment.

Because Zeus would sentence her to something, for sure, during that meeting. His demeanor showed he wasn't pleased with her—and she'd deny nothing. She condemned the humans, too.

But she had Lukus to thank. *He* drove her to see her issues. Without lifting a finger, he pushed her to work on her behavior, to be a better goddess. To prove deities weren't all snide, self-absorbed pricks.

It pinched her insides to admit she *cared* for him. That was why she dismissed Ares; but were these feelings those of a friend, a mother, or a *lover?* Her heart beat for him, and Ares figuring it out terrified her. Jealous as he was, he'd find the man and execute him—for existing.

Craning her neck to peek at the ceiling, she let out a moan. "This migraine must *end!"* She massaged her temples as she turned on her heels and lunged to her bed where she ripped off the satin sheets and shredded them. She cackled—maniacal—as she tore into the fabric, squealing in delight with every rip, every tear.

Her once peaceful, ocean-themed room was soon stripped bare. The golden bordered paintings—she broke them in sections and threw them into a growing pile of luxurious debris. She added centuries-old priceless ornaments, bronze statuettes of herself, hand-carved wooden doves, seashells left lying on mantles and nightstands. Each treasured possession *had* to leave her sight. She blew up, burned, destroyed them until she had nothing left.

Crossing her arms, exhausted, she glanced at her plain walls. Her empty bed. Sensing her soul, naked, reborn, renewed; rid of the guilt she felt for centuries. A necessary *spring-cleaning,* as the mortals called it.

Now she'd start a new collection from scratch, only with things of true value—not monetary, not over-the-top. Only sentimental.

Returning to her dresser, she reached for the last item in the jewelry box; a golden bracelet. Blowing out her cheeks, she snapped it in half—and nearly bumped her head on the ceiling as she jumped from a knock on her door.

The meeting? Already?

She would have growled, expecting Hebe or some other cupbearer she couldn't stand; but she reminded herself of her resolutions.

"One moment!" Fixing her messy mane, she arched her back and opened the door. Her jaw dropped at the sight of her visitor. "H-Hades?"

He blinked at her; concern plastered all over his expression. "I... hate to disturb you, Aphrodite, but... I need to speak with you. *Before* going to my brother." He leaned forward, pointing into the room, intent on coming in.

Aphrodite backed away, letting him enter and closing the door behind him. "What is it?" She pressed her spine against the wooden barrier. "... Majesty?" He was a king, after-all; and even in the safety of her chambers, she had to mind her manners.

The god of the Underworld's nose wrinkled as he pivoted, gaze wandering over the mess. Ashes, pearls cut into tiny pieces, golden strands and parts of silver cluttered in corners, atop the bed. Charred portraits and paintings, pale and shredded sheets.

"I, uh..." She rushed to where he stood, cheeks reddening. "... I'm cleaning. My apologies for my *unwelcoming* decor."

So much for making a good impression with my family.

She kicked some clutter under her bed frame, reminding herself to call for someone to tidy up during the assembly.

Hades shrugged. "Not my business. I'll make this quick; Zeus has likely sensed my presence." He darted to the window, gaping out as if checking their surroundings. He spun around and beckoned Aphrodite to his side.

She obeyed. "What is the matter?" She followed his gaze outside but saw nothing but the gardens.

"My talk with Persephone... she didn't want to drink the potion, but she remembered something; the night Eros visited. It happened to be... the same night I was away, visiting with Poseidon, discussing important matters." He kept his voice low, his eyes alert as he scanned outside still. He'd always been strange, for sure. Solemn, quiet, often absent but a prominent figure among the gods. A clear king. So why did he seem so worried?

Is someone listening in? Spying?

Hades' neck cracked to her as he nodded, pupils widening in response to her thoughts.

Oh... crap.

She gulped, unsure what to do, how to respond. If someone watched them, did that person... also hear her thoughts?

Again, Hades nodded, more insistent. "I'll inform my brother of this, too," he said, his tone louder, as if on purpose. "I believe whatever got Eros... also hit Persephone. Through *food*. They—and likely Psyche and Hedone—were poisoned. Different strands, though, for different reactions." He glanced outside, then back at Aphrodite. Again. And again. But if he wanted her to *do* something, she had no clue what; she read nothing in his thoughts.

Has he masked them?

He acquiesced, then grabbed her by the upper arms and spun her to face her window.

Her suite had a view of one of the many garden courtyards. Now, nearing nighttime, and with everyone preparing for the meeting, not a sound fluttered in the bushes. None of the usual nymph melodies flitted about the air. No one would be out there, listening to them. Plus, her window was closed.

And yet Hades' features only scrunched further as he narrowed his eyes. "*Someone* is definitely planning something. First, by turning Eros against us. Now that that has failed, I fear what this person plans to do next." He mouthed a word under his breath. One Aphrodite didn't decipher no matter how hard she stared at his lips. She had no clue what he mumbled, and still had no access to his mind.

"So... a plot against the gods." Hades bowed his head. "The Titans, you think? Getting help from someone on the outside?"

Hades smacked his palm over her mouth and dragged her from the window. "*Quiet!*"

Panting, his rough skin pressed against her lips, she moaned, the sound muffled. "*I'm sorry!*"

Nervously glancing about, he dropped his hand. "Zeus will want to investigate." He hunched to her level—he was several inches taller—and wrapped his fingers around her shoulders, gaze piercing into her soul. "In the meantime, no one is safe. Be on your guard, Aphrodite. Eros is the safest, right now—everyone else is in danger of corruption." His whispers filled her insides with ice.

The god of the Underworld was scared—how were all the other gods supposed to feel?

She bit her lip.

Lukus.

She peeked at Hades, chin trembling, desperate for him to understand what passed through her brain.

Zeus told me he was important! Needed protection at all costs.

He rubbed his temples with one hand, keeping the other around her biceps. "You erased his memories, yes?" Aphrodite nodded. "Then he is of no concern. He won't have extensive knowledge to give whoever the culprit is. I hope. You needn't worry about him."

Flinching at his breath, hot, heavy, she pulled out of his grasp. *"What in Tartarus is going on?"* she said sotto-voce, holding back a groan. His cryptic ways and odd mannerisms made her skin crawl.

"I'm trying to figure that out. I've begun *my* interrogation, but I... can't finish without hearing what Zeus wants to do first." Arms tensing at his sides, he pulled away and slid to the door. "Beware, remember. I'll see you shortly." He inclined his head and left.

As panic swelled in her ribcage, Aphrodite sat on her mattress. Her thoughts scrambled more than before. Eros. Lukus. Her family. All were in danger, and that terrified the king of the Underworld.

Fed-up with her human emotions, she huffed. And huffed harder understanding *all* their answers rested with the one who had disappeared, who escaped their grasp and who might, for all she knew, be dead.

Psyche knew it all. It all... came down to her.

‖37. LUKUS‖
LUKUS

Two weeks later

A deafening wind blasted through the window, prying his lids apart.

Lukus stood to close the glass pane and wrench the curtains over it. He thought of returning to the warmth of his bed, but the damage was done; and anyway, his doctor advised activity. To live normally again now that his injury had healed. Time to move forward. But from what?

Walking down the main corridor of his apartment, in his high-rise complex, he headed for the kitchen and straight for the coffee machine. He filled the engine with water, tossed in one too many scoops of his favorite blend, pressed the start button—and waited.

No, he wasn't supposed to drink caffeine; the doctor feared it would trigger the injury. But Lukus didn't care. He chuckled, picturing a world in which he didn't consume coffee— and assumed any who came in contact with him would die.

"Catastrophic." The bold scent slithered into his nostrils. "I'd rather make myself sick than deprive my body of what it wants."

Stomach rumbling, he opened the fridge. He had everything he needed to cook himself a healthy meal—but he sneered, slamming the door shut.

"Eat healthy, he said." He snorted. "Did this dude even *know* me?" The doctor was well acquainted with Lukus, knew his habits; so why would he prescribe a routine that would kill him?

He seized his cell phone from the kitchen counter and dialed his favorite pizza place in DC, ordering his usual triple-meat-threat with extra cheese.

At nine pm, the joint was busy; but when the clerk on the other end got Lukus' name, he promised they would rush the order.

"I am a high-tipping regular," he said aloud, hanging up. "And a fucking FBI agent, for crying out loud."

The image of dripping red sauce on the pizza made his mouth water. And at the same time, a slight nausea bubbled in his lower pelvis.

"Whoa, that's weird." He rubbed his stomach. "Probably just *too* hungry."

He shrugged, dismissing the discomfort as he moved to his office a few doors down from his bedroom. Did he need a place so big for himself alone? No. But he enjoyed the luxury.

Reanimating his computer, he found the page he left off before napping—a database of female names, blinking at him, begging for attention. A project that fooled with his head almost more than his concussion had. He sighed, sank into the chair, stretched, then typed a few words into the search engine, leaning back as the results loaded.

Everything messed with his head, if he was being honest. His vision often went in and out of focus; as if all he looked at, or everything he did, brought flashes of scenes and pictures that made no sense.

Like the time they served him spaghetti at the clinic, and one meatball rolled off his plate and onto the ground. He watched it, becoming sicker as it bounced, squished, splattered, splashing red sauce all over the floor, leaving a trail that brought bile to settle in his mouth.

"Ew," he mumbled, glaring at the computer screen.

Or the time his sister visited, hoping to inspect his wounds and report to their mother. Once she was satisfied with his progress, she described her last heart surgery, in detail—something Lukus would usually enjoy listening to.

He recoiled. That day, her words made him want to puke. Even she found his attitude odd and asked the doctors for another MRI scan. It revealed nothing, but she left with a weight on her shoulders, curious about just how hard he hit his head.

But he was fine. They *all* told him.

So why don't I feel like it?

He clicked on a few links and compared some articles to the notes jotted in a notebook next to his keyboard. Once he gathered what he needed, he closed all the tabs but the database, and typed something else into the search bar.

They all informed him that he solved the case he was working on, too; except he didn't remember what that was. A week ago, they released him—after seven days of recovery from an *unknown blunt force to the skull*—and still, too much mystery shrouded the past month of his life.

"Unknown, my ass!"

They knew, the boss knew—but the latter wasn't taking his calls. *No one* would give him straight answers… so he had to take matters into his own hands.

He again clicked on links generated from his search and cross-referenced them with his notes—to no avail.

"I'm getting nowhere." Glancing at the time—nine-thirty—his insides rumbled, eager to eat. The pizza would arrive in fifteen minutes, if they rushed the order as promised. Maybe he needed air, despite the crazy wind. Something to soothe him, relax his thoughts.

Determined, he marched to his balcony and stepped outside. The crisp breeze, though a little *too* cool for his taste, lapped against his cheeks, sending jolts of cold into his veins. He liked it.

He meandered to the table in the corner and sat on a patio chair. The wind hadn't moved his pack of cigarettes and lighter—so he smirked, snatching them, getting out one of his favorite guilty pleasures.

No, the doctor didn't want him smoking, either. "Fuck that." He brought the chosen cigarette to his mouth, lit it, and sucked in the nicotine, letting it fill his lungs. He didn't care that it hurt him; it was the only thing keeping him sane. That and booze.

Sex *would* be his third option, but since he woke up in the hospital, his libido... diminished. A feat he'd never expected—

Lukus had always been insatiable. But he refused to tell his doctor about it. He didn't want to find out he had an actual issue that would impact his mental health *more*.

With a few drags, he admired the nighttime view from his fifteenth-floor patio. A calm, cold Wednesday night, with few cars roaming about, nothing going on. Yet a nagging in his belly, a pinch in his ribcage, kept him on edge at all times. Lately, he heard sounds *not* occurring, saw things that weren't there and couldn't describe, and feared the invisible. The shadows, the darkness, the unknown. He found himself needing to keep the lights on—even in the spare bedroom that he never used—and struggled to watch TV or listen to music, wary the actions would distract him... from intruders.

But he never worried about intruders. Did something traumatizing affect him during his case? Was he beaten, assaulted, wounded within inches of his life? If only he remembered. The vivid but unclear flashbacks led him to think brutal violence wrapped around his investigation. But no one would confirm it. No one would help him cure the obvious PTSD he developed from whatever happened.

A strong gust extinguished his cigarette. "Argh, dammit." He fought with the lighter, desperate to finish the nicotine he so craved. But after what felt like fifty tries, it wouldn't reignite. With a grunt he threw the thing and smooshed it with his foot, stomping back inside to wait for his delivery.

The doorbell rang as he poured java into his favorite mug. "Shit," he nearly spilled, "Coming, *coming!*"

He snatched his wallet from the buffet on the way and pulled the heavy door open.

His jaw fell at the sight before him. "You're... not the usual person."

A young woman, luscious blond hair parted on either side of her face, smiled. "Sorry, I'm new!" Her emerald eyes twinkled as she beamed, her skin so fair, so delicate, it almost glowed. "They told me you were a regular, and I had to hurry, but I got lost." She chuckled—a sound that made Lukus weak in the knees. "I'm not used to this town, I just moved here!"

She had to be eighteen, nineteen at the most. Incredibly beautiful, radiant, a vision. *Why* was she a pizza delivery person? She had to be a model.

A surge of images in his head caught him off guard. The girl talked, rambling on, as Lukus squinted at her, wondering why she appeared so familiar. Why she triggered a picture of a lady, her exact twin, speaking to him and pointing at bodies on rainy concrete and showing everyone an FBI badge—

"—and they told me I'd get in trouble because you're with the FBI and... is that some kind of rookie joke, or is that true? Cause I can't have issues already, I just started, I can't lose my job—"

She blabbered as Lukus stared at her, then the pizza box, then her again. His lucidity fizzled and electricity shot to his temples. Her hair, eyes, skin. All blinked like flashing police-car lights, begging him to pay attention.

Shit... they match THAT description. The database—

He snapped his fingers, shutting her up. "You won't get in trouble." He forked out some money from his wallet. "Tell them I said you did great." She took the bills and handed him the box. "Thank you... for your service."

She frowned, but he shut the door before she spoke again, though her voice echoed in his mind and brought him back to his research.

His insides growled louder with every step, but he abandoned the pizza on the kitchen counter, grabbed his coffee, and scurried to his office. Picking up his notebook of scribbles and inconclusive theories, he flipped the pages to the beginning.

"*She had strawberry-blonde hair.*" He sipped his caffeine, hand trembling as it held the mug. "*Striking green eyes. Pearly, porcelain skin. Wore a long golden dress, cute sandals on her feet.*" He gasped. "Yeah, yeah *that's* why she triggered me— that chick is... was... the same as this."

Minus the outfit, the delivery girl matched the woman in his notes.

"But... no, it's not the same person, right? She would have... recognized me? Did I know her?" His fingers slipped, losing grip on his cup. "Would have said something if she... if she was... the visitor."

The notebook slid from his grasp as shivers racked every inch of his body. Goosebumps littered his arms, sweat formed above his brow.

"What the fuck is wrong with me?" He slammed his drink down so hard on the desk, the porcelain encasing it almost shattered. A few drops flew out and stained his pants.

He bent over, putting his cranium in his hands, breathing in and out, in and out.

"It... wasn't... her." In and out. In and out. "Just a coincidence. Couldn't have been her."

He lifted his chin, swiped the notebook from the floor, studied the rest of his scribbles. "*Only appeared for a moment, don't think anyone else saw her*... weird, a woman like that... one would notice." He scratched his cheek. The witness—the person whose words he read—was definitely confused, Lukus recalled. "*Lingered by the door while you slept. That was that. Must have gone when I left, because no one noticed her or anyone else enter or leave your room after that.*" He was a hospital janitor, the *only* person who saw the mystery lady hanging around Lukus' door after he landed in the ICU. Lukus knew he told the truth. No one else spoke up—and even when he flashed his badge in their face and promised to report them if they lied, they insisted. She had no name, no identity, but the custodian was *certain*. Persistent. And none of the staff called him crazy. And then his own flashback soon after that matched the janitor's description...

It was no coincidence.

Though the delivery chick was, for sure.

He scoffed, remembering the situation. Barely recovering, in his hospital gown, meandering around his ICU wing interrogating nurses and doctors. "Must have looked super convincing."

He stood up, pinching the bridge of his nose. "Chill out, Lukus, jeez."

Taking his drink and his notes, he returned to the kitchen. He opened the pizza box, sniffed the air, let the delicious aroma creep up his nostrils and tingle his senses.

"*Yes,* that's all I need. Pizza and coffee and cigarettes."

As he got a paper plate from a cupboard, he realized he'd likely never recover his memory... but he'd try as hard as he could. "I will figure this shit out." He selected a few slices, slid them onto his plate, then went to the dining room table where he set his meal, beverage, and notebook. He turned the page.

Case: no recollection.

Bosses have no recollection, either. Refuse to talk.

He took a bite—cheesy deliciousness numbed him with satisfaction. Then the three meats, bacon, sausage, pepperoni, exploding in his mouth. The savory, thick sauce, coating it all in bliss.

He hiccupped. Something boiled in his gut. "Oh... oh shit, no, not again." Queasy, he exhaled. No, he wouldn't let that weird disgust settle again, not while eating the *best* pizza in town. He took another bite, ignoring his stomach.

Past two, three, four weeks: no recollection. Linked to case?

He struggled to finish the slice without gagging. The texture, the colors, all created an acidic flavor on his tongue, only worsening the more he ate.

He gawked at his fridge. "No... I can't eat that healthy shit." He gagged again. "Ugh, I can't eat *at all.*"

Maybe the coffee, or the cigarette—something wasn't sitting well with him.

A sudden trigger pulsated through his brain. Him, stuffing his face. Lips stained crimson, eyes glacial, an inhuman groan escaping him.

"What the—" He slid off the chair, knocking his coffee over in the process as he came to his knees. His favorite mug plunged... and shattered. "*Shit!*"

Limp, he gaped at the puddle of brown liquid expanding before him.

Another flash.

The same puddle—but bright scarlet. Pieces of meat floating in it, decomposing, rotting. A putrid stench. A pile of ash, cut-up chunks of *something* nestled inside.

He choked, squealing, gasping for air; so loud he *had* to have roused the entire floor. "That's... *enough!*" He shoved the chair onto the caffeine, splashing it all over the counters. Seething, he got to his feet, trotted to a cabinet by the fridge, extracted a large blue bottle, uncapped it—and chugged. The smooth yet violent alcohol—vodka—drizzled down his throat, setting it on fire, cooling his organs, spinning his head.

That's more like it.

He took his plate, the bottle, and the notebook, and wandered over to his couch where he fell. Another swig of the booze and he licked his lips, holding the book up to his eyes. "I bet *she* knows what's going on."

He hadn't had a drop of liquor since the hospital, so the vodka would affect him fast.

Good.

"I... *have* to find her. Strawberry-blonde woman. Emerald eyes. Somewhere... on this planet. Has *all* the answers." Another few gulps. "I have to find her."

The bottle slipped from his grip, luckily remaining upright against the couch. The notebook tumbled to his torso. Every ounce of reality left him as he plunged into a deep sleep. A comatose rest where he saw *her*. The mystery woman.

She whispered in his ear. "Lukus, oh destined one..."

‖38. POISONOUS PLOTS‖
???

It had been weeks, but she recalled it as if it were happening all over again. The Olympian throne room rearranged for a godly meeting. The night sky outside contrasted with the candle-lit space. Though the marble pillars illuminated like millions of fireflies, and the oversized seats scintillated as diamonds, the usual festive music paused, leaving place for a calm atmosphere, perfect for reflection and meditation. It seemed a nice space to relax, but it was an illusion; for once the gods settled in their seats, their eyes narrowed, the Olympian throne room came off more as a dangerous boxing ring.

Here, most appeared of similar strength, thrones set up in a circle at equal distances from each other. Their differing personalities were ready to shine as they debated, expressed their opinions, weighed the options placed before them—few realized the entire world's safety depended on their rationalism and calm.

Many would share their opinion in the throne room, but that night, the gods all agreed—including Hades and Hestia, who rarely took part in Olympian meetings. Both were requested to attend—especially Hades, who gave the news of his wife's similar affliction to Aphrodite's son. His revelation caused much tumult and rage amongst the deities, and it was difficult for Zeus to quiet them, gain their attention.

Hades readjusted his seating, Poseidon stopped stomping his foot, and Demeter attempted to wipe her tears, afraid for her daughter.

"Persephone is fine, dear sister," said the king of the sky. "And Eros will remain locked up to purge for his crimes. Hopefully, whatever spell ensorcelled him will wear off if he's kept away from those blood arrows." His voice bellowed, piercing, awe-inspiring. "And far from memory potions, brother." He glared at Hades, who bowed his head.

Demeter sniffled; Aphrodite hiccupped.

I'd never expect their kids to share similar situations.

Zeus leaned against the cushions of his throne. "At this point, our only explanation for his behavior—and Persephone's participation—was a curse, or a poison. Maybe something more thorough, who knows. We may never discern the whole truth."

Everyone was on edge, suspicious and suspected, wary of consequences.

"I've assigned lesser beings to assist with the duties he abandoned to pursue his personal vendetta. Though he murdered humans, I cannot eliminate his post. His role is *still* important, and I'll return it to him once I deem him fit," said the ruler of the gods, tone strained, concern in every word.

He watched his constituency as they watched him; features reflecting worry, lips sucked between teeth, hands wringing in laps.

"Now that we have a minimum of details, we must focus on the real problem." His commanding voice laced with something no one was used to hearing in his voice.

Fear? Or something else? I can't tell.

A few gods shifted in their chairs.

He angled to Hades. "Brother, would you care to share the other... information you gave me moments ago?"

Hades cleared his throat, and all spun to him. "Persephone has little recollection of encountering Eros in the Underworld, yet *he* remembers meeting her. Though I believe they were both poisoned, they didn't suffer the same effects. She... remembers coming close to Cerberus, taking his blood without effort; but she has no idea what she whispered to him to do so."

Speech solemn, calm, Hades never showed emotion. Not even to his family.

More shifting came from his audience.

"She agrees that a spell may have been cast on her, albeit temporary, as she never lost control or had a crazy killing spree. She is cured of malice, and I don't believe her to be harmful, but... I made sure someone supervised her as I left, just in case."

Demeter sobbed again. "M-my... *baby...*"

Zeus inclined his head. "Thank you, Brother." He peered at his staff, his family, his friends. "It's clear we have an offender *among* us. An invisible criminal. How else would two of our own get poisoned, right under our noses?"

Whispers, murmurs, obvious distress floated among the attendees.

He must use more tact; they'll all lose their minds from such accusations.

"*Someone* is rendering the gods mad. And I believe that *same* someone is responsible for Psyche's and Hedone's disappearances. Because they... knew something?" He fiddled with his beard. "These are lesser goddesses, but they *are* direct Olympian family. Eros is a descendant of royalty, and Psyche is his bride. Hedone is their daughter. Something like this doesn't go uninvestigated, ladies and gentlemen. Nor does it go unpunished. Does anyone disagree?"

All shook their heads.

Aphrodite's usually lustful expression turned to gray. With her son in a negative spotlight, something *different* radiated in her aura that night; maturity, understanding.

Odd—does she fear for Psyche? Or did she learn something from the humans?

The goddess of love fingered a few strands of her shimmering curls behind her ears.

"Hades, you must interrogate your constituents in the Underworld. I'll send someone else down there to help, at some point. You and Persephone have access to realms and people we don't, and *they* might have answers. Leave no stone unturned."

Hades bowed. "At once, Majesty." He waved his hands and with a *pop,* he disappeared in a cloud of black smoke.

Zeus rubbed his forehead. Someone cleared their throat, requesting his attention—and he obliged, twisting to the goddess in question.

"We're all in danger as long as this unknown culprit roams," said Hera, her fingertips wrapping around the arm of her throne. "Should we suggest all Olympians pursue their activities and jobs from the safety of Olympus?"

A few gazes wandered to her, likely curious about her speaking up without being addressed. She was the queen, yes; but her opinions rarely mattered.

Even she is afraid... but I don't trust her. She'll hide behind his tunic, cower like a coward.

Hera batted her lashes at her husband, waiting for his reply.

I can't rule her out. She's a suspect, too.

Zeus pushed off his seat. "I agree." He nodded at his wife, who beamed. "You're all confined to the palace unless otherwise stated by me. And pay attention to anyone you encounter; this being uses dark spells and may be able to shape-shift and take on another's appearance. If anything feels *off*... assume it *is* and locate me at once." He paced in the circle formed by the thrones.

More worried than I've seen him in centuries. We really are in danger. But... why Eros, first?

Zeus stopped before each god, analyzing their presence, digging his sight into their skulls. Soon, he halted before Hera and exchanged a glance with her that differed from all others. In response she squinted, features troubled, chin tipping down. Her nostrils flared, and she gave a quick nod before slouching back in her spot.

Zeus resumed marching. "I need my strongest out on the field investigating the situation. Someone on earth, checking every location, interrogating lesser gods, searching through all possibilities. We *must* find Psyche and Hedone, and I trust they may be somewhere down there."

He strolled up to Ares. On either side of the war god were Athena and Hermes.

"You three…"

He'll choose Ares. Vengeful war-god. Eros is his son.

Zeus pondered the angry deity, inching closer to inspect him.

The best option. His daughter-in-law and granddaughter are the ones missing.

"Hmm." Zeus sniffed the air, causing Ares to flinch.

I hate it, but he's a fantastic fighter. The best for fast answers, ruthless tactics.

"Perhaps, perhaps..." Zeus stiffened, still scrutinizing Ares.

That's what Father wants, right?

Zeus snapped his gaze to Athena.

Me? No... Father, no. Choose Ares.

A grin formed across his lips. "No, Athena." She went limp, frozen under Zeus' piercing glance. "My strongest and *wisest.* And that, dear child, would be *you.*"

All gazes rested on her, and she gulped.

He... listened to my thoughts? He said he'd tune everyone out tonight!

Zeus' smile expanded. "Sorry, but I couldn't help it." The air around became suffocating as he brought the tip of his nose within millimeters of hers. "I need *you* to be the envoy roaming down there in search of our missing goddesses. To gather clues on our culprit. You're the best for the job, and you won't let me down."

Grumbles of agreement echoed in the space—including Ares.

"Me?"

Did he really find her up to the task? She hadn't been to Earth in centuries, she only watched from afar.

I'm not the wisest anymore. I'm not sure I'm up for this.

Everyone ogled Athena as she debated. They expected her to step up to the plate, to save them all; and she winced at the responsibility on her shoulders.

"Dear daughter, though I commend your humility, I require you to be the goddess you once were, in the old days. The judge. The investigator, the one who knew all, understood all, and punished when necessary. I'm counting on you. We *all* are." Zeus' eyes darkened, a storm of thunder and lightning and orders.

She had no choice. She couldn't show her weakness and never revealed her flaws, dealt with issues as her wisdom never failed. Because she judged fairly, found solutions... and *was* the appropriate deity for the task.

Father is right. Accept this—or I'll criticize whoever else he chooses in my stead.

The powerful magic cloaking the room concealed her internal words; only Zeus had access, though he promised *not* to use his ability. Yet now, he chuckled at her, his gaze returning to normal. "*That's* my girl. The Athena we all remember. So, what say you?"

It wasn't really a question.

"Yes, Father." She dipped her head, submitting to his will, but begging him not to reveal the struggles in her mind. "I will investigate this and recover the missing goddesses. And the culprit. For Olympus."

All cheered. "For Olympus!"

Athena blinked and her family rose from their seats. In a blur, they congratulated her acceptance, proud of her mission. But *could* she solve it? Recover two lost goddesses and catch the miscreant who started this? She hadn't dealt with anything like this since the Titans.

Her temples throbbed. She shivered as all chatted, preparing to turn in for the night. She exchanged a quick glance with Aphrodite—they both witnessed Eros' attitude change in the dungeons. No matter how much she hated her, Athena owed her.

A mother shouldn't carry such a burden. Never clear on what attacked her son, and why he didn't remember.

Same for Uncle Hades; I must find answers for he and Persephone.

As she got up, her light tunic flowed to the ground, one she would have to toss and replace with her war gear. For weapons on her back, and a heavy burden she'd haul around with them.

Who took Psyche and Hedone? Who was the new evil among the Greek gods?

And am I ready to find out?

To be continued in book TWO

POISONOUS PSYCHE

#2 in the "Angry Greek Gods" series

ABOUT THE AUTHOR

Stephanie Rose is an author based in Nevada, but her heart lives in Paris, France, where she resided for almost twelve years. When she's not writing, she spends her time playing video-games with her boyfriend, catching up on TV-shows, or snuggling her black cat, Onyx.

"CARNIVOROUS CUPID" is the first in a four-book series, inspired by her obsession with Greek mythology. For updates on upcoming works, visit her website: www.stephanierose.online